A VANISHING IN GREENWICH VILLAGE

by

Elisabeth Amaral

CENTRAL PARK SOUTH PUBLISHING

Publisher: Central Park South Publishing

website: www.langtonsinternational.com

Book Layout © 2020 Central Park South Publishing

A Vanishing in Greenwich Village by Elisabeth Amaral - 1st ed.

ISBN: 978-1-0878-8298-7

For my granddaughter, Elodie.

You give me such joy, but I need a pinky swear that you won't read this book until you're in college.

CHAPTER ONE

Summer 2015

My marriage ended during my husband Patrick's fiftieth birthday party. Our home was filled with friends. When Patrick finally appeared, dinner had been eaten and cake served. His lateness was awkward, made more so when he approached me reeking of Chanel No. 5, which is not my scent. I turned my head as he tried to kiss me, not caring how the gesture might seem. I'd used up my embarrassment a long time ago. What I felt on that warm summer evening was relief. No more pretense or false hope. No more marriage.

I'd spent the day with Betsy and Louisa preparing the house and the food. Salad, sirloin, salmon. Beautifully ripe melon. Music. Flowers. I shouldn't have bothered. I should have gone for a walk, or to a movie, or taken one of my cast iron pans and smashed it into Patrick's handsome, duplicitous face.

Our son Jonathan had been standing by my side. Eighteen years old, tall and thin with a mop of dark, wavy hair. A younger, more intellectual-looking version of Patrick, but kinder. More thoughtful. In touch with his feminine side, thanks to me. He was on his way to England, then college, then the rest of his life. But first, this night. The sight of his father's embarrassed grin and the stink of one of his sluts. I murmured that I was fine. That we'd be fine. I believed it to be true.

My beautiful brownstone was filled with guests sophisticated enough to act nonchalant as they stood, wine glasses or cake plates in well-manicured hands. They handled themselves well. So did I. Louisa and Betsy, our tenants for so many years they felt like family, looked at me with concern. They needn't have. Patrick's late, aromatic arrival had given me a comforting determination I hadn't felt in years. I stood straight and proud in my slim summer dress and bid the guests goodnight. I walked up the dining room stairs that led to our living quarters and changed into my kimono, then left the master bedroom, passed the hall bathroom, Jonathan's room and entered the miniscule guest room at the end of the hall. The twin bed with its rose-colored chenille bedspread beckoned. The moon shed minimal illumination through the single window into the cramped quarters. A small fan sat atop a low bookcase filled with old *New Yorkers*, but summer heat soothed. I closed my eyes, took deep breaths. Om, rippling pond, weeping willows dancing in the wind, idiot leaning on a car horn, Om.

For so long I'd pretended that long, lonely nights over long, loveless years didn't bother me. Nights in which Patrick came home, undressed, climbed into bed and fell into deep, immediate slumber. Sometimes I wasn't bothered because I was so busy selling real estate, so tired, that I welcomed his absences and our lack of intimacy. Other times, I despised him. This party was such a time and it carried with it the added insult of having the state of my marriage so visible. So naked.

So what.

Jonathan entered the room.

"Mom, are you okay?"

"I will be, honey." I looked at my son and a flood of love washed over me. "I just want to sleep this day off."

He grabbed my hand and squeezed it, then left the door slightly ajar as he left me alone.

Faint sounds from downstairs. Guests saying their goodbyes. Then Patrick, knocking on the door. I ignored him. He walked in, admitting sufficient light from the hallway that the continents on the globe near the window were clear enough for me to find a focus. I settled on Greenland.

"It's not what you think, sweetheart," he said, taking a few steps toward me. "Come back to our room."

"I'm comfortable here," I said. He knelt and took my hands in his. He leaned over to kiss me. I turned my face away. Away from him and away from Greenland, the latter of which had attained some importance to my sense of control. He sat, struggled to find purchase for his broad frame on the narrow bed.

"Can you move over?" I moved closer to the edge, forcing him off. I could barely look at him as words spewed out.

"Don't even try to explain," I said. "I've put up with your crap for years. Tonight was it. To come home stinking of another woman, in front of our son. Our guests." I was beyond rage, yet when I saw the raw pain on his face, the tears that threatened to spill, it was so unexpected that my breath caught.

Don't you dare, you bastard.

"No matter how badly I've acted, El, I love only you."

Words, from a mouth that's been who knows where.

"You'll pay for this, Patrick. If you don't, I will hurt you. Now leave me alone. I'm tired."

That was the night I removed my wedding ring. I don't even remember where I put it. Threw it. I slept better than I had in a long while. When I awoke to a dazzling sunny morning I felt an unexpected fondness for the narrow bed, the cozy room. When I peered past the open door of the master bedroom on my way downstairs I saw that the room was neat, the bed made, none of Patrick's clothes strewn about. Downstairs, all signs of the party were cleared away in the living and dining rooms. Jonathan, Betsy and Louisa were having breakfast at the kitchen table. They'd been talking, but an awkward silence fell when they saw me.

"Oh, please," I said. "I'm fine. Hungry. I hardly had a thing to eat last night." I sat down and helped myself to coffee, a slice of French toast, syrup, fresh fruit. "Thanks for the breakfast."

"Betsy made it," Jonathan said. I smiled at Betsy, my mouth full. I nodded my thanks.

"*De nada*," she said.

"Dad cleaned up from the party before he left to work. You look rested."

"I slept well," I said. My eye lit on the dome-covered cake plate that held the remains of the birthday cake. Devil's food with white frosting from Amy's Bread in Chelsea Market. I cut myself a thick slice, placed it on my plate. One hundred percent maple syrup lapped at the icing.

"It's eight-thirty in the morning, Mom."

Betsy handed me a clean fork.

"I don't know how you stay so thin, the crap you've been eating," Louisa said. "It'll catch up to you, one of these days." I thrust a fork into the cake and eyed it, swallowed it, pushed the plate away. I was stronger than sugar cravings.

No I wasn't. I picked up the piece of cake and stuffed it in my mouth. Crumbs and a glob of seven-minute icing found their way onto the kimono. I wondered what to do with the rest of the day. With the rest of my life. There was no reason to go to the office. Business was slow. Real estate was usually slow in the summer, at least with higher-end clients. Most either traveled or were at their weekend homes. Whatever I had to do I could do from home, including a search for a divorce attorney. I'd make a list of all the ones I knew through deals I'd done. I would choose one when I felt like it. But first, a movie on TV. A French one. *Papillion.* Butterflies. Prison. Escape. This was great. I had a plan. I stood, tightened the obi on the pale yellow and lime green silk kimono I'd slept in.

"Patrick bought this for me when he was at a convention," I said. "In Japan."

"We know that kimono. You've worn it for years," Louisa said. Jonathan fidgeted in his chair.

"What," I said.

"Nothing." He looked miserable.

"Oh please."

"It wasn't a convention," he blurted.

"Of course it was. A dental convention in Tokyo. Dad's a dentist and everyone has teeth, all over the world."

"*No es verdad*," said Betsy, shaking her head. Her dark braid danced across her back. "I have an auntie who has no teeth." She paused for a minute. "*Dos.* I think she has *dos.*"

"Well, I'm sorry for her but she shouldn't have neglected them," I said.

"It's not easy when you don't have money," Jonathan said. "Or access to a dentist."

"She has money," Betsy said. "She doesn't have teeth." I found that difficult to understand. I turned to Jonathan.

"What were you saying, honey? Before the teeth."

"Remember Dad's new bowling ball when he was on that Port Authority team? Years ago. I was only about ten. He kept it in a plaid bag and I checked it out. There were plane tickets for Tokyo inside, for him and someone named Cindy."

I nodded, a wise maternal nod, even as I fought a rising fury. Patrick had been cheating on me for eight years. At least eight years.

"Oh, Cindy," I said nonchalantly. "I remember her. She was his bookkeeper. She had implants."

"Did Dad do them?"

"Not that kind, honey," I said. "Think Dolly Parton." I fought to keep my voice calm but couldn't stop clenching and un-clenching my fists. I wanted to punch something.

Jonathan's face turned red. "Her breasts? She had fake breasts?"

"She had bowling balls!" I let out a sound that resembled the cry of a moderately-sized safari animal in distress. I left the kitchen and entered the powder room. Faced the copper framed mirror above the sink, untied the kimono. My breasts were still firm and they were mine. I returned to the kitchen. "My breasts are better than Cindy's," I announced proudly. Louisa and Betsy said nothing but it seemed to me that Louisa was trying hard not to laugh. Jonathan looked uncomfortable but he'd get over it. He'd have to. Besides, city kids are tough.

So are their mothers, I assured myself, even as sudden pathetic sobs escaped my mouth like hiccups.

"Patrick slept with Cindy because of silicone," I cried. "That's just wrong!" My nose began to run. "Oh, shit!" Louisa handed me a napkin. As I reached for it my arm flailed about in the wide sleeve of the kimono. It was an unintentionally dramatic gesture, something Maria Callas might have done in *Madame Butterfly*. I blew my nose. "This kimono is hideous, isn't it? And it clashes with my skin tones. I hate that!" I ran upstairs to the master bedroom, tore it off and threw it in the decoupage waste basket. I walked to the window and looked down at the garden. The riotous colors of the blooms below gave me hope. I cupped my bare breasts. "We'll be fine," I promised.

CHAPTER TWO

No one was downstairs when I returned to the kitchen. There was a note, to call if I needed something, they were all there for me. Except that they weren't. I reached into a cupboard and took out an unopened box of Mallomars, carried it into the living room. I searched for the *Papillon* DVD I'd bought from a man on Astor Place years ago for two dollars, but couldn't find it. No worries. There was *The Lower Depths*. Even better. I sat back and watched misery unfold, calm me. I was well into it when I heard the clop of Louisa's clogs on the hallway stairs.

"I'm coming in," she called, walking through the open floor-to-ceiling double doors. Her platinum hair was streaked with pink this morning. It had been blue for the party. Her clogs were yellow. She glanced at the screen. "What's the movie?"

"Shh," I said, thoroughly engrossed. Louisa picked up the cover and stared at me.

"You're kidding. You have nothing better to do than watch this shit at ten a.m.?"

"It puts life in perspective."

Louisa grabbed the remote and paused the film.

"Jonathan went to meet his girlfriend. He said to tell you they're going to Coney Island. Betsy is visiting friends, somewhere in Queens. We're going for a walk. You have nothing to say about it, so get up." I understood. She'd been chosen to babysit me and from her I'm not kidding voice I knew she intended to honor her commitment. I found my sandals, slipped into them, checked my bag for wallet, keys and phone. All that took energy, so I sat back down on the sofa and hugged my bag to my chest. "Get up," she said. "Again."

"I don't want to."

"I don't care." She pulled me up, her thin arms surprisingly powerful.

It's not that easy just walking out of a brownstone. I had to open the door, lock it behind us as we stood in the tiny vestibule, unlock the heavy front door, lock it behind us. In my state of mind it was exhausting. I stood on the top stoop and wondered why I'd agreed to leave my house. Besides, it was hot outside. Muggy. But I walked with Louisa as she led the way to Ninth Avenue. We walked north, against sparse summer traffic.

"If you feel like talking..." Louisa said. "I'm here." I took her hand briefly to acknowledge her sensitivity - her quiet, solid friendship. We walked, past Chelsea Market, past the projects. No kids in the playground, only two adults asleep on benches, brown paper bags clutched in their hands. Rotgut for breakfast. Small storefronts, buildings as familiar as the mood that at unexpected moments draped me like a shroud.

A siren wailed as a fire truck sped down Ninth Avenue. Louisa covered her ears. We turned on West 22nd Street. Block Beautiful. On Tenth Avenue we entered Clement Clarke Moore Park. "'Twas the Night Before Christmas" Clement Clarke Moore. He and James N. Wells developed Chelsea in the 1830s, something I learned my first week in real estate. I bent down to smell the roses in the park named after him. I'd planted flowers there years ago, along with other brokers from my firm. These were different flowers, different colors. Ours had been prettier. These seemed sturdier. Expensively dressed kids played while chic parents and casually clothed nannies watched over them. Images of Jonathan as a toddler. Memories of a young, virile Patrick pushing him in a swing, arms strong and tan. Images of Patrick pushing himself inside a woman, any woman, her legs spread wide on the padded arms of his black leather dental chair. Maybe that mother in black capris and halter top standing by the jungle gym. Or the bleached blonde au pair by the sandbox. I fought nausea, along with a rising dislike for anyone who appeared to be the least bit happy.

"Let's go," I said, feeling a sudden, powerful urge to leave.

We walked down Tenth Avenue and I wondered what percentage of drivers were headed uptown to the nearby Lincoln Tunnel entrance. Not that I cared, I was just mildly curious. We passed the back of the magnificent General Theological Seminary, which was now a hotel. Before that it was the Desmond Tutu Center. Before that it was all just seminary, except for the condos built on the Ninth Avenue part. We turned onto West 20th, the Seminary building and its gardens to our left, townhouses across the street. I'd sold several of them over the years, both one-family and those divided into co-ops - some big and beautiful and others small and sweet. I once showed a famous Irish model the top floor of a Federal-style home turned into a four-unit co-op. When I opened the door to the luxurious bathroom a fat, wet rat stared at us from inside the toilet bowl. The model and I stared at each other in horror, then ran around the apartment screaming like crazy people, until we realized we could simply leave.

Mid-block, Louisa and I watched a man back out of a parking space large enough that a waiting car was able to pull right into it. The lucky driver shot us a triumphant grin and why not? It was a big deal.

Back on Ninth Avenue we entered La Bergamote, or rather I entered and Louisa followed. She sat at a table while I studied miniature fruit tarts behind a glass case in the patisserie. They sparkled like jewels. I ordered a multi-berry tart, an almond croissant and two iced coffees and brought them in two trips over to the table where Louisa sat. I recognized the only other customer as a tough-guy actor from *Law and Order*. He was reading the *New York Times* folded neatly into long halves. A chocolate mouse sat on a small plate in front of him, partially dismembered. When he saw me looking at him he winked. It was so unexpected that I not only smiled at him, I felt a surprise tingle between my thighs. A momentary reminder of pleasures long forgotten, of how my body used to feel before numbness settled in with more ease than was fair. He folded the paper again and took out a pen. He started the crossword puzzle.

I do the puzzle. He used a pen. I use a pen. There is, I believe, an unspoken bond between crossword puzzle people. I wondered what would happen if I asked him if he wanted to fool around. There was no way I could lose. If he said yes, it might be good or it might be lousy. I was used to lousy and I was used to nothing so it was a win-win scenario for me. If he said lady are you out of your mind, so what? I'd be back where I started but really one step ahead because doing something is better than doing nothing.

What happened was that after a while he looked at his watch, refolded the paper, stood up and was about to pass our table when I reached out and touched his arm.

"Thank you for reading the *Times* so neatly," I said. I meant it. Things like that matter. He grinned, took my hand and kissed it. I smiled back, reminded once again of why I love this city so very much. Depending on how one chooses to view life, a kiss on the hand from a *Law and Order* actor can be just another day in the city or it can be a promise of good things to come. That's what it was to me. A promise of more.

"Thank you for reading the *Times* so neatly?" Louisa said, after the actor left.

"It says something about a person. He's even better looking in real life."

"Who is he, anyway? Should I know him?"

"Maybe it was my fault with Patrick," I said. Working so hard, for so many years."

"You were doing your job. What should you have done, ignore your clients?"

"Now and then, for the sake of the marriage."

"Screw that," Louisa said. "You had a living to make, especially after the lean years following the recession. You did what you had to do."

"All that work for his party. What a waste of our time."

"No it wasn't. It was fun. You, me and Betsy in the kitchen. And that woman we met while we were shopping. How pathetic was that."

I smiled at the reminder, then wondered why, because there was nothing funny about our encounter with Janet. She was a former client of mine who Louisa and I bumped into while shopping for Patrick's party. I hadn't seen her since I'd sold her Bank Street townhouse five years ago. She never would have left that house, or Manhattan for that matter, until her husband Pete fell in love with his dream house in South Orange, New Jersey. She loved Pete so she reluctantly agreed to the move. Two years later, she returned to their six bedroom, five bathroom Tudor home after driving her kids to school and found a note propped against the espresso machine: Darlings, I've found my true calling and am going to spend the rest of my life in a monastery in Galicia. Everything I own is yours.

Everything included an enormous mortgage, Mercedes and Volvo loan payments, taxes on the property and to the IRS, maxed out credit cards and an upcoming and obscenely expensive Bat Mitzvah. Janet had given up her lucrative Manhattan career to be a suburban mom. Learned to drive so she could carpool. Learned bridge and canasta to have something to do. I'll never forget the bitterness in her voice as she reminded me how she'd had to sell the Bank Street house at a loss while overpaying for the suburban Tudor due to a five-way bidding war.

"What her husband did to her is worse than Patrick cheating on me, isn't it," I said.

"Way worse," Louisa said. "You can always cheat on Patrick and be even. She'd have to become a nun." She looked at me with curiosity. "Did you ever?"

"Did I ever what?"

"Cheat on Patrick."

"I never even thought of it."

Even as I said the words I wondered what was wrong with me, that I hadn't ever thought about being unfaithful. What had happened to my sexuality? I thought about the actor who had just left and realized I wanted it back. The feeling of a body on top of me. Under me. In me.

Louisa was looking at me, a bit strangely.

"Where are you? she asked. I smiled.

"A nice place," I said.

"I'm glad for you. Hey, how about that scene at the Short Hills Mall."

What was she talking about? Oh, yes. Janet. We had been talking about Janet. How after she had read the note from her husband about joining the monastery, she walked out of the house and drove to the mall. She walked aimlessly about until she found Hanro panties on sale, three for the price of two. It gave her a sense of victory which vanished as she stood in line to pay. Her small sense of victory turned into a meltdown as she began screaming 'fucking asshole, fucking asshole.'

"At least it happened in Nordstrom," I said. "In Lingerie. People understood." I paused, looked at Louisa. "You realize, don't you, that what happened to her could just as easily happen to me."

"You wear Hanro?"

"That's not the point," I said. "But yes, I do, sometimes. They're great."

"I didn't know that. You want another croissant?" I shook my head. We paid, then walked toward home. "Don't worry," Louisa said, a few blocks later. "We'll get through this."

"How?"

CHAPTER THREE

A few days later I was in a small nail salon in the Far West Village when my cell phone rang. Irma was polishing my toenails I'm Not Really a Waitress Red.

"Hi. Are you Ellie Allington?" In the background I heard a Bach partita. Outside, car horns honked behind a garbage truck. "I'm Valeria Mandel. I live in a loft on Jane Street that I have to leave, by the end of September. Maybe we could meet."

I'd sent many mailings to many buildings over the years, especially in the West Village, so I assumed I'd sent a postcard to her building that boasted of my real estate experience. Or maybe she found me on the internet, or heard of me through friends. I didn't ask because I didn't care. Instead, I marveled at how my toes looked happier than I felt. They were almost dry. I could put on my sandals and walk to her place if that's what she wanted, even though it wasn't what I wanted.

"Now?" I asked, hoping she didn't hear the reluctance in my voice.

"I was thinking tomorrow for lunch. We can see the loft another time, if you want." I thought that was an odd thing for a potential seller to say but had so little motivation for anything that I was barely listening. She surprised me by suggesting that we meet the following day at Moustache, at noon. Since it was one of my favorite restaurants, I agreed. I hung up, relieved to have the rest of the day to myself.

"Change feet," Irma said. A short time later she sprayed my toes and I slipped into my sandals, paid and walked outside into blinding summer sun. I had a momentary wish that it would melt me into oblivion. I crossed Hudson, took Bleecker to Bank to Greenwich Avenue, then Seventh Avenue and the tumult of West 14th. The walk up my stoop, key in hand. The quiet of my elegant home. The comfort of my kitchen. I poured myself a tall glass of cold lemonade and carried it into the living room. I curled up onto the sofa and settled down to watch Max von Sydow in *Pelle the Conqueror*. He tore my heart to shreds every time I watched it. Patrick came home during the last few minutes and knew not to say a word until the credits ran.

"I miss you," he said. He sat next to me, took one of my feet and began massaging it. "Nice polish. Sparkly."

It felt good. Very good, but it was my foot. He had no right to it. He no longer had rights to any part of me. I yanked my foot away and went up to the guest room, wondering as I climbed the stairs why I chose there instead of the garden, remembered how hot it was outside and felt a surge of satisfaction at my cleverness. I plopped down on the edge of my new bed, feet on the floor. Patrick followed me into the room. I looked at him, sensed his longing, saw it in his dark brown eyes. I felt my own. He reached out and pulled me up. I sobbed against his broad chest. His smell. Familiar. Musky. To be held again. Touched again. He kissed me. Slipped his hands under my tee shirt, put his hands on my breasts. I felt long-suppressed desire flood through me. My need was raw.

Blatant images of him with other women. If I gave in now I'd hate myself later. Passion ebbed as rage returned and I pushed him away. He seemed stricken, but he left. I closed the door, discarded my clothes and lay on the bed. Spread my legs.

I didn't need him.

*

I met Valeria at Moustache the following day. It is a small ethnic restaurant on Bedford Street and on a slow summer day it was almost empty. She was already seated when I arrived, a delicately built blue-eyed blonde, her long, blonde hair wavy and loose. For the first time in years I thought of my late sister. It almost overwhelmed me. This is how Sally might have looked, had she lived past childhood. I felt momentarily weak with the unexpectedness of memories long suppressed and fought an urge to leave. Leave the sudden onrush of pain. But an even stronger urge pulled me toward her.

"You're much more attractive in person than you are on your postcard photograph," she said. I sat down and tried not to stare at her, was relieved when a waiter walked over with menus.

"I don't need one," she said.

"I don't either."

We both ordered lamb pitzas. We made small talk for a while and then I asked if she was thinking of selling her loft. She smiled a strange little smile.

"It's not mine. I just live there, but I have to move out soon. By the end of September. You can see it if you like, though. Come for lunch on Friday." She smiled at me. It was such a warm, gracious smile. "Please do. It'll be fun."

I wanted a listing, not a friend, but there was something about her. Her grace, her charm. Her delicate beauty. Her need for a place to live. I asked what her plans were after she moved out but her answer was ambiguous. Maybe she'd need a place, she said, or maybe not, but if she did, of course she'd ask me.

I told her I don't do rentals but if that's what she decided she wanted I would find her a rental agent.

I was wasting my time here. And Valeria had pulled me back into my past. To Sally and my mother. When Sally was born it was like the second coming of Christ. Then one day she died.

Sitting across from Valeria brought it all back. It was a relief when our conversation led us to discover that we both enjoyed long, solitary walks, unassuming ethnic restaurants, foreign films in almost empty art theatres.

"But not totally empty," she said.

"No," I agreed. "Then it's creepy."

Valeria nodded. "Exactly! Maybe we can go together. Have movie dates."

"That would be great," I said. "And maybe we can see your place today, after lunch," I said. "It's so close."

"You look a bit like Pier Angeli. Do you know her?"

That was her answer.

After lunch we walked east and found ourselves on St. Luke's Place. A park on one side, teens playing ball in the heat. On our side large, elegant houses on a beautiful street. "Remember when that playground was sometimes referred to as Hell Park," I asked.

Valeria shook her head. "No. When was that?"

"A long time ago."

"A long time ago was bad for me," she said. "One day I'll tell you about it."

I wasn't sure I wanted to hear, but I don't walk away from people or their stories. You never know who has what in this city. Who knows whom. The sale of a modest studio once owned by a struggling writer turned, many years and several best sellers later, into her purchase of a ten room terraced duplex on Fifth Avenue with Central Park views. I made a small fortune in commissions over the years by working with her, her friends, family, publisher, ex-husband. The same with a once struggling gallery owner. She became a success, bought a house, stayed loyal to me and recommended me to all her friends. That's why I made time for everyone, except that lately I didn't give a damn.

We walked together uptown and parted on Hudson and Jane. She walked west and I walked north. I turned to look at her once more, watched her walk away light and graceful as a dancer and felt a strange, unexpected sense of loss.

CHAPTER FOUR

I was scrambling eggs when Jonathan entered the kitchen.

"Hi, honey. Ready for your trip?" I asked.

"We have the whole route planned." He and his girlfriend were taking a hiking vacation in Cornwall, England. After his return we'd have just a few days to shop for college and then the move into his dorm room at Columbia.

"What are you doing today? Seeing Maggie?"

"Nothing planned 'til tonight. I'll text her later." A desire to spend the day with him took hold. I watched him pour a tall glass of milk and gulp it down, marveled that he was mine. "You seem better today, Mom."

"I feel better. Want to do something together? Get on a train and see what happens?"

There was only a brief hesitation on Jonathan's part before he grinned at me.

"Yeah, sure. Like old times."

Fighting back the relief and happiness I felt, I gave attention to the eggs as though I hadn't scrambled hundreds of them in my lifetime. Probably thousands. A momentary wish that I had written down each egg I'd ever broken, scrambled, fried, poached. An egg list.

We ate quickly and got ready even faster. For Jonathan it was grabbing his phone and keys. For me, it wasn't much more. Basically, checking that I had cash and my phone. In case a client called.

"Eighth Avenue or Seventh," I asked.

"Seventh." We walked east.

"Uptown or down?"

"Down."

We took the 2 train to Clark Street in Brooklyn Heights. I quickly found my bearings and led the way.

There is a timeless beauty in those quiet streets and graceful buildings. The exquisite views of lower Manhattan and the Statue of Liberty from the Promenade. I could live here.

We shopped for spices at Sahadi's on Atlantic Avenue, had a light lunch of potato pierogi at a Polish restaurant on Montague Street, bought chocolates in DUMBO. Walked back to Manhattan across the Brooklyn Bridge, one of the wonders of my world. The stunning, larger than life skyline of lower Manhattan loomed closer with each step, a perfect counterpoint to the gentle, poetic view from the Heights. A young couple admired the view mid-bridge. She had a short mop of curly red hair and with her red summer dress made me think of a grown-up *Annie*. The sight of them with their arms around each other reminded me of Patrick and me on our first date on the Staten Island Ferry. I felt certain then that we'd be together forever. Be happy forever. As Jonathan and I walked past the couple I fought an urge to warn the girl that nothing lasts.

"Let's have soup dumplings at Joe's Shanghai," Jonathan said when we left the bridge. We passed a Chinese wedding party. The splashes of gold, red and purple clothing were like flowers on trash-strewn streets.

We had to wait outside the restaurant on Pell Street until a table opened up inside.

"Why do you stay with Dad," Jonathan asked. I looked at him, surprised at the unexpected intensity in his voice.

Here we were, on this narrow little street, leaning against the wall of the restaurant, waiting to be called inside. Maybe it was the perfect place for a long overdue conversation and my son was old enough for this conversation.

"First it was promises to stop his, um, indiscretions. Then the recession. I wasn't making money, not for a year and a half. Two. Your father's business slowed down, too, but not by much. Plus there was no no-fault divorce in New York until 2010."

"It's 2015, Mom. I was the reason Dad used, wasn't I? Wait until Jonathan goes to college." I nodded "It's so stupid, that way of thinking," he said. "How do parents not get that there's nothing worse for a kid than living with a shitty marriage?" I looked at him in surprise. Lots of worse things crossed my mind. Starvation. Mudslides. Earthquakes. Mad Cow Disease. That flesh-eating thing.

"I know there are, sweetheart. Sex trafficking, the Syrian crisis."

"World hunger. Bedbugs. Remember 2011? That horrible summer with all the mattresses wrapped in plastic? When we even hesitated about going to the movies. So what's a divorce compared to all that," he said.

"You think bedbugs are worse than divorce?" I looked at him, both stunned and amused at his remark.

"I'm just saying, if a marriage is over, it's over. At least you tried. At least you have a choice."

At least we have you.

Our name was called and we were shown two seats that had just been vacated at a table for eight. A large round table with a lazy Susan in the center, plates half-filled with food. Our table mates nodded, ignored us, continued their meal. We ordered soup dumplings, pan-friend noodles with everything, and dry sautéed string beans, but my appetite was gone. It was almost three o'clock and the restaurant was beginning to empty out. I waited until most of our tablemates had gone, not that any of them would have been the slightest bit interested in our conversation.

"I once met with a divorce attorney," I said. "In 2008, soon after the election." Jonathan seemed surprised. He was even more surprised to learn that my decision to see a lawyer occurred following an Obama call party. "Linetta, she's the lawyer, told me to think about a legal separation until no-fault divorce became legal. That it could become really ugly otherwise. Your father refused the separation. It was a terrible time. The market was dead because of the recession, so I had plenty of time to be depressed."

"Tell me about it," Jonathan said.

"I know, honey. I must have been a misery to live with. And I still have those moments. But I'm almost back now. I can feel it."

"So could everyone at the party, Mom. You were magnificent. Your strength was there for everyone to see." He paused.

"Especially Dad." I looked at my son and nodded.

"That strength came from anger. I have a fight ahead of me and I'm ready for it. Finally. But even now, no-fault's not the complete answer. There's the house. Your father won't leave it and I can't afford to buy him out, not with what it's worth in this market." I put my hand on Jonathan's arm. The sinewy muscles startled me. I wondered how far he and Maggie had gone. Then wondered why I wondered. "And I don't know if I could ever leave that house."

"It's just a house," he said.

CHAPTER FIVE

The real beginning of the end of my marriage, 2008

The first time I was an actual witness to Patrick's wandering eye was at an Obama call party in the West Village. He and I had gone together, to a terraced duplex penthouse a short walk from our house. We signed in with the doorman and rode the elevator filled with other volunteers. There was an excited energy that permeated the atmosphere the moment we'd stepped into the lobby and only grew as the evening progressed. A steady stream of volunteers streamed into the massive, exquisitely appointed apartment.

We signed in at a table that read Obama for America and were handed a prompt sheet with instructions on how to make our calls. We took call sheets for swing states. I had Indiana, Florida and Ohio. I didn't pay much attention to Patrick, I was too busy looking around. Ahead of us was an enormous kitchen, the island laden with platters of food. Nova on black bread, small sandwiches, large fruit bowls, crudités. Sparkling and flat water, soda, cookies, miniature brownies. A catered call party with enough class to match Obama's.

Every inch of the wide staircase leading up to the bedrooms was occupied by people of all ages looking at their call sheets, speaking on their cell phones. In the living room, dining and den every chair, love seat, inch of sofa space was taken up. Almost every spare section of brick wall on each of the three enormous terraces had people standing or sitting against it for back support as they made their calls. It was an amazing, exhilarating sight. A delirium of dedicated Obama fans. I found space against a brick wall that faced west, into the setting sun. Eventually, Patrick joined me.

"Did you ever see anything like this, El?" He was looking at his prompt sheet. "You go first. You're better with this kind of thing." So I called the first name on my Indiana list. My first attempt hung up on me. The next few calls went fairly well.

"Hi, I'm calling for Ob..."

"Shhh," said the woman in Indiana. "I'm a yes, but my husband can't know."

Another one answered, "Okay, yes. We can. Gotta go."

"Die, bitch, die,"

Patrick had some luck with Florida and seemed extremely proud of himself. After he finished Florida but before he began Ohio he volunteered to bring us some food. I continued with my calls. And continued. I finally went to look for him. He was standing between the living room and den, his back to me. When he turned his head I saw that he was laughing. It was the way he was laughing. That flirty way he held his head. He stepped to the side as a tall, slender young man in cargo shorts walked past Patrick and the person he was with. If it hadn't been for that young man I might not have seen the voluptuous redhead in a pale blue sundress who was the cause of my husband's apparent delight. That was when I finally admitted to myself what I'd long suspected, when things fell into place with a visual certainty I hadn't seen before. I felt faint. Mortified. I looked around to see if there were any familiar faces. Clients, friends, anyone. Amazingly, gratefully, there weren't. I held on to the fat armrest of a nearby loveseat to steady myself and took a few deep breaths.

"It's overwhelming, isn't it," the woman on the nearest half asked me.

"It certainly is," I said, anger slowly replacing my momentary mortification. Not only was Patrick disrespecting me, he was disrespecting Obama.

Maybe it wasn't a new conquest. Maybe the redhead in the blue dress was an old lover and she and Patrick were rekindling their lust. Laughing at how much fun they'd had and could have again.

I looked away from them to all the other people surrounding me. Such devotion, excitement, joy for the upcoming election. I'd felt it, too. Now I felt like hurting someone. I had to leave. I handed in my call sheets and walked home, knowing with certainty that Patrick's bowling nights and late-night emergency appointments had been anything but. When he came home not so much later that evening and said he'd looked everywhere for me, was worried about me, I told him he disgusted me and never ever try to touch me again. At that moment I hated him more than I ever had. I could have killed him. It wasn't the first time, nor would it be the last that I had such thoughts, but this time we were in the kitchen and the rack with its array of chef knives was within arm's reach.

If only that feeling had manifested itself earlier, it might have overtaken the depression I suffered on and off over the years of our marriage, a depression sometimes so unbearable that I wanted to disappear. Felt myself, the essence of me, begin to disappear. Melt from the outside in until I was a blob, then nothing at all. Invisible. The vanishing of Ellie. During those times I willed my mind to follow my body, willed my thoughts to disappear into nothingness. A melancholy so profound that it eventually began to comfort, like a second home in a serene glade. Not a big, imposing brownstone, but a cozy, rose-covered cottage that embraced me in warmth. Through it all I continued to work, make deals, build a client base. As though a part of that ghostly figure operated on its own. A hidden me, who emerged to make deals.

I loved making deals. I loved seeing properties, representing them, selling them, making money, but then I went home and slid into something else, someone else who was dead inside. What began to bring me back was the financial crash. Work slowed, then stopped. Lehmann Brothers, the banks going under, all the hell that followed gave me time I hadn't had in years. It proved both my enemy and my salvation. My enemy because it gave me endless hours in which to wallow in misery and my salvation, because self-pity eventually became boring. When, in the midst of the desert that real estate had become, I received a phone call from a former client, it proved the very boost I needed. I'd shown him several properties a few years back. He hadn't bought then but promised one day that he would. His moment was the recession and he grabbed it. He knew of two distressed multi-unit buildings in Queens and wanted them both. The only thing I had to do was represent him and pocket the commission checks. I never even saw the properties. There I was, in a dead market, seated at a conference table drinking tea and being handed a commission check for slightly over six hundred thousand dollars, sixty-five percent of which would be mine. I opened a bank account apart from the joint account with Patrick, a bank into which I would put all future commissions. I might have been depressed, but I was nobody's fool. I bought two small one-bedroom condos in East Harlem, renovated and rented them to tenants with impeccable references and credits. I sold them a few years after the market picked up and almost tripled my investment, and Patrick knew nothing of it.

Patrick remained acceptably busy during those lean years, bonding and laminating the teeth of Muffy and Buffy and their beautiful, always perfectly groomed private school children. He took care of all the household bills, knowing that the real estate market was on hiatus and unknowing of my new bank account. Betsy remained busy with her almost-famous and already famous clients, cleaning their apartments two and three times a week. The men who frequented the salon in which Louisa worked continued to get waxed, buffed, polished, massaged. I had the luxury of them filling in for me with Jonathan whenever I asked, so in all the years they lived with us I never raised their minimal rent. They had become more important to me than my husband.

I slowly and steadily began to feel not only stronger but also completely in control. One day when I had an unexpected set-back I was able to easily recover, such as the day I'd gone to see a martial arts triple-feature in a Chinatown theatre with no arms on the seats. I'd felt I could kick anybody's ass. On my way back home I stopped at a café. I was the only customer. Hi, I'm Abdul, the thin, young waiter had said. I'll be your server today. He bowed. I smiled. I ordered mint tea. He brought it to the table after it had steeped just long enough, held the teapot high and poured it into the small glass in a lovely arc.

The smell of mint.

I told Abdul I had a son about his age. He said his mother lived in Beirut with four cats, one of which had three legs. He missed her. Because I seemed nice he felt he could be honest with me.

"Of course you can," I said.

"You seem a bit fragile," he said. "If I wasn't alone here I'd walk you home and make sure you were safe." I would have preferred that he punch me in the stomach. His unexpected concern and kindness, my pathetically obvious vulnerability, cut through me and threatened my new-found strength. Tears stung, threatened to spill over. Stupid tears that had started to show up during my bouts of self-pity. Sometimes they just showed up. During dinner, in the shower, talking to a buyer, a seller, receiving a commission check. Like uninvited guests, they came and they left when they felt like it. I told people it was eye drops, an allergy, ocular sensitivity. The last vestiges of a few unhappy years and nothing I couldn't handle. Abdul handed me a few small, beige, recycled napkins. They said "recycled" in proud red letters. Then he brought me a piece of cake. It was yellow, with fudge icing.

"Thank you. I love this kind of cake," I said. "Like an old-fashioned birthday cake. But it's huge. Share it with me." So he went to get another fork and sat across the small table from me. I took a bite. He took a bite. We looked at each other.

"It's stale, isn't it?" he said.

"Yes."

And it was over, that moment of vulnerability. Abdul was sweet, but he was just a kid. What did he know of life? I walked home, powerful again. In control. I could do anything.

One day, as I walked home from the Angelica Theatre, I began to worry that I'd forget the films I'd seen and began a mental list. *Ninotchka. The Girl from Paris. Le Corbeau. Mongol.* So many titles to remember. So many scenes. The actors. The settings. It became imperative to write them down. I entered a stationery store on Sixth Avenue and bought thirteen identical slender notebooks with red covers. I was going to buy an even dozen but felt sorry for the last one sitting all alone on the shelf, so I bought it, plus a box of pens. I agonized over what color ink to use, wavering between purple and turquoise for so long that I bought a box of each plus one of black. I could use different colored pens for different lists. I began what would become a ritual. Ellie's Lists of Important Information. This is how I began.

Notebook No. 1: Turquoise ink.

Page 1: Films I've seen with actors' and actresses' names as I remembered them.

Page 6: Films I wanted to see, with an asterisk next to the ones I had to see.

Page 9: Cities, towns, states and countries I visited.

Page 11: Cities, towns, states and countries I plan to visit.

Page 13: Cities, towns, states and countries I will never visit.

Page 14: Teas I like: Hu Kwa, Earl Grey, Russian Caravan, Typhoo.

Page 15: Albinoni, Bach, Couperin, Dieter von Dittersdorf, Elgar, fuck you Patrick.

Page 17: Interesting fact # one. If you take away the "at" in Patrick it becomes prick.

Page 20: Azalea, Begonia, Carnation, Daffodil, Edelweiss, Fuchsia, Gardenia.

Hyacinth, Iris, Jasmine. Blank space for K. Lily of the valley. Marigold.

Narcissus. Opium poppy. Petunia. Queen Anne's Lace. Roses. Sunflowers.

Tiger Lily. Umbrella plant, Violet, Wildflower, X won't stop me, Yellow roses, Zinnia.

Page 21: Lawyers.

I felt positively euphoric when I completed the flowers list. I knew it was out of proportion to the minimal feat but it was in fact a major steppingstone to serious control of my marital situation. When Patrick came home from work that night before heading out for 'bowling,' I greeted him by saying I'd decided on an attorney. I didn't say 'from my list' because I didn't want him to know about them.

"We already have an attorney. Sam." But I didn't need Sam. I needed Linetta Wilton. She had been on my short list of possibilities until Patrick came home and walked into the kitchen. Something about the weight of his foot on the wooden floor reminded me of her, not in a bad way. Just a way.

"A divorce attorney."

"Oh." Patrick sat down. "What do you want me to do, El? Tell me. I'll do it."

"You've already done it," I said. "With everyone but me, for years. Not that I give a damn anymore. I hate your guts."

"No you don't."

"Yes I do." But at that exact moment I didn't hate him. I just wished he hadn't come home.

Linetta had been a client of mine and was one of the smartest and toughest people I knew. It had taken me over two years to find a home to suit her exacting tastes. I finally found it for her, a two-bedroom upper duplex in a Federal style house on East 7th Street. Beamed ceilings, wide plank floors, brick walls, fireplace, and a deck overlooking a garden shared by the owner of the lower two floors. It was one of the few partnership arrangements left in the city and I'd had to track down one of the absentee partners for a meeting with the others. No one knew exactly where he was but one of the partners thought he had the ex-wife's number. He found it, called her, she thought he might be in Madagascar. That was a blow until she called back to say no, what was wrong with her head? She meant Michigan. Madagascar was last year. The partner came back from fishing in the Upper Peninsula and the deal was done. All cash, because mortgages weren't available for partnerships. They still aren't, if, in fact, there are any more partnerships like that still in the city.

Later that afternoon I called Linetta. No-fault divorce was now legal in New York and had been for a while, but the timing never seemed right to start proceedings. Jonathan was in middle school, then high school. The economy showed faint signs of improvement along with me, then boom years returned. I became busy again, slowly at first and then crazy busy, able to push back the reality of my marriage until the night of the party.

"Whenever you're ready," Linetta said.

CHAPTER SIX

Back to the Present

Valeria called to confirm my visit the following day. She seemed anxious until I assured her I would be there.

Friday was extremely warm. I dressed in a floral cotton halter dress with large side pockets for my keys, phone, and cash, shocking pink sandals that I refer to as Schiaparelli pink, and a large-brimmed straw hat, then walked west to Greenwich Street and south to Jane Street. Twelve minutes, door to door, walking slowly.

I was familiar with her building, having almost sold one of the first units when it converted from a rental to a co-op in the late 1980s. The eight-story building had little exterior personality. A small, drab entry led to an ornate birdcage elevator whose metal doors had to be operated manually. I stepped in, pulled the door shut and pressed the button for the top floor. The slow elevator opened onto a small private hallway lined with bold-colored paintings. Colorful scarves draped over a hat rack. Valeria stood in the doorway to the left, a wide smile on her face. She was wearing a knee-length black jersey dress and pale pink ballet slippers and looked almost ethereal, with her delicate build and pale features.

Like my sister.

Like my mother.

An enormous, sun-flooded square corner living room. An oversized sofa strewn with kilim pillows in the center. Windows with wide views south and west with a vast swath of the Hudson River. White, polished concrete floors glowed in a small patch with washed out splotches of pink and orange that seemed almost otherworldly in the sunlight. I've seen views from countless apartments over the years, but these were exceptional. Expansive, poetic views of lower Manhattan that captured the Jefferson Clock Tower, church steeples, small boats and large yachts on the river. For so many years the only boats on the Hudson had been garbage-filled barges looking for homes in other states. The piers along this part of the Hudson, until fairly recently frequented by dubious characters congregating on rotted wood, were now recreational wonderlands. Bicycle paths ran parallel to a wide swath of verdant lawn that led to the water. My gaze went from that to the rooftops and water towers. On the roof deck of a small building, a woman with long white hair took off her bikini top and oiled her well-muscled body. Next to her a long, thin bald man lying on a matching lounge chair reached out his hand to her.

Valeria led me to a bar stool at the kitchen island and took the lid off a medium sized cobalt blue Le Creuset pot.

"*Soupe au pistou,*" she said.

She served it in small bowls.

"It's delicious." I said, taking a sip. It was also lovely to look at, with the vegetables all cut to the same small sizes.

"I love to cook," she said. "I work as a caterer."

We talked easily. Silly things. I was enjoying myself. Enjoying her company. Taking a certain pleasure when I looked at her face and remembered Sally. It had begun to give me an unexpected sense of comfort. I almost mentioned her to Valeria but something held me back. I wasn't ready to share. Instead

I thought of the endless mailings to countless buildings I sent over the years, to the owners. This building. "Kevin Drake used to own this apartment. I met him years ago at the White Horse Tavern."

"That's odd," Valeria said. She had unwrapped a loaf of dessert bread, was about to slice it when she paused, arm poised mid-air, the knife steady in her manicured hand. Pale pink polish. Pale blue eyes that seemed to stare right through me. It was unsettling. "You know Kevin," she said again. "That's remarkable." But it wasn't. Downtown had been a small market in the early nineties when I'd met him. So many years ago, when I was just starting out in real estate. Before the condo conversions and new buildings, downtown brokers knew each other and we knew all the properties. There weren't that many. Kevin had been Board President of the building at the time and I'd needed him to give me information about the mechanicals, for a potential sale.

"He's a writer, isn't he?"

"Yes. That's all he does, write, write, write. Romance novels under the name Karen Drake." She poured the tea. Sliced thin pieces of the loaf with almost surgical precision and placed them on a small platter. Gave each of us a matching dessert plate with two slices of zucchini bread loaded with bitter-sweet chocolate chips.

"It's delicious," I said. I could have devoured the entire thing.

"I know. I sell it. Kevin can eat a loaf at a time. It's disgusting." Her blonde head tilted, as though deciding whether to continue. Nodded, her mind made up. "He left here, maybe two months ago. He had a deadline for his latest book and said I made it impossible for him to concentrate. That there's something wrong with me for not allowing him to work, among other things." She looked at me and in a split second the expression on her face changed from annoyance to unexpected vulnerability. Her lower lip trembled. I almost reached out to comfort her but stopped myself. Wondered what I was doing there.

"These views are amazing, aren't they," she said. "They make me feel safe. And that's what's important, isn't it, Ellie? To be safe."

"What's wrong," I asked, but she shook her head. I looked around the living room, noticed things I hadn't earlier. A tall, thin bookcase filled with books. A spinet piano that seemed almost lost in the large room.

"Do you play?" I asked.

"No. It's Kevin's. Do you?"

"I used to." There's a piano in our house, in the neglected garden apartment. Untuned and unused for years, but for many years it had given me much pleasure. Valeria stood and took me by the hand, walked me over.

"Play something. Please. For me."

"It's been so long. I know nothing from memory."

"Oh, that's no problem," Valeria said. She opened the piano bench to show two piles of music, one of classical compilations and another of popular sheet music. I rummaged for something familiar. Something easy. I ignored the collections of Bach and Chopin, the familiar red bound book of Favorite Classic Pieces and took out a handful of popular songs in their brightly colored covers. "Deep Purple." I lifted it from the rest and placed it on the stand, sat down and tentatively played the right-hand chords. The left. I looked at Valeria and she smiled, a shy smile that touched me in spite of myself. Chords came back to me and I began to play, tentatively. She sat next to me and surprised me by singing along as I played.

I felt a strange, discomforting intimacy as she sat close to me on the narrow bench. The moment I was finished with the piece I slid off and walked back to the kitchen, wanting to leave, not understanding why I was there.

Valeria began to clear the few dishes we'd used.

"Feel free to look around while I clean up," she offered and the broker in me couldn't refuse. I walked past the kitchen to a short hallway. On the right was a large, windowed bathroom with separate tub and shower. To the left, a room outfitted with an L-shaped desk that held both a red IBM Selectric typewriter and a MacBook Air. Neat piles of paper everywhere. A single long bookshelf overhead was filled with multiple copies of romance books, all by Karen Drake. The master bedroom had a king-sized bed and a long, low Art Deco dresser that held a single empty silver frame.

I walked back to the living room. Valeria was sitting on the sofa. I walked over to her and thanked her for a lovely lunch. "Call if you need help in finding a place."

"Oh no. Please don't go," Valeria said. But I had already walked out the open front door into the small hallway. She followed me, blocked the elevator so that I couldn't reach for the button. I was forced against the far wall. The intimate space that had felt so welcoming when I'd arrived now felt claustrophobic. Thick walls, cement floors, high ceilings. No neighbors within hearing distance, an ancient elevator the only escape but for fire stairs and Valeria blocking my access to it. There was no reason to fear her, yet I had a growing sense of unease.

"Come back, Ellie. Please. I have something to tell you."

There was something so pleading in her tone that I reluctantly followed her back inside. The look of relief on her face made me feel proud of myself. Even to myself I thought that was a strange response, but that's what I felt.

"Kevin's coming home today," she said. "That's why I need you to stay, at least until he arrives. I can't do this alone." I looked at the clock on her stove. One-thirty. I'd been there over an hour and there was no reason to stay any longer, except for her plea. There was also no reason not to stay. Really, none at all. "I don't think he'll be too much longer. He's driving down from Maine and he would have left early enough to beat Friday afternoon traffic. When he left here he was so furious with me. I know he had every right to be. I threw a vase at him so how can I blame him, but what if he's still mad? Look."

She pointed to the washed-out stains on the white floor in front of us. "That's blood. I tried to wash it out but it just got a bit faded and mushed around. But it's actually lovely when the late afternoon sun hits it at a certain angle. Anyway, that's where he bled. He needed fifteen stitches. He had to go to Beth

Israel since St. Vincent's closed and he acted like even that was my fault. I mean the stitches were but not Beth Israel." I tuned out her nervous talking and sat on a stool by the kitchen counter, let the hypnotically lovely views calm me. My garden had nothing on these views and I wondered what it would be like to live in such a place, where the city beckoned, its arms open wide. My beautiful brownstone sheltered. Maybe it was time for me to break free of its hold. "After the hospital he came back here and packed his bag. I've hardly heard a word from him since. Just this."

Valeria's voice startled me out of my thoughts. I watched as she opened a drawer, pulled something out and pushed a postcard in front of my face. It had a large red lobster on the front and a few words on back. Home Friday afternoon. K.

"That's all I've heard the entire time he's been gone. It arrived early this week. Monday. I've dreaded each day as it passed. He wants me out of here, Ellie, and I have nowhere else to go." She looked at me and then shrugged. "Well, maybe somewhere. I'll let you know."

"He wants you out because you threw the vase?" She looked at me as though I were crazy, even though who could blame him.

"I threw the vase because he wants me out."

She was visibly upset. The terse message Kevin had mailed from Maine would have upset me, too, though I understood that when you throw a vase at someone's head you can't expect much more than a few abrupt words on a lobster postcard.

"You need time, you know, even with rentals," I said. "There's credit checks, paperwork." She nodded. She knew. Okay. I was a broker and she was about to be homeless but she didn't need me for anything other than a buffer between her and Kevin.

"I'm going to make a fruit salad," she said.

"I'll help," I said, relieved to have something to do while we waited.

"No, you just relax." So I sat on the bar stool and took turns looking out the window and at Valeria as she quickly, expertly washed, cut, sliced and filled a large bowl with melons, mangos, pineapple, berries, cherries, all at a perfect point of ripeness. When we heard the groan of the elevator door she wiped her hand on a dish towel and looked at me.

"Oh God, that's him," she said. "I'm so glad you're here."

Men's voices. Plural. Footsteps. Valeria came to stand at my side, her grip tight on my arm as we watched a tall, broad man with reddish-brown hair and grey beard enter the room, a large duffle bag in each hand. He dropped them on the floor. I assumed that the bag slung across his chest held his computer because that one he placed down gently. He glanced at me in surprise before his eyes rested briefly on Valeria. Her face paled when he refused to move toward her. Her eyes blinked away tears. Bastard, I thought. He could have at least acknowledged her but he turned his attention to me. "I know you," he said.

"From years ago," I said, standing up, wondering why I did. Annoyed at myself for doing so. "Ellie Allington. You told me all about the boiler." He laughed.

"God-damn. The broker. You sure had a lot of questions back then." He glanced at Valeria and then back to me. "Not that it's not a pleasure to see you after so many years, but what's going on? Valeria trying to sell the place out from under me?" He continued to ignore her and I was glad for her sake that I'd stayed. This would be hard on anybody. He walked past her into the kitchen. Called out. "Tony, c'mon in." That's when I saw the man who had arrived with him, who had been standing behind him in the narrow hallway. Who now entered the loft.

He was magnificent.

Tony. I wanted to be his Maria. He walked towards us, long legs in tight black jeans. Bronzed skin, a chiseled face with high cheekbones and long, almond-shaped eyes. Green eyes that were a shock. Dark hair brushed back from a wide forehead. He resembled Jimmy Smits. Gregory Peck. Jack Palance but handsome. How was that even possible? He gave Valeria a hug. I wanted it to be me. I could almost feel myself in his arms.

"Hi, gorgeous," he said to Valeria. Even his voice. Deep and mellow. I wanted to thank him for being so decent. I wanted to take my clothes off and straddle him, stunned at myself, at my overwhelming attraction to him.

"Antonio. I didn't know you were with Kevin," Valeria said.

"I joined him for a week after he finished his manuscript."

"I'm so glad to see you. Stay for some food. There's plenty," she said. She turned to me. "You, too, Ellie. Please." She looked at me, eyes pleading. It was an awkward situation, like a surprise double date where anything might happen and none of it good.

"No thanks. I'll be on my way," he said. "It was a long drive. See you, pal," he called to Kevin. "Thanks for the fishing trip."

"Yeah, buddy. Good times," Kevin said. "And good to see you after all these years, Ellie. Still in the business?" I nodded. I needed to pee but the timing felt awkward. I could wait until I was home. Antonio caught my eye and I nodded. I hugged Valeria goodbye, shook Kevin's hand and walked out of the loft. Antonio grabbed his bag from the hallway and we took the few steps to the elevator. He pulled the door shut, pressed the ground floor button.

"That was rough," Antonio said. Then he looked at me as though seeing me for the first time. He seemed startled. I could barely take my eyes off him.

"I feel guilty leaving her," I said.

"Nothing we can do. Where are you headed?"

"Fourteenth Street."

"I'm headed north, too."

We walked a few blocks in silence. When my hand accidently brushed against his it felt like a jolt of electricity. At the northern end of Greenwich Street, where it meets Gansevoort and Ninth Avenue, I stopped. "This used to be my favorite little section in the city," I said, because it was true. "Right here. It was magnificent. Now the soul is gone."

"So is the crime," he said. "But I agree."

We walked the few blocks north to West 14th Street, stopped in front of the Apple store. I said I lived across Ninth Avenue and held out my hand. He took it but didn't shake. He held it.

"Have lunch with me," he said, his green eyes meeting mine. "I haven't eaten since early this morning. I'd love your company."

Your company, he said. Not simply company. I'd done almost nothing but eat while I was with Valeria, but I nodded. Our hands disengaged and we looked at each other. Looked away. Looked again. It was like *Sleepless in Seattle* at the very end of the movie when Sam is alone on top of the Empire State Building and Meg Ryan finds him and then Tom Hanks shows up, frantically looking for his son. This was kind of the same, without a kid or a backpack or the Empire State Building. Tony asked me if Old Homestead was okay for lunch. I said sure. I would have gone to lunch with him in Mongolia.

The restaurant, an old downtown standby, is a steakhouse about a five-minute walk from my house, but I hadn't eaten there in years. Antonio obviously had. The waiters greeted him like a long-lost brother. One of them showed us to a table toward the rear and brought over menus. I excused myself to use the ladies' room. When I walked back to the table and saw him watching me, I felt I was walking into my future.

I'd forgotten how warm and welcoming the restaurant was. I felt I was exactly where I was supposed be at that moment. A Gershwin song, leather seats, subdued conversations from other diners. I looked at Antonio.

"This is nice," I said, a smile spreading across my face.

"She smiles," he said.

"Very rarely. You're lucky to catch the moment." I looked at him and could barely look away. I thought then that I would never tire of looking at his face. "Do you think things will work out between them? Valeria and Kevin?"

"Not a chance. All he talked about on the drive back was how it was time for her to move out."

"She has nowhere to go."

"Then she probably shouldn't have split his head open."

"Probably not," I agreed.

"You look a bit like Ida Lupino," he said. I thought back to movies with her.

"I can only remember *High Sierra*. She's dead. But she was gorgeous."

"I agree." He was looking at me as he spoke. He had said, in so many words, that he thought I was gorgeous. Oh my God. My cheeks felt as though they were on fire.

"Is my face red?"

"Yes."

"Well, it's not menopause," I said. He laughed again but I didn't. Menopause was right around the corner for me, but then our eyes met again and held and there was no more laughing or flushed cheeks or anything but the sense that time had stopped. There was something happening and I could swear it wasn't just to me. It was as though I were being pulled underwater, out of my depth, yet I wasn't afraid.

Is this how it happens? The coup de foudre? I closed my eyes, counted silently to ten. I opened them and looked at him. I lost my heart to him at that exact moment.

*

He had recently retired from the New York Police Department and celebrated by spending the week at Kevin's cabin in Penobscot. They hiked and fished, two childhood friends from Alphabet City. I watched his mouth as he spoke, realized what I was doing and made myself look away.

"You don't look like a cop," I finally said.

"I can try harder," he grinned. He reached for his wallet and handed me a card. Antonio Wu. Detective First Grade, retired.

"Detective. Okay, I believe you. Did you catch a lot of bad guys?"

"Too many to count," he said. He took a bite of his hamburger. I'd never seen anyone look sexy eating a hamburger before.

It had been so long, years since I'd felt even the slightest stirring of desire and what I felt toward him then was not slight. I pushed the salad away and tried to quiet my thoughts. My feelings.

He had coffee, I had tea. I didn't want this time with him to end. He insisted on paying for lunch. We walked outside and again he reached for my hand. I smiled inside. It was as though I'd entered some new universe where confusion, peace and the hint of happiness met. He walked me home. I wished I lived miles away, to have more time with him. I ascended the bottom stoop and turned to him. Our faces were level. Kiss level. He looked at the house and then at me.

"You have this whole place?"

"We have two rent stabilized tenants," I said, instantly regretting that I'd said 'we.'

He turned to walk away. Turned back.

"I'd like..." he said.

"So would I."

He put his hand to my cheek before leaving. I sank down on the stoop and watched him walk west. I put my hand to my face, the way he had done and sat for a few minutes before I pulled his card from my bag. His name, his status. His phone number. I tried to fight the urge to call him but couldn't help myself. I punched in the numbers, wondered what I was doing. Knew exactly what I was doing. I thanked him for lunch.

"My pleasure." I wanted to keep hearing his voice. Hold on to the feeling of being alive. Hold on to him. Be held by him.

There was an uncomfortable silence before he said, "this has to be up to you."

"I know."

.

CHAPTER SEVEN

I had a closing scheduled for a prewar Gramercy Park apartment. My buyers, Dan and Susan, had been having conflicting reactions during the entire process. Dan refused to submit the required financial papers and back-up required when purchasing a co-op apartment in Manhattan. The Board Package. When he finally left it in my office to go over, he left out personal information on the Purchase Application sheet. I couldn't submit an incomplete package. Finally, Susan hand-delivered a complete package along with copies for each of the Board members. I spend several hours going over everything, making sure their financial information was complete and matched the Asset and Liability statement. I called a messenger to deliver it to the Managing Agent. About three weeks later, after they'd been approved and had a date for the closing, I called Susan to let her know. She told me she'd forged Dan's name on everything.

The morning of the closing we had the walk-through. Dan ran the faucets in the kitchen and both bathrooms, set the timer on his iPhone for fifteen minutes and let the shower run the entire time. He popped popcorn in the microwave, checked the lightbulbs in all the fixtures and happily found a single burned out bulb in a bedroom closet. He insisted it be replaced before the closing, which was in half an hour. I left him, his mortified wife and the selling broker in the apartment and went to a local hardware store to buy a dozen lightbulbs. Then the four of us shared a cab to the Managing Agent's midtown office. I paid the cabbie before Dan had a chance to have another little tantrum.

At the conference table he pretended to read every single word of every single paper, even though that's what he and Susan had a lawyer for. When he wasn't reluctantly signing he sat with his arms crossed on his chest like an adolescent girl shielding budding breasts. Susan, his trust fund wife, sat through it all gripping her Mont Blanc pen. I gave their marriage two years. Or maybe through lunch.

"Tell me I'm not the only schmuck buying in this market," he said.

"You're not the only schmuck," Mona, the closing agent, said. Every now and then she took a pile of papers, left to make copies, came back. The sellers, Melissa and Michael, were expecting their third child. Any minute. About halfway through the closing when Melissa started periodically making little gaspy sounds I began to watch the clock on my iPhone. Five minutes between grimaces and grunts.

"Oh, God," she said at the exact moment the pay-off banker arrived. "My water broke!" She looked at Michael. "Let's go."

It was interesting to see how differently people reacted. Dan and Susan looked frightened, the bankers horrified. The attorneys looked at each other and shrugged. Only Mona, the closing agent, seemed relaxed.

"Should I call a car service?" she asked calmly. "An ambulance?"

"We've got a driver downstairs," Melissa said. "I'll call the doctor." She called on her cell phone and left a message for her doctor that they were on their way to Lenox Hill Hospital. Then she and her husband signed everything they needed to sign, she leaned her arms against the table and struggled to get up. Michael stood behind her, hands under her arms. It must have tickled. "Honey," she said to Michael, "give someone the deposit slip for our check, please." Surprisingly, it was Dan who volunteered to deposit the check into their account.

"Are you kidding me?" Melissa said. "Anyone but you. But thank you." It was an entirely useless exchange as everyone understood their attorney would deposit the five million dollar check, minus closing costs, into her and Michael's account. Dan's face paled and I thought he might cry. I had the feeling that he grew up a little bit there in the conference room. Like oh, wow, it's not all about me.

I'd worked hard for this deal, showed Susan and Dan more than ninety apartments over almost two years before they bought Melissa and Michael's Gramercy Park co-op. I felt a sudden sympathy for Dan. He was a young man married to a wealthy wife. He needed to prove himself worthy. And the truth was, the market was overpriced and changing. Real estate prices had gone through the roof since the recovery of the 2008 recession. I looked at Dan and thought of Jonathan. This could be him one day, buying his first house, though doubtfully with a trust fund wife. I almost wanted to hug Dan, tell him that everything would be fine even though I had no idea how things would be. Look how my happily-ever-after life was going.

When the piles of paper were finally signed and placed in neatly stacked piles, when I held the hundred fifty thousand dollar commission check in my hand, I did hug Dan. "It's a beautiful home," I said. "Be happy." I walked down Fifth Avenue the mile or so to my office to drop off the check and then went home. Ten minutes after I arrived, Patrick texted. Did I want to go out to dinner? I thanked him but said I was planning to watch *Traviata*.

"Again?"

"Zeffirelli's a genius."

Patrick walked through the front door just as Violetta was dying. I hated him for that. I replayed the last half hour while he went to the kitchen. Heard him open and close the refrigerator and the cabinets looking for something to eat. After she died again I joined him. He was seated at the table looking at an old *People* magazine. It was the top one in a large pile that I'd gathered from the garden apartment, home to large collections of old magazines and outgrown clothes brought up to either recycle or donate. I sat down. He leaned over to kiss me before I was able to stop him.

"Just on the cheek, El," he said. He pointed to a photo. "Look how sad Katie Holmes looks here."

"Who can blame her? What she went through was so brave." I paused, remembering her flight from Tom Cruise. "Heroic, when you think about it."

"Yeah, I guess." Patrick turned the page. "I don't get this woman." He pointed to Victoria Beckham. "She looks like an anorexic alien."

"She's stunning." I said. "I saw her on a talk show once. She was funny and smart."

"Really? She's funny?"

"She was that time. Maybe it was the only time in her life, but I liked her." He reached over and grabbed my hand.

"You have to give me a chance, honey."

"No I don't," I said. "I gave you lots of them. Years. I can't do it anymore; I can't live like this. It's time for you to move out. Jonathan thinks so, too."

"That's not going to happen and I don't believe Jonathan feels the way you just said. But his opinion in this doesn't matter here. He'll be living uptown for the next four years, so it's you and me."

"You think this marriage has a chance? With you screwing half of Manhattan!" I felt anger take hold as intrusive, painful memories surface. "I'll never let you humiliate me again, or hurt me, or disappoint me. Or touch me. We're done." I grabbed the People issue and threw it on the kitchen floor. I ripped Victoria Beckham's face by accident. "I'm sorry," I said to her face.

"That's decent of you, to at least have some regret."

"What are you talking about?"

He stood up and placed his hands on my shoulders. Rubbed them. It felt good, which annoyed me. I had only myself to blame for not kicking him out the night of the party. He would have been shamed into leaving. Stupid stupid stupid. I left the kitchen and walked out to the garden. Lay on a chaise longue. He followed. Lay on a neighboring chair. "I deserve better than you," I said. I closed my eyes against the sun and let it burn into me until I felt it through my clothes, let its heat burn away some of my anger. But he didn't give me a chance. He knelt at my side.

"I love you, sweetheart." I turned on my side and faced him, wanted to smack him. Sort of.

"What the hell do you know about me? What I waited for, from you. For years!" My voice cracked with remembered pain. "You think I can just forget about your women? Did you ever think about me when you were with them? That I have needs, too?" Tears of rage started down my face as I forced myself out of the chaise, went back to the kitchen, grabbed my bag and left the house. I walked up Tenth Avenue, not knowing if I was angrier with him or myself for letting our farce of a marriage go on for so many years. Years in which frustration, desire, hurt, pain had built up and destroyed not only my happiness but my belief in it.

My once comfortable world was crumbling. Even our enormous house had begun to feel claustrophobic with its almost open layout of the parlor floor. There was no private place just for me unless I locked myself in the small guest room I'd idiotically banished myself to.

No. Not true. There was the empty garden apartment. It was time to spend some money on renovation, clear it out, buy some furniture and have my own place.

Screw that. Why should I live downstairs with the tiny bath and kitchen instead of the sun-flooded duplex apartment I'd brought lovingly to life over the years? No matter the consequence, it was my time now and I would grab it. I sat on a bench and opened my bag. My hand touched the Art Deco card case inside it. I loved the feel of it. The size of it. I pulled it out and snapped it open. I had Antonio's number in my phone, had memorized it, but I took out his card and looked at it. My heart beat faster just holding it. I envisioned every feature of his face. His smile. The sound of his voice. For the second time since we first met, I called him.

"Hi," I said. "It's Ellie."

"I know. Caller ID. It's good to hear from you."

"Do you want to see me?"

"Yes."

"Then please wait for me. I'm almost ready."

CHAPTER EIGHT

The next morning, Patrick walked into the kitchen as I was having breakfast.

"Do you really hate me?" he asked.

"Sometimes. Sometimes I have despised you so much that I thought of killing you."

He poured himself some coffee and sat down.

"Now?" I shook my head. He smiled. "How would you do it?"

"It would depend on my mood. I could poison you or stab you to death while you're sleeping, or crush your head with something heavy, like that Le Creuset pot on the stove. Or we could try again."

"Move back to our room, honey. Please. I miss you." I took a bit of my omelet and chewed it before answering.

"How do you have time to miss me, with all your other women?"

"There haven't been that many." I pushed my plate away, pushed away from the table and stood to face him.

"What about Cindy? Was she the first, or can't you remember?"

"Who?"

"You know, Cindy with the bowling ball breasts. The one you went to Japan with. Who probably picked out that hideous kimono for me. Where was she on your roster?"

The lingering scent on his shirt collars when I took them to the cleaners. A phone number written on a scrap of paper. A barrette. A pair of pink thong panties the size of my pinky, wedged into a jacket pocket. I wasn't a snoop. That's not my thing, but when a person takes things to the cleaners, they check pockets. After the thong incident I not only stopped checking pockets, I stopped taking Patrick's clothes to the cleaners. If he wanted clean clothes, let him take care of them.

There were other signs, too. The way he looked at me the morning after, or when he averted his eyes. It took a while before I almost found humor in his attempts to hide guilt. The joviality. "Good morning, sweetheart. How's everything with my girl?"

"Which girl, Patrick?"

That question worked. Whether he looked away, or at me as though I were crazy, that was what I began to almost look forward to. I'd more or less conquered my depression and was able to handle almost anything thrown my way, so it was just idle conversation on my part that morning, while having a little breakfast chat with Patrick.

"Seriously. How many? But wait. Leave that for a minute. Was Cindy the first?" He seemed uncomfortable but didn't flinch. Didn't deny.

"I think she might have been."

"You think? The first of what? Several? A dozen? Several dozen?" I was feeling good. My voice hadn't ratcheted up at all. It stayed nice and even as I looked straight at him, his virile, handsome, rugged face with the hint of a five o'clock shadow even this early in the day.

"That's all over, I swear it."

"Not for me, it's not. You say you want me to move back into our bedroom. For what? Old times' sake?" Uh oh. I heard my voice become nasty. My words began to match. Feelings I'd fought long and hard flooded back in a rush. "Just so you know,

Patrick, our old times' sake never did anything for me. You must save your moves for your bimbos because they left me wanting. Worse off than if we'd done nothing, so leave me alone."

The hostility in my voice. The hatred seeping in. But when I saw the look on Patrick's face, I felt awful. The pain. His pain. He stood still and stared at me in disbelief, then turned and went to the fridge. He poured a glass of orange juice. Put two slices of seven-grain bread in the toaster. Waited for it pop to up. He sat down, his face neutral, his voice controlled as he talked to me standing across the table from him.

"They weren't bimbos, El. They were lovely, smart women."

"Cindy was a bimbo."

"Okay, Cindy. I slept with other women because you never had time for me. When you weren't out with clients you were on the computer, or on the phone, or setting up appointments. Or making deals, having meetings, checking out new listings. Every day, every night, for years. You weren't there for me and you weren't there for Jonathan, so give me a break. I don't know how I would have managed without Louisa and Betsy to help out." He spread three-berry jam from Sarabeth's Kitchen on his toast and ate almost half of it in one bite. "What was I supposed to do, jerk off every night?"

"You never complained about my commission checks," I said. "We needed them, for the house. And for when you expanded your practice."

"I needed you." He glanced at the large, round wall clock. "I can't have this conversation now. I have a nine-thirty."

He left and I was alone in the house with the truth. The mess of our marriage was as much my fault as it was Patrick's. How we got to this terrible place had been a long, seductive road. The years following the recession of the early nineties had given birth to an incredible period of change in downtown's real estate market. My market. Downtown had always been the poor cousin to uptown's real estate inventory and prices until it began to change mid-decade. At first just a few scattered condo conversions from former commercial and industrial buildings into large loft spaces. Countless others quickly followed. Each conversion was more luxurious than the last. Toto toilets, Italian kitchens. Doormen. Pools. Parking spaces. Yoga classes. Play areas for kids. It changed everything, brought uptown people downtown, increased prices so fast it was hard to keep up. The conversion of the Mercantile Building, home to Chelsea's Whole Foods Market and also for a while to Katie Holmes and Suri, saw prices rise at least a dozen times. More. Who kept track? Who wanted to? It was hectic, fun, thrilling, lucrative. Lunches, dinners, parties. Clients who bought, often from nothing more than a floorplan or a table model, flipped, made money and on to the next. And each time, a big, fat commission. Tribeca, the Village, Chelsea. Prices of traditional inventory rose also, even as newer, glossier, glassier buildings went up. Famed architects. Starchitects with their designer buildings. Should I have let it pass me by just as Patrick's business was taking off? If I hadn't taken the eight a.m. showings, the late night phone calls, another broker would have. So what if it was Patrick who attended Jonathan's recitals, Betsy who left large pots of food on the stove, Louisa there for Jonathan when Patrick wasn't. Was it selfish? No. It was business.

Plus, at the end of a long and tiring day when I hadn't felt like making love, it wasn't simply because of exhaustion. Patrick might have been an ardent lover, but he wasn't an attentive one. "Slower. More gently. There. Now." Nothing I said made a difference. Ever. So, after spending long days running all over Manhattan with clients, why put myself through that. Why bother.

That's how it had been. We'd both failed our marriage, yet here he was, willing to try. At least saying that he was willing to try.

I wasn't. I no longer trusted him. I probably never would. Too much damage had been done and I didn't have the strength to fight for a damaged marriage. Didn't have what it took to try. The realization was crushing. I sat at the kitchen table and stared as the second hand of the kitchen clock ticked by. Tick-tock, tick-tock, tick-tock. Another useless mantra.

Louisa stood in the doorway. She seemed exhausted.

"Get up and come with me."

I shook my head. "I'm comfortable."

"I don't care."

"Where are we going?"

"My grandma's. She doesn't have much time left, so I've been spending my free time there."

"I had no idea," I said.

"Betsy's engaged." I had no idea about that, either.

"Is he a good guy?"

"I only met him a few times," she said. "Eduardo, from Uruguay. He has his own contracting firm in Queens. You'll meet him Labor Day, at our picnic."

"I'm not up for the party this year."

"So don't come. Just keep wallowing in your misery. The rest of us will try to have a good time."

We walked across town to Second Avenue and then south, with Louisa stopping in several small stores to pick up treats.

"Betsy has a boyfriend?" I asked. Louisa turned toward me and shook her head. "Have I been that self-centered?"

"Oh, please."

Louisa's grandmother lived in a second floor walk-up on East 4th Street between Second and Third Avenues. It was an old building whose fire escape hung like a broken arm, almost to the sidewalk. It was a hot day. A hydrant was open, spewing water onto two young kids while their mother watched from a folding chair. A small piece of the city that had managed to remain unspoiled, despite new condos and boutiques stuck rudely between tenements, altering forever the soul of the East Village and the Lower East Side.

"I have the keys," Louisa said, as she rang the downstairs buzzer. "But I like to let them know when I arrive." We heard a click and she pushed open the front door. A second click and then we were in the sparse but clean hall. There was a front apartment and a back apartment on each floor. Cecilia's was the first-floor front.

A tiny Filipino woman opened the door, a wide smile on her sweet face. She couldn't have been more than five feet tall or weighed more than ninety pounds. Fay was Cecilia's live-in help. She and Louisa hugged and I followed them into the apartment. Into the long kitchen, all the appliances against the left wall, the open bathroom beyond. There were two bedrooms, a living room and the front room that faced the street. Large, framed movie posters and Mucha prints covered the walls.

Cecilia was seated in the front room, seated on one of a pair of turquoise velvet covered love seats, a cup of tea in her surprisingly graceful hand. She was elegant in her floral summer dress and low-heeled, bone colored shoes that were resting on a small, tufted ottoman. Her wispy white hair was tied back with a large turquoise and coral barrette. I felt as though I had stepped into a stage set. Her face beamed when she saw Louisa. She must have been stunning, I thought. Louisa went to hug her and Cecilia smiled joyfully.

"She's my favorite," she said to me. She pointed toward a side table at a photograph and Louisa reached for it, handed it to me. It was of a gorgeous young woman with an incredible figure. She was dressed in a showgirl outfit, a bare leg kicked high.

"Grandma was a Copa girl," Louisa said.

"The Copacabana," Cecilia said, a proud smile on her face. "I was really something back then."

"You still are," Louisa said. This was a Louisa I'd never seen. The love between her and her grandmother was so tangible I felt a deep ache for never having felt that towards my own parents. For my even more aloof grandparents. Closeness hadn't been part of my upbringing. It hadn't been given to me. Nor had I given it, except to my son, and that was only when I made the time. It was there in that East Village apartment that it hit home. I'd been a so-so mother, a workaholic wife, an indifferent friend. I couldn't let myself care because it could either devastate me or not, and if the latter, then what was I.

"Here, dear," Cecilia was saying to me. She took off one of the several rings worn on each manicured hand and handed it to me. Louisa told me to put it on. I struggled it onto my ring finger, looked more closely at it. Diamonds, surrounding a deep blue sapphire. I looked at them, at Fay. She was standing next to Cecilia, a wide grin on her sweet face. Patrick would have approved of her teeth. They were perfect.

"I can't accept this," I said.

"It's fake," Cecilia said, laughing. Her face was a mass of crinkles and wrinkles, yet the beauty she once was showed through. "I have boxes of it, top quality crap. I knew people. Take what you want. I don't need it anymore. Louisa, show her." Fay poured iced tea and cut small slices of the marble sponge cake while Louisa brought over a few jewelry boxes and placed them next to me on the love seat. Glittery piles of bracelets and necklaces, earrings, chokers, anklets, rings, each of the boxes bursting with baubles. I felt like a little girl, enchanted by all the glitter. Ran my fingers through the piles. My mother's jewelry was real, but she never let me touch them.

"Who are you?" Cecilia asked. "Why are you wearing my favorite ring?" I looked around, realized she was talking to me. I had no idea what I should do. Say. Louisa looked at me, pleaded silently with me not to screw up.

"I'm your granddaughter's friend," I said. "I was just admiring your jewelry. I hope you don't mind. You have such exquisite taste." I took the ring off and placed it on the table. Cecilia was patting Louisa's hand. I poured myself a glass of lemonade from the pitcher on the small table that stood between the loveseats.

"I'm tired now, dear. Please go away. Where's that girl who lives with me, I have to use the bathroom."

"I'll take you, Grandma," Louisa said. She helped Cecilia up. "Take my hand." And they walked out of the living room towards the bathroom. I put the jewelry back in boxes and walked to the kitchen. Fay was there, her eye on the open bathroom door.

"She needs to nap," she said. I nodded. She walked into the bathroom. "I'll take over now," she told Louisa, who walked out with an ashen face.

"She peed, then she took some cold cream and put it in her vagina. I told her not to do that and she told me I had no right to tell her anything, that it was Ponds and everyone knows that Ponds is good for you. Fay cleaned her up." I looked back towards the bathroom, at Cecilia being supported by Fay into her bedroom.

We were silent as we walked to Houston Street, Second Avenue, St. Mark's Place, the farmer's market at Union Square.

"I wish I'd known," I finally said. "From now on, I'll be with you every step of the way. I promise. And don't be upset about the Ponds. It's part of a lifetime ritual for her. She just forgot where to put it. I'm half her age and forget where I put my keys. It's all just a matter of time."

"Everything is, isn't it? You'll handle the listing when she dies."

CHAPTER NINE

The visit with Cecilia greatly affected me. It clarified that we each have a certain amount of time, luck and love in this life and it is up to us to make it count in the way that we can accept. To look back and say, I tried. At least I tried. I showered, washed my hair, dressed in walking shorts and cotton shirt. Had melon and tea, then left the house. Antonio lived north of me so I walked up Ninth Avenue. I stopped on the northwest corner of West 22th Street, pulled out my phone and called him.

"It's Ellie," I said. "Would you happen to be free today?"

"I'm in the middle of something now," he said. "If you don't mind meeting at my place, I'm on West 38th.." He rattled off his address.

I hadn't counted on that. The thought of going to his apartment startled me and I hesitated, not exactly sure why. I've been in countless apartments with plenty of strangers, buyers, sellers, contractors, supers. Locked on the roof of a building under construction in pre-cell phone days. In a loft where a body had been found hanging from the bathroom ceiling, cut down and removed prior to my arrival. Handcuffs still screwed into the bathroom ceiling, dried blood still staining the floor. It hadn't mattered to the downtown trader who bought it that very day.

He liked the price as much as he liked the light pouring in from eleven windows. The doorway of a Murray Hill apartment where the seller with diplomatic immunity stood stark naked and at full mast, holding a bottle of champagne. I looked him in the eye, not easy to do as he was impressively endowed. I flat-out lied and said I was a recovering alcoholic, then walked away as quickly as I could. Real estate in the city. I was able to handle it, but I wasn't sure I could handle myself with Antonio.

"No," I finally told him. "I don't mind." He repeated the address. I said I knew where it was. He said of course I did. I thought briefly of walking to Tenth to take the bus but ended up walking the rest of the way, even though it was in the mid-nineties and I was perspiring. So what? It's summer. People sweat in summer, at least normal people. I walked past London Terrace, the Penn South houses across the avenue, the Health Building around West 28th Street. A short stretch of ugly, lonely streets at odds with glass towers rising behind impenetrable wooden walls. Hudson Yards, the future city within the city for the wealthy. The traffic heading into the Lincoln tunnel.

I stood in front of a live-work building manned by a security guard. A bike messenger rushed out, a model or at least someone who looked like a model walked in. I followed her. She apparently lived there as she strode past the guard directly to the elevator. I had to be cleared. I rode the oversized key-lock freight elevator to the fifth floor and walked down a long hallway. Antonio stood in his doorway wearing a pair of red satin boxing trunks and nothing else. His lean, muscular body glistened with sweat.

He pushed a lock of damp hair from my face. I reached out and touched his bare chest. The sweat and muscle and dark matted hair. The beat of his heart. I realized what I was doing and took my hand away.

"I don't think I should stay," I said.

"Where will you go?"

"Somewhere safer."

Just the hint of a smile on his full, beautifully shaped mouth.

"I'll go with you. Give me ten minutes to shower."

I looked around, wondering how he managed to have such a nice place on a cop's salary. A retired cop's salary. The main room was squarely proportioned, with windows facing west and south. The view was of industrial buildings and, as real estate ads say, a sliver of river. A clean, sparse, masculine space with a large open kitchen to the right of the entry. Worn brick walls and thirteen-foot ceilings. Wide-planked worn maple floors. A desk piled with neat stacks of papers, a wall of shelves heavily laden with books. An enormous tobacco-colored leather sofa and an old steamer truck that served as coffee table. Opposite the sofa was a long ebony piece housing stereo equipment, a turntable, shelves of vinyl records. Near a corner was a judo mat, punching bag, weights. There was a motorcycle. A shoji screen toward the back shielded what I assumed to be the sleeping area and bathroom.

He was out of the shower and dressed in less than the ten minutes he'd said he needed. Black T, blue jeans, a belt with a magnificent turquoise and coral buckle.

"You bought this place for the freight elevator, didn't you?" I said. "So the motorcycle would fit."

"It helped."

"What year?"

"Ninety-three. This and a small building in northwest Tribeca." That surprised me. One family owned many of those buildings and had held onto them, at least until recently.

"Were you a crooked cop?" I was serious. "Or I know what. You did someone a favor. A big one. Do you still own the Tribeca place?"

"I'd like to kiss you," he said.

"That's not an answer."

"I sold it."

"When?"

"The last few years."

"To a developer?" When he said nothing I knew that he had. That he'd made a killing. An outhouse in Tribeca would have made someone wealthy. How had a cop managed that? I looked at him, saw him watching me, a slow smile on his face. I desired him in a way I'd never desired anyone before – a deep, damp, elemental yearning, but seduction was not my game. I took my bag from where I'd placed it on the stainless kitchen counter. He was right behind me. I turned, reached up. Brushed my lips across his. To taste him, to touch him, because what if I never saw him again.

"What was that?" he said, his voice low.

"A kiss. You said you wanted one."

"That wasn't a kiss."

"Yes it was."

He pulled me to him and I felt the heat of his body. The heft of it. He took my face in his hands and I literally swooned. Closed my eyes as his lips explored mine, a kiss so lingering and sweet and full of promise I almost cried. He held me and I did cry, just a few tears. It was more than my attraction to him, more than realizing I was capable again of feeling. I felt safe with him, safer than I ever had. It was terrifying.

We went to MoMA. The Museum of Modern Art. We walked through the galleries and somewhere among the Impressionists I felt a peace settle over me that astonished me. If I never saw him again, I thought, this moment, this day, would be more than I could have hoped for. My hand reached for his like it was the most natural thing in the world.

We had lunch in the second floor cafeteria, seated across a long, narrow, communal table from one another.

"I'm married," I said.

"I thought you might be. That house."

"It's been over for years," I said.

"I just retired," he said. "I start teaching at John Jay soon."

"So the last thing you need in your life is a complication," I said, preparing myself. "I understand."

"It depends on the complication." Our eyes met and I looked away because it was almost too much for me. It was a relief when we were interrupted by a slim, elegant woman with auburn hair, wearing a yellow sundress. She had squeezed her way between the closely placed tables and stood next to Antonio. Smiled at me.

"Ellie! Fancy seeing you here." She took a good look at Antonio and then at me. I felt heat rise on my face. She winked at me, held out her hand to Antonio. "Kate Patterson," she said. "Gallery owner."

"Antonio Wu," Antonio said. "Retired cop."

"Really? A cop? Is Ellie in trouble?" Kate was grinning now.

"Not yet," Antonio said, grinning back at her.

"That's good news, because I need her." She turned again to me. "I've decided to sell. The house for sure. Maybe the gallery in a few years. It's time to simplify. I was going to call but you know how things are. Summer. Travel. How's your family? Your son?"

"He's starting Columbia," I said, wishing that this conversation wasn't happening, but at least Kate was tactful. She never mentioned Patrick.

"Are you still with the same firm?" I nodded. "Come to the house. After Labor Day. You'll see how I've renovated. You have the exclusive, of course." Kate looked from one of us to the other. "Wonderful to see you again, Ellie. Sorry to have interrupted your meal."

"That happen often?" Antonio asked when she left. "A listing just falls into your lap?"

"Not often enough. I've sold Kate several properties over the years. I wish everyone was as loyal."

His hands. One holding a lemonade, the other on the table. Strong and square. I wanted to feel them, all over my body. Inside me. "I sold in your building years ago," I said, after an awkward pause. "Nineteen hundred square feet for three seventy-five. He was a photographer. She ran off with her yoga instructor to start a naked retreat somewhere in the tropics."

"I remember that," Antonio said. "After that early nineties recession, right? She got dengue fever. He met an heiress in line at Zabar's and they fell in love."

I hadn't known that part of the story.

"Imagine," I said. "Falling in love at Zabar's." My voice sounded wistful, even to me. Something was happening inside me that was not simply attraction or need. I no longer just wanted him. I wanted to be with him. I knew the difference. I was unashamed of tears that threatened, of the words I said as I looked at him. "I'm not afraid."

I will never forget the expression on his face. The intensity of it.

We went outside to the Sculpture Garden. Our thighs touched on the bench. We moved closer. He put his arm around me and I leaned my head on his broad shoulder. Later, he walked most of the way home with me. Over two miles, hand in hand. Beneath a streetlamp near the Penn South Houses, a quiet stretch of Ninth Avenue, he pulled me toward him and kissed me with a slow passion that I felt from my toes up through every inch of me. My hardened nipples beneath my thin clothing ached for his touch. I ached for him to lose himself in me.

"Come home with me," he said.

"Soon," I promised.

CHAPTER TEN

Everything is close to where I live, even funeral parlors. Louisa and I just had to cross the street and walk a short distance to Redden's, where it took us over an hour to agree on an urn.

"I was with her when she died," Louisa said. "One last tiny, raspy breath and she was gone." Louisa fought unsuccessfully to hold back tears. In all the years I'd known her, this was just the second time I'd seen her cry. The first was under considerably different circumstances. She'd waxed a weightlifter's back and he broke out in a bad rash. Even though he told her he had unusually sensitive skin and that it wasn't her fault, it took time for her to get over it.

She finally chose the first urn we'd looked at. It was simple and elegant, made out of fir wood. She paid. We were told to either wait or return the following day.

"Wait for what?" Louisa asked.

"The ashes," the funeral director said. "They already left the crematorium. They're probably in the Brooklyn Battery Tunnel by now."

"They're in a tunnel?" Louisa asked, incredulous.

"We use the crematorium at Green-Wood Cemetery in Brooklyn. It's magnificent. A National Historic Monument."

Louisa nodded, as though unable to believe there was anything beautiful in Brooklyn. I filed away the information for future need.

"I'm going to keep the ashes with me once I have them," Louisa said. "Cecilia's all the family I have, besides you, Betsy and Jonathan. I had an aunt, but she died choking on a chicken bone in a Chinese restaurant. On East Broadway. Not one person in the fucking place knew the Heimlich Maneuver."

"You've told me that story," I said.

"But it's a good one, don't you think?"

"It's very good."

The ashes arrived about half an hour later. The director took them into another room, poured them into the urn and handed it to Louisa. She placed the urn in a Bendel's shopping bag she'd brought with her and walked home with it nestled in the crook of her arm, as if it was a newborn baby.

"Your message machine is blinking," Louisa said, once we were back in my kitchen. She seemed anxious to have something other than her grandmother's ashes occupy her thoughts so I listened to the messages. One was from Antonio. I called him back.

"I tried your cell," he said.

"I turned it off. I was in a funeral home. My tenant's grandmother just died and we had to pick out an urn. They're both here now."

"Both?"

"My tenant and the ashes."

"Oh. Please give your tenant my condolences."

"She was a Copa dancer."

"The grandmother?"

"Yes. The Copacabana."

"Maybe this isn't the time to talk," he said, "but I'd like to see you again."

"Me too. When?"

"Now. Tomorrow. I think maybe all the time."

Oh my God. I was so stunned by his words that I could barely answer. I almost didn't.

"I feel the same way," I finally said and hung up. I walked back into the kitchen, dazed. I sat down and stared into space.

"Okay, who was that," Louisa said.

"Someone I recently met."

"Tell me!"

"A retired cop."

"Really? Does he have handcuffs?" I stared at her. "Okay, sorry. Anyway, how is he? You know." She was looking at me in the way she has when she demands an answer. I could barely think straight.

"He wants to see me again."

"What about you? You feel the same way?"

I looked at her, my heart still racing from Antonio's words. From mine.

"I do," I said. "More than I think I've ever wanted anything else." I nodded at the paper bag holding the urn. "But now isn't the time to talk about stuff like this."

"Are you kidding me? Grandmother had tons of lovers. Just be careful, okay? You're pretty vulnerable." I nodded. "It's odd, isn't it? We've all met someone. That oboist. I like him even though his feet are awfully long and narrow. Betsy's engaged. You and this cop. Maybe he can arrest Patrick for making your life so miserable and then we can all live here with our new men and have parties all the time. We can have weddings in the garden. All we have to do is find someone for Patrick so he doesn't make our lives hellish."

"Great idea," I said, grinning. Louisa stood and took the bag.

"I'm going upstairs to find a resting place for grandma."

CHAPTER ELEVEN

Valeria called the next day. She was at Chelsea Market and knew I lived nearby. She asked if she could stop by. I was about to say no, then wondered why. I also wondered how she knew where I lived. I heard myself invite her over and gave her the address, then sat on the stoop and waited for her. It wasn't long.

"You have this whole house?" she asked in disbelief as she walked up.

"We have tenants."

I led the way to the kitchen, poured two glasses of lemonade and we went to the garden.

"I didn't know people lived like this in New York," she said. "I mean I knew, but I never thought I'd know any."

"How did you know where I live?" She shrugged.

"Didn't you tell me? The day you visited me?"

We reclined on chaise longues and I thought, if anyone ever looked like an advertisement for leisurely living, it was Valeria, relaxing in my garden. She was exquisite in her sundress and peach sandals, long blonde hair in a single braid. I handed her some suntan lotion for her pale skin. She rubbed it on absentmindedly.

"I never get freckles," she said. "Kevin says I'm crazy. Not because I don't get freckles. Just that I'm crazy. Sometimes he scares me."

"Has he ever hurt you?"

"No, but there have been times..."

"What are you saying?"

"Nothing, not really. He's been good to me. But he has quite a temper."

"You still have to leave by the end of September?"

"Don't worry about that. I have an idea I'm working on. What I need is help finding my husband, to make things right. I have to make things right."

"You're married," I said. She nodded. "You don't know where he is." She nodded again. "You don't have a place but you don't need one." She shrugged. "You just want me to find your husband, but what I do is find apartments. Where should I look, in a broom closet?" Valeria giggled. I realized I'd never heard her laugh before. For that matter, she probably never heard me laugh, either. It seemed odd and then it didn't, but her visit seemed odd, how she knew where I lived, that she suddenly wanted to find her husband. Wanted me to help her find him.

"That's funny," she said. "Could he have divorced me without my knowing?"

"I don't know. Let's Google." I picked up my phone. "Okay, it says here you'd have to be notified of a filing."

"What if I was dead?"

"But you're not."

"Where would a filing be sent if he had no idea of where I'm living?"

"Oh my God, how would I know? And why this sudden interest in finding a man you haven't been with for years?" She didn't answer me but the fleeting look of sadness on her face was sobering. "Don't you have any family you could ask? Or his family?"

"I don't think he has any. I'm not sure, but I haven't had family since high school." She sat there looking as though she'd walked off the pages of a magazine ad for the perfect woman and told me a story that I tried to believe was true. She lost both parents during her senior year of high school. Her mother died of cancer and her alcoholic father burned to death while in a drunken stupor. The fire destroyed the house. "On the day I graduated from high school, Ellie! Imagine coming home to find fire trucks where your house had been. Not exactly a house. It was a shack in one of those sad, neglected upstate towns. Dolgeville. I'm sure you never heard of it. No one has. My father was already drunk by the time I left for the ceremony. It was morning! Anyway, I was relieved he didn't come. I would have been mortified having my classmates see him." Classmates. Not friends. "But to come home to no one. No house. If I hadn't known about the safety deposit box in town I would have had nothing. But there was my father's life insurance policy and some personal items that I've kept."

"Is this true?" I said, staring at her. Seventeen, eighteen years old, orphaned and homeless. Looking at her pale, elegant beauty, it was hard to imagine her in such straits. I wasn't sure I believed a word she said.

"Of course. Do you remember the day we met? I told you my childhood was hell. I had no friends. How could I invite anyone to a hovel?" She looked at me and reached for my hand. "Aside from Grace, the teacher who took me in afterwards, you're the only real friend I've ever had." Her comment made me uncomfortable, burdened with a responsibility toward her that I didn't want or need. I was pulled to her, to her story, but just to a degree.

Grace had not only taken her in, she'd recognized Valeria's strengths and had her enroll in culinary school. She also had Valeria invest a portion of her father's twenty thousand dollar life insurance policy in the stock market. The rest was to tide her over until she started earning a living.

"She was wonderful to me," Valeria said. "Like an older, wiser sister. She was thirty-six, exactly twice as old as I was. She seemed so old then. Well, she could have been my mother, if she'd had me when she was a teen. I felt sorry for her that she wasn't married. As if marriage was the answer to everything."

She lived with Grace for over a decade, catering small parties, baking cakes and cookies that she delivered to specialty stores in the more established towns on both sides of the Hudson River further downstate. Then Grace went to visit a cousin in Ottawa and fell in love with a recently widowed Royal Canadian Mountie. They married. She moved north.

"So I was abandoned again, even though they invited me to live with them. I stayed on in her house, able to pay the monthly charges from my catering but after a few years Grace wanted to sell the house. She found a local broker and from the sale gave me a small percentage of the proceeds to help me settle into the next stage of my life. I hated her for leaving me but eventually forgave her." Valeria paused and looked at me. "Imagine. I forgave the woman who took me in and nurtured me. I forgave her for falling in love and wanting to be happy." She started pulling at a napkin, tearing little pieces off and piling them neatly one atop the other.

Royal Canadian Mountie? Seriously?

"What about your husband," I asked. "How did you meet him?"

Once the house sold, Valeria moved to Burlington, Vermont. She found a room over a bookstore in town and was offered a part-time job there. Once she felt settled, she catered here and there. One of her first jobs was for a poetry reading at the bookstore. Max was the featured poet. He was a professor at the college and a friend of the store's owner. Kind, handsome, considerably older than Valeria, she found it hard to believe he had an interest in her, but they fell in love and were married.

"Max was the best part of my life, but I hurt him. Badly. I was frightened, so I ran away. I came here."

"You still love him?"

"Always."

"What about Kevin?"

She hesitated before answering. "I have a lot to thank him for. He gave me a place to live. I'll always be grateful."

"But do you love him?" I asked. "Did you? Ever?"

"Not the way I love Max. I like Kevin, but he made it clear that I was never the big love of his life. I'm too needy for him, plus he has this on and off thing with a woman he met in Maine years ago. She's one of those outdoorsy, independent artist types. They see each other only now and then but she's it for him. He's not it for her, though, so he took me in. If you want to know about our sex life, it's occasional. It's okay. Not because of him, I'm just not that into it. It's so messy, don't you think?" I almost said I don't remember. "Kevin likes having a woman in his life. It helps him with his romance books. A brawny guy like Kevin writing from a woman's point of view can use a female perspective."

"I guess," I said.

I was confused by my feelings for Valeria. I could barely pull myself away from looking at her face, the exquisiteness of it. The delicacy. The pain of thinking about Sally, imagining her grown up. I looked at Valeria and imagined my dead sister alive, the things we might have shared. The fun we might have had. It colored my feelings for Valeria from warmth and a sense of responsibility to near hostility for forcing me into painful reminiscence.

"Kevin's actually doing me a favor by making me move out and stand on my own. I'm forty-two. I want to do it right and to do that I have to square things with Max." I heard Valeria's voice, realized she was still talking while I had veered off into some fantasy of what might have been. "Help me find him, Ellie. His name is Maxwell Mandel. He's no longer teaching at the university. I called and they told me that but refused to give me any other information." She touched my arm. "Call Antonio Wu. You remember him, don't you? Of course you do, you two left here together, remember? I feel funny asking him since he and Kevin are such good friends, but he'll help you. Please." Her pale eyes pleaded with me.

"This is weird," I said. "Does Kevin know that you're still legally married?"

"I must have mentioned it to him at some point. Why?"

"Just curious." Suddenly I was worried about her. "Do you have any money," I asked. I regretted the words as soon as I said them. If she had none I had just opened myself up to be a part of her problems, which was the last thing I wanted or needed. And yet, what if she didn't have money or a place to stay. I couldn't help but think of my enormous house, my support system, my substantial commissions tucked away in a private account. I couldn't not think of Valeria and her situation. I couldn't imagine her homeless. And yet I almost could.

"I have the stock that Grace made me buy. I never sold it. It's in Apple."

"That's what you bought with your father's insurance money?"

Valeria nodded. "Ten thousand dollars' worth. Half the policy amount."

"When?"

"Sometime in the mid-to-late 90's. Maybe '97. Whatever it's worth now could disappear with another crash." She reached into her bag and handed me a card. Antonio's card, as if I needed it. "Here. He's a good guy. Nicer than Kevin." She paused, "Of course, Antonio never had to live with me."

"There is that," I said, smiling.

"Text him. He'll get back to you. He's another one whose marriage went down the tubes."

"That's too bad," I said, hoping she'd say more.

"His job. Antonio was a kind of a big shot, you know. Cracked some really big cases. Kevin says he's lucky to be alive." She stood. "I have to leave now. I have a catering job on the Upper West Side. It's a biggie. Six of us working tonight."

She meant nothing to me, I told myself, but I knew it wasn't true. It was timing. In my world, centered as it was either at home or at work, there remained little time for idle relationships. Time was money, at least it had been, for many lucrative years. But it no longer was enough. I began to realize that after meeting Antonio. There had to be time left to find myself. Finding apartments for other people was no longer enough, nor should it ever have been. Feelings and thoughts whirled as I walked Valeria to the front door. Then I sat on the sofa with Antonio's card in my hand. It felt alive. I reached for my phone.

"How about a picnic in Central Park on Saturday," he said.

"Like a date?"

"Like a date."

"Then yes. Do you know that Valeria is married? She wants you to find her husband."

"He's lost?"

CHAPTER TWELVE

When I had moved out of the master bedroom into the guest room I told Patrick I would still be using the master bathroom. I wanted the use of the large walk-in shower, the deep soaking tub, the bidet. He said sure, he'd leave the bedroom door open when he was gone so I'd know the bathroom was free to use. He also asked me again to move back to our room. I said it would never again be ours and he started a whole big apology, honey this and honey that and I told him to shut up. What had been our room should have become my room. Bursting with sunlight, spacious, comfortable, beautiful, overlooking the garden. I'd been a fool. Now I felt like an intruder every time I used the bathroom that I'd had completely renovated. I'd chosen the fixtures, the fittings, the towels, the bathmat, the soaps, the lighting. What had Patrick done? Plopped down on the king-sized bed on the nights he came home, absent-mindedly pawed me before sinking into a sex-with-other-women induced sleep. I'd handed the master bedroom and bathroom to Patrick like it was nothing. It had been a gesture of idiocy on the night of his birthday party just over a month ago.

I walked into the bedroom and looked out the window to the summer flowers, rich with bloom. I loved this room and I would take it back. It and the bathroom. I pulled myself from the tranquil view and went into the bathroom, leaned into the shower to turn on the water. I stood under the large showerhead, washed myself, shampooed, then just stood beneath the showerhead wondering how things had come to this. Me, feeling almost grateful to be able to use *my* bathroom. Wrapped in a towel, my body still damp, I walked into the bedroom toward the open door when I heard Patrick's heavy footsteps on the stairs. In another instant he was in the bedroom, breathless. We stared at each other in surprise. My hair was damp and loose, the towel looser. It fell to the floor and I stood naked, speechless, as droplets of water dripped from my hair onto my shoulders, down my breasts After an uncomfortable silence, Patrick picked the towel up and handed it to me. I covered myself, he retrieved his cell phone from the night table, held it up for me to see and left the room. Bounded down the stairs. I heard the front door slam behind him. His abrupt departure left me almost as shaken as if he'd grabbed me.

I walked to the large, mirrored armoire, curious to see how I looked to my husband after all this time. I let the towel fall to the floor and looked at myself. To me, my body looked the same as it always had. Full breasts, narrow waist, long legs.

The body that had given birth to Jonathan.

The day rushed back as vividly as if it were yesterday. The images. The joy. The insane pride. My water broke on West 14th Street. I'd been steps from home, carrying a bag of food. I looked down at the filthy sidewalk and saw the growing puddle in front of me. I stood in surprise and clutched the groceries to my belly for support. Had I just peed on the street?

Two teenaged boys sitting on a nearby stoop ran into a bodega and pulled a middle-aged woman outside. She didn't speak a word of English but she screamed to a man inside the store, *cuidado con la tienda.* Careful with the store. She ran to me, took the bag of groceries, flagged down a cab and gingerly helped me in. She ran around the back of the cab, impressively dodged traffic, opened the door and slid in, all so that it wasn't necessary for me to slide over. Then she started issuing commands to the driver in rapid Spanish, "al oh spee tal, al oh spee tal," and I kept saying, "*por favor*, New York Hospital, *calle* 68th and York." The driver's ID card gave his name as Russian, so it surprised me when he looked through the rear view mirror and said, "*Si, señora. Con gusto y con mucho cuidado.*" With pleasure and much care. It was comforting, a lovely touch that could only happen in New York. It was also a lovely thought that soon I would be with my doctor in familiar surroundings. But of course when we got to the hospital he wasn't there. A freckle-faced, tow-headed doctor who looked about bar mitzvah age took over. By the time my doctor and Patrick arrived, so had Jonathan. Two hours after giving birth I was sitting cross-legged in Rooming-In, a grin so wide on my face I thought it might crack.

This body. I might be interested in how it appeared to Patrick but I didn't care what he thought or felt about it. Antonio was another story. One day, hopefully, I would lose my fear and make love with him. But I was terrified of failure. Not his failure as a lover but our failure together. If we tried and it was a disappointment, what chance would I have with anyone, ever?

I took a deep breath and stood straight in front of the armoire mirror. Stretched my arms over my head. To the side. Watched the movement of my full, still firm breasts. Turned around. Bent over and looked at myself through open legs, glad I was still agile enough. Sat on the carpet and opened my thighs, wide. Thought briefly of getting a Brazilian and dismissed the thought. This body belonged to a natural woman and whoever didn't like it could go to hell and that included Antonio. Of that I was certain. I wouldn't subject myself to unnecessary pain because a man wanted to see more of me. It was my choice and my choice was to be natural. Years of neglect, of want and self-doubt were over. I would handle my future and my needs on my terms. I lay down on the rug, thighs still spread, and imagined Antonio inside me. It was easy to do. I closed my eyes and felt him. His hands, his mouth, him engorged, inside me. I knew then that I would pursue happiness no matter the cost. I would even sell this house if it stood in the way of the rest of my life.

CHAPTER THIRTEEN

This house. The first time I saw it was 1993, over twenty years ago, during the recession of the early nineties. AIDS, crime and homelessness were rampant. Patrick's dental practice and my real estate career were in their early years. The housing market was slow, but there were investors ready to buy blocks of condo units to rent or to flip. Bottom feeders who wanted a steal, even if it was over someone's limp, lifeless body.

Stu Whitterman was such an investor. A property on West 14th Street hadn't yet hit the market. I picked up the keys from the estate attorney. The owner's duplex was vacant but three rent-stabilized tenants still lived there. They might agree to be bought out of their protected leases, making an otherwise tough sale on an undesirable street considerably more attractive.

I met Stu across the street from the house on a hot, humid morning as the stink from the Meatpacking district wafted our way. The block was dotted with bodegas, an OTB parlor, church, fortune teller, fast food restaurants, tiny storefronts selling umbrellas, valises, sunglasses. Also a handful of great big beautiful brownstones.

"That's it," I said, pointing to a building across from us. "Twenty-five feet wide."

"There's a bum on the stoop," Stu said. "There'll always be a bum on the stoop. Besides, what do I do with it? I condo it, what kinda people will pay to live on 14th? It's a pit." Investors all respond the same way. The price is too high, the place needs too much work. The area sucks. We crossed the street during a break in the traffic. The man on the stoop was lifeless, his pants filthy and his sneakers laceless. "You'd think the smell from the Meatpacking would get to him. At least there's no breeze off the river today to make it worse."

The smell never bothered me. What bothered me was the dwindling number of meatpackers. The area was changing, slowly beginning to lose its soul. I loved watching enormous forequarters and hindquarters carried by luggers, fat dripping from the beef onto the cobblestones, the loading docks. From the trucks to the streets to the docks, then inside to be hung up. For a long time I thought it was the meat that smelled. I learned it was the fat, melting, dripping, slippery, hosed away over and over again in an early morning ritual. A rough, eerie, late night, early morning world shared with S&M clubs. Where transvestite prostitutes worked the same dark, uneven streets tooth and jowl with the truckers and the luggers and the butchers in their bloodied aprons. And when the setting sun cast a glow on the old brick warehouses and the nearly deserted cobblestone streets it seemed as lovely as an Impressionist painting.

Stu and I stepped over the man on the stoop.

"I hope he's just sleeping," I said.

"Sleeping. Dead. Whatever. I don't have all day."

The front door opened with a single key. I had to work three locks to the steel inner door in the cramped vestibule. A wide hall, staircase on the left. To our right, large double doors to the living room. Twelve-foot high medallion ceilings, fireplace, bay windows. Dining room, eat-in kitchen, powder room. A staircase that replicated the one in the entry hall ascended from the dining room. We climbed it to what had obviously been the rest of the owner's quarters. Master bedroom and bath. Two other bedrooms and small hall bathroom.

"Let's get this straight," Stu said. "These entry hall stairs lead to the tenants' quarters while the dining room stairs lead to the owner's bedrooms."

"Yes. The top two floors and street level garden apartment for tenants, plus basement."

"Brilliant. It is a hell of a house but three tenants, all of them paying bupkis." We returned downstairs to the hall staircase and climbed to the fifth floor. With every step my heart pounded faster. Niches on wide landings, stained glass windows, chandeliers. "I have another appointment," Stu said. I ignored him. He always had another appointment. As we approached the top floor landing we heard King Pleasure and Annie Ross, *Jumpin' With Symphony Sid*. The door opened and a slender man in a striped djellabah and fez walked out.

"Best waxer downtown," he said as he nodded toward the woman in the doorway. She was thin, her short platinum hair steaked with purple. She wore bib shorts and a tank top. Purple clogs.

"Which one's the broker?" she asked.

"I am," I said.

"I'm Louisa. No one's buying me out. Betsy either. But the guy in the garden apartment, he's getting married and moving. Alaska, or maybe it's Canada. Someplace cold."

"Is Betsy home?" I asked, trying to look over Louisa's shoulder into her apartment. She shrugged, left her door ajar and led us down one flight. She knocked and soon a sweet-faced woman opened the door. Louisa introduced us.

"Good luck *con la casa*," Betsy said. "But I'm not moving."

Stu and I left. The man on the step was mumbling to himself.

"He's alive," I said, relieved.

"Great house," Stu said. "For someone else." My heart raced with possibilities. I kept the keys long enough to show the house to Patrick. I put in the offer that day, pending inspection. It took the estate attorney a few days to reach all the family members. If Patrick and I agreed to keep the tenants, both of whom were cherished by the lately deceased owner, the house was ours for six hundred seventy-five thousand dollars. It was a no-brainer.

The house was in the highly rated Greenwich Village school district. We had the ten percent deposit needed at contract signing but needed more in order to qualify for a mortgage and not be hit with Personal Mortgage Interest. I knew better than to ask my country-club parents for a loan but Patrick's father Jack, a contractor, lent it to us at zero interest until we could repay him. Jack then proceeded to spend countless hours uncovering the original beauty of the house. He stripped paint off the mantel, the hearth, the floors. Marble. Portuguese tiles. Glass-beveled pocket doors. Maple flooring. He started the work as a widower, but one day while having lunch at B&H Dairy over on Second Avenue, he struck up a conversation with the woman seated on a neighboring stool. They fell in love over bowls of borscht. Within months they moved to Miami to be near her ailing parents. A colleague of his finished the work and Patrick and I moved in, our pride of ownership overwhelming. In the twenty plus years we'd lived here I never considered the possibility of selling. Until now. If that's what it took to move on with my life, I'd do it.

CHAPTER FOURTEEN

Antonio called while I was in the garden, thoroughly engrossed in an old Robert Ludlum. *The Matarese Circle.*

"I found him," he said.

"Okay great. Who?"

"Valeria's husband. He's living here. He teaches at Brooklyn College."

Things clicked. "Valeria's husband lives here? In the city?"

"Yes." He rattled off an address. I grabbed for a pen and asked him to repeat it, to give me the phone number, scribbled it all down.

"Don't call him," Antonio said. "That's for Valeria to do."

"Don't worry. I'll just give her the information." I paused. "Thank you."

"You're welcome. I miss you."

"I miss you, too."

I picked up the Ludlum again but was unable to concentrate. Hearing Antonio's voice was enough to take my mind off everything but seeing him again. Just a few more days. I looked at the paper with Max's contact information, stared at it to take my mind off Antonio, then used it as a bookmark and closed the book. I'd promised I wouldn't call Max.

I never said for how long I wouldn't call. And Max had a 347 number. I'd never called a 347 number before. My few contacts in Brooklyn were 718. I figured it was time to widen my area code horizon.

His phone rang long enough that I was about to hang up when a man picked up. It was Max. He said so. He picked up the phone saying "Max here." I introduced myself and explained my relationship to Valeria, tried to ignore the silence on the other end. I asked if I might pay him a short visit today or any day that was convenient. Again, silence for what felt a long time. Then he said what the hell, he was free until three-thirty that day. After that he might change his mind. I glanced at the time on my cell phone. Almost eleven. I said okay. He asked if I was familiar with Ditmas Park. I said no, what was it. He said that's what he said the first time he'd heard of it. It was where he lived in Brooklyn. He gave me directions, told me when I arrived at the Newkirk Plaza station to exit the Newkirk Avenue side.

"As opposed to what?" I asked.

"As opposed to Foster. You'll come out of the subway which is in a little building in the center of a plaza. Stores line both sides."

"Oh. Sort of like Broadway and West 72nd Street."

"Not really."

I freshened up and left the house half an hour later. A few blocks walk took me to Union Square where I waited on the sweltering platform for the Q train to Brooklyn. The first Q of my life. I felt as though I were on an adventure when the train arrived. I grabbed a seat between two manspreading men.

"Excuse me," I said firmly. One of them stared at me in surprise. I met his gaze but he didn't budge. The other moved his legs closer together so I was able to sit between them. There were other free seats but I was feeling assertive. The ride was faster than I thought it would be, about half an hour. At the Newkirk Plaza stop I walked up a few stairs to an actual waiting room with benches on either side, then walked through the turnstiles to a manned booth. There were two entrance/exit doors on either side and I took the one marked Newkirk. I faced a long line of stores. Curious, I walked to the other side of the Plaza and there was the same amount of stores, the little subway house smack in the middle. There were donuts, Mexican food, 99 cent stores, a hardware store, jerk chicken place, pizza, a Subway, a coffee shop, Chase and Santander banks. A large clock. I checked my cell against it. It had the correct time. I was impressed. Then I noticed that I was the only white face in the Plaza. No, there was another. Three women in hijabs. One in a burka, but mostly there were African Americans. No, there were more white faces, mostly young parents pushing strollers. It felt a bit like Manhattan years ago, before gentrification. It was both comforting and discomforting because in every other way it was totally unlike Manhattan. I thought how fitting a Cuban-Chinese restaurant would be here, the kind that used to line Eighth Avenue in the teens and low twenties. I missed them. Losing those restaurants was the start to losing Chelsea as it was before the fancy, expensive condos and big box stores. I doubted that a big box store would ever come to Newkirk Plaza. I decided, since I had some time, to walk around the neighborhood.

It was a strange mixture of feelings that I experienced as I walked around. It felt a bit like walking on the edge and also quite comfortable. I started by turning left on Newkirk and the change in demographics was startling. What appeared to be a largely Caribbean population suddenly changed and store signs were in Arabic. There were more women in hajibs, lots of kids running around. A few unhealthy looking health clinics, at least from the outside. Soon, an upscale corner restaurant with out-door tables, each chair taken. I went inside to see homey so-phistication and an appealing menu. Lots of young people and small children. I didn't stay, but I bought two chocolate cigars and two almond croissants to take to Max. Almost everyone in the restaurant was white. I walked across the street to a public school with a large front yard. Wait. Was that a chicken coop on the lawn?

The school was a beautiful red brick building and had a large playground to the side. Plenty of kids running around, climbing, sliding while mothers in burkas and saris and hajibs and jeans and shorts sat around keeping watch in the summer heat. It was like an international playground. I checked my phone, realized I'd walked in the wrong direction from the subway. I started to walk back the way I'd come but after checking the map app more carefully I made a left on Rugby Road. Cute houses, one after the other, some painted different, bright, happy colors. When I turned right on Ditmas Avenue the houses appeared larger, more opulent, some with wrap-around porches, turrets, driveways, lawns, only half an hour subway ride from Union Square. Bucolic, despite the traffic. I walked on Ditmas as street names gave way to numbers. Sixteenth Street was first. I needed 19th. Few people were on the streets, which I found a bit disconcerting. I'm used to crowded streets. I feel safe on them.

On East 19th I turned left and looked at house numbers. A man waved from the porch. I waved back, assuming it was Max and not a superficially friendly axe murderer. If something bad happened to me, who would ever find me out here? He wore a light blue Izod shirt and khaki shorts. He was attractive in the way quiet, academic men often are. We sat on the porch at a small table drinking lemonade with fresh mint, in French jelly glasses. I handed him the bag of desserts. He went inside and came out with two plates, a knife, some napkins.

Not another person in the streets for long moments, then a young woman pushing a stroller. Isolated people, in no hurry.

Max seemed uncomfortable, so I talked about real estate, something everyone in this city loves to talk about. When had he bought the house, what condition was it in, what was the neighborhood like. He relaxed into the wicker chair.

He bought the house shortly after moving to the city for the job at Brooklyn College, after he accepted that Valeria wasn't coming back. Maybe four or five years ago, he wasn't sure. The neighborhood had been a bit like a war zone then – gangs, shootings, robberies. It was changing rapidly. Gentrifying. Great neighbors. Writers, musicians, lots of young families. Signs of small new condos going up. Decent restaurants, not exactly around the corner, but close enough. His favorite was a Tibetan café. I should try it. He found it a fascinating area. I asked about the classes he taught at the college.

"You're here to talk about Valeria," he said. "Let's get it over with."

"She asked me to find you."

"That's something she would do. Ask someone to do her bidding. You found me easily enough. Why couldn't she?" I told him that a retired detective found him for me after Valeria could get no information from the Vermont college he had worked out.

He nodded. "No, I guess they wouldn't. Can't blame them for that."

"She still loves you," I said.

"Bullcrappy."

I couldn't hold back my laugh, "Bullcrappy?"

He grinned. "Strange word, I guess. But the truth is, Valeria means maybe half of what she says. Not that she's a liar. She's confused. It was my fault, marrying someone so much younger. So troubled. I shouldn't have expected much." A wistful look crossed his face. "But she was so lovely."

"She still is," I said. "She thinks you despise her, the way you kicked her out."

"You know about that?" I nodded. "You know how she left me with my foot impaled to the kitchen floor?"

"Excuse me," I said, thrown completely off-guard.

"Tell me, since you're here. What's the guy like she's living with, because there must be someone. She's too needy to be on her own."

This wasn't going exactly as I had hoped, but I told him what I knew about Kevin, that it seemed to me their relationship was based more on convenience than affection. Or rather, had been based. When I mentioned that Valeria seemed to be in a particularly vulnerable spot, Max said she does vulnerable very well. His sarcasm didn't escape me.

"I'm sorry," I said. "This is none of my business. The last thing I want to do is bring up unpleasant memories."

"Unpleasant?" Max laughed. It almost sounded like a bark. "Oh, what the hell. You came all the way out here..."

"It's easy," I said.

"It is, isn't it. Tell my wife that I'm alive and kicking at fifty-seven. I'd seem an old man to her now."

"You don't seem like one to me."

"No? How do you see me?" I looked at him thoughtfully, to reaffirm my initial impression.

"A bearded Sam Shepard."

He looked pleased. "Damn fine writer," he said. "So I guess that's good."

"That's very good," I said, smiling. He did too. He began to collect the plates. I took what he wasn't able to carry in one trip and followed him inside, through a double parlor with floor to ceiling bookcases, into a large country kitchen.

"You've done a great job."

"Thank you. The work helped me get over her." He turned his back and started washing the dishes by hand, despite the Miele dishwasher. "It hurt to think about her for a long time," he said. "She left me in a bad way, but it was partly my fault." He turned off the faucet and straddled a chair at the round kitchen table. Nodded for me to join him. "I screamed at her to leave, that I never wanted to see her again. I only said it because I was in agony. But there's a bit of a back story you might as well know. We'd been trying to have a child before I was too old. Then one day I saw her birth control pills, clearly visible in her open pocketbook." He remained quiet about it for weeks, though her deception devastated him. One afternoon while they were in the kitchen, he had the nerve to mention it. He was peeling apples for a German raw apple cake and she was unloading the dishwasher. He so startled her with his accusation that she loosened her hold on the cutlery basket and the contents spilled helter-skelter, including a large chef's knife. It flew out and then flipped over, straight down into his bare foot, impaling it to the floor.

"Oh God," I gasped, imagining the horror of it. The agony.

"You can't believe something like that as it's happening," he said. "Like a slow-motion horror film. Valeria and I stared as the knife arched up, then straight down. There was so much blood." He slid his right foot out of a soft, tobacco-colored moccasin and showed me the scar that ran from the center of his foot down to the tip of his middle toe. "I'll never forget her screams. Her running around asking how she could help, but she didn't even think to call for an ambulance while I bled all over the place. She brought me towels. White towels that immediately became saturated with blood, like winter roses on snow, until the blood covered almost the entire towel. It soaked into the floorboards. She bent over me, staring. Hysterical. She was completely useless. I yelled at her to get help and then get out of my life, forever." He paused, brushed the air, as if shooing away a fly. His voice softened. "The look she gave me was of complete despair. I'll never forgive myself. It was the last time I saw her."

It was a terrible story, told in a monotone. The voice of a man who had covered his emotions for a long time.

"She left you like that?"

"I must have blacked out because the next thing I knew I was in the hospital. Neighbors were there. She'd run to them for help. They told me that while I was being tended to, she got on a bus. Someone said that the bus was headed for Manchester so when I was home again I tried to locate her. Nothing. I thought she'd get in touch with me if she needed more money. She had taken a few blank checks from our joint account. I didn't put a stop on them. I think it was a few thousand that she finally cashed. I don't remember. I don't care."

"You never divorced."

"I didn't want the hassle."

"You still love her."

"Sure I do. I also hate her." He slipped his foot back into the moccasin. "Mostly I hate her for not coming back. I thought she would. I waited for her about a year and gave up. I needed a change, so I sent out applications. I was offered a job here.

I thought it would help me heal. It did, eventually. I met someone..."

I wrote down both my contact information and Valeria's. He walked me to the door. A slim book of poetry on a small table caught my eye. Brooklyn Streets. Poetry Volume No. 9, Maxwell M. Mandel.

"It's not my newest, but take it. I have plenty."

I walked back to the subway. It wasn't a long wait and I found a seat on the mostly empty train. I pulled out Max's book, surprised to see that it was dedicated to Valeria. I read the first few poems before the power of his words hit me. My reaction must have been obvious, because the young, muscled man on the opposite bench kept looking at me. Do-rag, gold tooth, enormous red high-top sneakers, large silver cross on a thick chain that fell onto a bare chest beneath a thin, unzipped jacket. When the train pulled into Atlantic Avenue he rose from his seat and bent down briefly to look at the title.

"Huh," he said. "Maybe I'll get me some of that."

CHAPTER FIFTEEN

On Saturday as I walked up Ninth Avenue to see Antonio, he texted me, asking where I was.

"Ten blocks away."

"We won't be alone. I'm sorry."

Kevin was seated on Antonio's sofa with another man who had a shaved head and a hard face that was somewhat softened by a welcoming smile. He introduced himself as Cliff, Antonio's ex-partner. Kevin nodded to me.

"Hi, Ellie. We're here because Valeria's gone," Kevin said. "No sign of her for a few days."

"What about her clothes," I asked.

"Some, I guess. Those skinny little dresses she wears. The size of a handkerchief. It's hard to say what she took but there's plenty still there. What I'm sure of is that she took over a thousand bucks from my desk."

"You had that much laying around?" I asked. Kevin simply stared at me without answering. "She did that to her husband, too, when she left him." I was unprepared for the startled looks I received from all three men.

"How do you know that?" Antonio finally asked. The look he gave me was not something to write home about.

"I went to see him," I said, looking at my shoes. "I took the Q." As though I'd been heroic. Instead, I'd been deceitful. I'd lied to Antonio when I told him I wouldn't call Max, only to call him minutes later. "He's a lovely man. A poet. Valeria left him after she dropped a chef's knife into his bare foot. Because of it, actually." I was babbling but stopped when I looked up and saw disbelief on Antonio and his friends' faces.

"She what?" Kevin asked. His face was so tense it seemed it might crack.

"He wanted a baby. She didn't. When he confronted her with her birth control pills, she dropped the dishwasher basket that holds the cutlery." I wanted to sink through the floor, aware of how idiotic this sounded. "It was an accident. She was devastated."

"I bet he was a bit upset too," Cliff said. "And he's not the only one." He glared at Antonio in such a way that I knew he had been the one to secure Max's contact information and give it to Antonio. To deflect attention from myself I turned to Kevin.

"Are you going to press charges, for the money?"

Kevin looked ill. "I don't want anything to happen to her," he said. "The money's no problem. I won it in a poker game. I don't want her to be penniless."

"She's not penniless," I said. "She has Apple stock. She bought ten thousand dollars' worth in the nineties, from her father's life insurance policy.

The change on Kevin's face. A dark shadow crossed it like a rain cloud about to burst. Cliff sat motionless. Antonio's eyes never left me. I sensed an absence of warmth and it seemed a good time for me to leave until I noticed the large picnic basket on the kitchen counter. There might still be the possibility of our afternoon date. Antonio walked over to his computer and a few minutes later said that accounting for splits and the actual year she bought it, Valeria must have well over a million dollars by now, perhaps even closer to two.

"What the hell?" Kevin said. "All those years living with me, not paying a fucking dime towards the loft." He glared at me as though it were my fault. I glared back. To cover my doubt, my growing discomfort, I rummaged in my bag and pulled out Max's book of poems. I stood there holding it, feeling awkward.

"Is there something you want to read," Antonio asked. Not a hint of a smile. I felt small. Silly. Angry, for being made to feel that way.

"No," I said. "I don't want to. I thought we'd be alone and you would read a few of Max's poems, see what you thought of them. But since your friends are here, worried about a few of Valeria's missing dresses and a thousand dollars won in a poker game, we might as well get this over with." I heard the sarcasm in my voice. What the hell, I thought as I turned to the first poem.

"Oh, geez. She's gonna read to us?" Cliff groaned. That really annoyed me.

"She's here," I said. "And yes, she's going to read. Leave if you don't like it." Antonio, leaning against a brick wall, showed the smallest hint of a smile. I brushed my hair back from my face and took a deep breath. I began to read and tried not to look at any of them, especially Antonio. It was impossible. I blushed, but forced myself to continue. When I was done I saw the men focused on me in a way that made me think my slip was showing, even though I haven't worn one for decades. Then Antonio surprised me by taking the book from me. He began to read from where I'd left off.

"Not bad," Kevin said, after hearing Antonio.

"Not great, either," Cliff said.

Antonio continued. With his more deliberate pace and obvious ease I heard the words more deeply. Saw his face tighten as he read a poem towards the end.

> *Golden hair, viper's soul,*
> *Empty heart, beyond control.*
> *A deadness 'neath the curve of breast*
> *Survival is the only quest...*

"I'm not into this stuff, but there's a shitload of anger in those words," Kevin said.

"There's also love," I said, "in those first poems." But I was doubting myself. My judgment. There was also hatred.

"What are you, crazy?" he said. Antonio turned to the front pages.

"He dedicated this to Valeria," he said.

"I never dedicated anything to her," Kevin said.

"You never loved her," I said.

"Hey! I let her live with me. Practically supported her, for years. Tony knows however long it's been, it's a record for me." He paused. "Any sense of what this Max is really like?"

"He's one pissed off motherfucker, that's what he is," Cliff said. "What about you, Tony. You're the scholar. How'd his words strike you?"

"They're powerful," Antonio said. "An almost uncontrolled passion. Obsession. I don't like it. This guy has a score to settle and we don't even know where Valeria is. Ellie, have you told her about your visit to Max?"

I shook my head. "No. But I don't think he ended up in Brooklyn by chance."

"Smart girl," Cliff said.

"Woman," I said.

"Anything's possible," Antonio said. "Cliff..."

"Yeah, I know. So Valeria doesn't have Max's address, unless she does. Unless she's known it all along." Cliff stood. "Unless he's known where she is from day one." He looked at Kevin. "Better watch yourself, buddy. Meanwhile, if no one hears from her by the end of the weekend I'll go to Brooklyn and have a talk with this guy. Last thing I want to do on my day off. Fuck."

Kevin looked confused, then mumbled. "Most of the time, she drove me nuts."

"And the other times?" I asked. Kevin took his time before answering.

"The other times she was lovely," he said. He seemed surprised at his words. "Christ, I hope she doesn't do something stupid."

"If her clothes are still at your place then she's coming back. She's probably just looking for a place to live. She said you want her out by the end of September."

"This poet," Kevin said. "He's not all pure love and noble heart."

"That's not bad," Antonio said, looking at his friend.

"It's from someone, right?"

"Yes."

Kevin and Cliff stood, walked toward the door. Kevin looked miserable as they left. Antonio and I were finally alone and it wasn't the mood I'd hoped for.

"You promised me you wouldn't call," he said.

"I know. I'm sorry. But..."

Without another word he picked up the picnic basket and handed me a lightweight navy blanket to carry. I had disappointed him. Killed whatever trust he might have had in me.

We walked uptown in silence, settled on the blanket beneath a shade tree in Central Park. I sat cross-legged in my walking shorts. Antonio stretched out on his back. We began to relax as we watched people doing their thing. Kids, couples, solitary readers, sunbathers. A man in very brief shorts performed impossible yoga positions which, no matter what anyone will ever say to try to convince me otherwise, is nothing more than showing off, especially when clad in such revealing clothing. A father and son tossed a softball back and forth. A couple walked with their arms around each other. We saw them at the same time. Our eyes locked for a quick moment and he looked away. The intense attraction we had, cut by disappointment.

"I'm sorry," I said. "Truly sorry." I looked at him, hoping not to see anger.

"You think he still loves her?"

"I do. I think he's suffered for years. But he said he's met someone. Please don't be angry with me for going to him." He reached for me and our eyes met. Then our lips.

"Maybe it wasn't such a good idea to leave my place," he said.

"It wouldn't have been fair. I was going to use you. Sexually."

He laughed. "That was your intention?"

"It was, before I saw your friends there."

I lay down next to him, took his hand and brought it to my heart. Covered my breast with it. After a while we had lunch, seated cross-legged on the blanket. I began to feel relaxed enough to lose feelings of guilt at having disappointed him, until the conversation turned again to Valeria.

"She's not your concern," Antonio said. "Or mine."

"That's the problem. She's no one's concern. Think how awful that must be, to go through life being no one's concern. No family, no ties, no real home." My alternating feelings toward Valeria. The unexpected sympathy for her sorry youth, even as I had doubts about its truthfulness. Not for the first time did thinking of her cause me an elusive unease. Not for the first time did I push it aside.

"Don't let her get to you," Antonio said.

"But she has."

A teenage boy with a boom box walked by. Almost danced by, to the strains of "Begin the Beguine." I smiled at him, at his surprising choice of music.

"I love that song," I said to Antonio.

"So do I." I looked at him, the most beautiful man I'd ever seen.

"The first time I saw Valeria I thought she was a ghost," I said, turning on my side to face him. "I could barely breathe she reminded me so much of my late sister. All I thought of was Sally, how she might have looked had she lived." Antonio met my eyes, held them. "We were riding bikes. She fell and scraped her knee. I took her inside, washed it, put on mercurochrome and a Band-Aid. Two days later she died in agony, of sepsis. She was nine. I was twelve."

"That's a horrible story," he said. "I'm sorry. But where were your parents?"

"Not home." I heard the anger in my voice. "My father was at his country club and my mother was having her hair dyed champagne color. They blamed me. At the hospital, in front of all the doctors and nurses, my mother screamed that they never should have had me. That I was irresponsible, that I not only looked like a gypsy child but was wild like one while Sally..." I caught a sob and pushed it back, then struggled to go on.

"And Sally what," Antonio asked, his voice gentle.

"She was delicate and blonde. Like my mother."

"Like Valeria," Antonio said. He touched his hand to my face.

"I missed Sally so much it was a constant ache, for years. Unlike my parents, she adored me. Looked to me to protect her. I don't blame myself for what happened to her. Even in the hospital they said I'd done everything possible to save her." I paused. "I hadn't thought of her in so long. Not really. Then I met Valeria and the resemblance..."

"You feel a desire to protect her." I nodded. He pulled me toward him and kissed me softly on the lips. "I know her story. Her mother died of cancer and her father in a fire. There was a big question about that fire, by the way. The cause was questionable."

"What does that mean?"

"One day Valeria mentioned it, casually," he said. "To talk that way of such a horrible event seemed strange to me. I made a few calls. They never arrested anyone, but arson was definitely considered. Then there's the ease with which she'd moved into Kevin's life just days after arriving in the city. The story with her husband. Wanting to find him after all this time." Antonio looked at me. "Every instinct in me says there's something off about her."

"There'd be something off about anyone with a story like hers," I said.

"If it's true," Antonio said. "And if it's not, that's a worry."

"Her moving in with Kevin so soon after her arrival in the city wasn't all on her. Kevin had something to say about it." I listened to myself defending Valeria when I had no idea of whether anything she said was even true. I didn't understand it.

"He'd recently ended a long-term relationship. He's always needed a muse. Here's this gorgeous woman who shows up at just the right time for both of them. She can help him get over his break-up. She can cook. She also might have deliberately started the fire that killed her father."

"You don't think that's a bit far-fetched?"

"Is it? A teenaged girl came back from high school gradua-
tion to find herself both parentless and homeless. She seemed
relieved. That's in the reports. Through you I find out that she
turned her father's small life insurance policy into what may be
worth well over a million bucks. Okay, the market was crazy
back then and anyone who had certain stocks and held on made
out well, but her father had to be dead for her to buy that stock."

'Teléfonos de Mexico," I said. "My broker kept telling me to
sell but I held on. From the pink sheets to the New York Stock
Exchange. It paid for my kitchen."

"Telmex was good to me, too. But back to Valeria. The vase
she threw at Kevin could have blinded him. The knife in Max's
foot. The rage in his poetry. I've known Valeria for years now.
She's lovely and charming and there's definitely something
very much off about her." He paused. "You matter to me, Ellie.
I don't want you mixed up with her."

"There's nothing wrong with her that a bit of security won't
cure," I said. "Besides, it's not your place to tell me who to see."

Oh God, the look on his face. I'll never forget it. I would have
given anything to retract my words. "I'm sorry," I said. "Really
sorry." I put my hand on his arm. He pulled away and I felt my
heart break in half.

"So am I," he said. He stood. I bit my lip to keep it from trem-
bling. I'd hurt him. Disappointed him a second time in a single
day. I tried to help him gather the basket and blanket but he
managed without me. We walked to Central Park West. No
handholding. No talking. A silence between us that stunned me.
I ached. On the corner of West 71st Street he handed the thin
blanket and picnic basket to a man whose sign read Homeless
Vietnam Vet. It felt as though Antonio wanted to rid himself
of anything that might remind him of our day together. As we
neared Lincoln Center I turned to him.

"You don't like me anymore," I said. His lack of response made
me want to sit on the sidewalk and sob. In front of Fordham
University, I said it again. When he still said nothing I felt tears

come, angrily wiped them away. "They don't mean anything. There's just something wrong with my tear ducts."

"Is that it?" His voice was gentle but why wasn't there a smile. A softening of that chiseled face. A kiss. A hug. A declaration of undying love. All I saw was Antonio looking at me as though he'd never seen me before. A block or so north of where we were, a number eleven bus was stopped at a red light before it would make its way towards us. The one that goes down Columbus Avenue, Ninth Avenue, leaves me practically at my front door.

"We owe her," I said. "You and I owe Valeria."

"How's that?"

"If it weren't for her, you and I wouldn't have met."

Please, kiss me. Smile. Something.

"That might have been for the best."

I almost doubled over from the pain of his words. I stared at him in disbelief. I reached up and touched my lips to his as the bus pulled up.

"Not for me," I said. "Never for me." When he said nothing else, did nothing else, I ran to the bus. My hand shook as I swiped my Metro Card and sank into a window seat, let tears stream down my face. Antonio stood there, looking at me through the window as the bus pulled away.

CHAPTER SIXTEEN

I was in a fog of confusion. Why had I defended Valeria? I owed her nothing. Nothing! I barely knew her. But no one has the right to tell me whom to see or not see. Who the hell is Antonio to think he has the right to boss me around?

Not the right, you idiot. He's a cop. A detective. He sees or senses something about Valeria that I am either unable or unwilling to see?

Only a few more bus stops to mine. And then I was in my large, lovely house that used to be filled with life, with laughter. Jonathan, Patrick, Louisa, Betsy, me. In and out of the kitchen, the living room, the garden. Sharing dinners, stories, disappointments, helping my son with his homework. Betsy making casseroles on the nights I worked. Louisa reading books backwards with Jonathan, both of them rolling on the floor laughing hysterically. Homework gone amok. Patrick playing catch with Jonathan in the garden. Me, walking into the activities, bone tired. Both the outsider and the heart of the house. Now, on this late Saturday afternoon, I heard nothing. No one. I didn't want to see Patrick, yet the idea of being alone for the entire evening felt unbearable. I went to the garden and stretched on a chaise, closed my eyes and wondered what the hell had happened.

My cell phone rang and my heart leapt, but it was Patrick telling me he'd be working late for a while so he could take the last weeks of August off. I wondered how many cosmetic dentists in Manhattan worked late on Saturdays during August, or even at all. It was ridiculous to wonder how many of Patrick's wealthy uptown clients were even in the city during the month. They weren't. They were at their other houses in the Hamptons, the North Shore, Connecticut, Maine, Cape Cod, Cape Ann, the Jersey shore. Whatever he was doing had nothing to do with laminates.

The kitchen phone was ringing. I fought the urge to rush inside. Then I had to know who it was, so I went in and played back the message. My mother, reminding me that my father's seventieth birthday was in two days and not to forget to call. A real phone call, not an email or a text. Oh, Ellie, dear, a thoughtful gift, please.

I'd get through this disappointing day with Antonio. Chinese food and a movie would help. I went upstairs to see if Betsy and Louisa were home. Louisa was. If I ordered Moo Shu pork with six pancakes just for her she'd join me for a movie as long as there were no subtitles. But first she needed an hour or so as she was going through some of her grandmother's papers. I went back outside and stretched out again on a chair. Om, tranquil garden, floral smells. Smack. A mosquito. And another. Fuck. Smack. Om.

Valeria texted, asked me to call. I did. She had finally acknowledged to herself that she had enough money to live modestly on her own. She had never done so before and knew that now was the time. She had to get out of the city to think, she said. She was upstate, in New Paltz. She used to live nearby when she went to culinary school so she felt comfortable there. Now her cooking and baking made sense to me. If she'd attended the Culinary Institute of America she had even more talent that I thought.

"There's a great hotel up there, Ellie. Mohonk Mountain House. It's on a lake, it's gorgeous."

"I know Mohonk," I said. "It's magical." Memories flooded back. Happy ones, with Patrick and then with Patrick and

Jonathan. The wide porch overlooking the lake, the long walks, the incredible eccentricity of the sprawling Victorian hotel. It was an enchantment of a place and I felt a strong pull towards seeing it again. To get out of the city for a few days, to avoid the crowds in the Meatpacking District, on the High Line, the art galleries, all of them just blocks from me. The years of quiet summer months when people deserted the city in droves had long gone. Walking on a few blocks of Ninth Avenue, just minutes from my house, was a battle, at least on the weekends. Chelsea Market, a nightmare of tourists who all walked slowly, blocking the ability to pass them. We live here, please get the fuck out of the way so we can go home, go shopping, get to wherever we're going.

"It would be great if you joined me up here for a few days," Valeria said. "They're booked, but my room has two beds and overlooks the lake. Please. I'm at a crossroads in my life." She paused. "Having a friend with me would mean so much and you're the only friend I have, in the whole, wide world."

The whole wide world? At another time in my life I would have thought this the most pathetic admission I'd ever heard, something I could never imagine myself say to another person. Another time I would have made an excuse so that I could sit at home and enjoy quiet moments of self- pity. But this was not another time. This was now and Valeria wasn't the only one facing a crossroads. I had reached the end of my marriage, the end of a possible beginning to a love affair, a growing disinterest in work, which had, fortunately, slowed as was usual during the summer months. I hadn't a clue as to what was ahead for me. I couldn't trust my husband, I didn't trust the markets, either real estate or stocks. I barely trusted my own instincts anymore. I felt suffocated with unknowns. The ache from disappointing Antonio, of losing him, was the worst of it.

"I'll come," I told Valeria.

"Oh my God. Really truly?"

"I'll take a morning bus." I felt my mood lift. Time away was exactly what I needed. "By the way, Kevin is worried about you. Let him know you're okay."

"I doubt he's worried. He's just mad that I borrowed money. I'll sell some stock to pay him back before moving out. I would have left a note for him but I had to rent a car, pick it up, actually drive it. It's been years." Valeria laughed.

"Give him a call," I said. There was a pause before she asked if I would do it because her mood would be destroyed if he sounded angry. I don't know why I agreed to call him. It wasn't my problem but it seemed the easiest thing to do. Valeria thanked me and ended the call before I could tell her of my visit with Max. I checked the Sunday schedule to New Paltz. Plenty of buses. Then I texted Kevin, to let him know Valeria was okay. That she was upstate. He texted back to thank me. A short while later, Antonio called.

"Kevin called to update me about Valeria," he said. His voice was low. "I'm sorry I upset you. It's the last thing I'd ever want to do. Seeing you cry like that..."

"Those stupid tears had nothing to do with you. They just happened, like with that Bush guy."

"That who?"

"The one who always cried, even when he was talking in front of the entire country. I can't think of his name."

"Boehner?"

"Yes! John Boehner. He wasn't really crying, it was just a thing." He laughed. "It's not funny."

"Yeah, it is. Listen, Ellie, I don't want today to be the end of us."

I didn't expect that, couldn't have hoped for it, but I wasn't built for this. It took me some time to be collected enough to answer.

"I don't want that either," I finally said. "But I'm not sure I'm strong enough to try again."

I hung up, proud of myself for being honest. Being strong. If Louisa hadn't been home, hadn't agreed to join me for dinner and a movie, I don't know if I would have been either of those things, but she was home. She even gave me one of her Moo Shu pancakes. Then she asked if instead of watching a movie, would I help with her grandmother's papers. She'd tried, but not only was it too emotional for her, she wasn't sure she understood what was what. I constantly dealt with financial papers for co-op Board Packages. We went upstairs and settled at her dining table, which was a card table covered with a waxed Mexican yellow and red floral tablecloth.

There was a Will. Aside from fifty-thousand dollars that Cecilia bequeathed to Fay, her aide, everything went to Louisa. That included the East Village apartment, furnishings, paintings, "fake" jewelry, and six hundred thousand dollars.

"Grandma had six hundred thousand?" Louisa asked, astonished. "I haven't made that much money all together in my whole life. If it's for real, I'll need you."

"What for?"

"You know. Stuff."

"If you want her apartment and the co-op board approves you, we can work on that. Otherwise you can sell it and buy another apartment for yourself."

"I want to stay right here and invest the money from the sale. How much do you think I could get for it?"

"More than you think," I said. "The market is decent now and the East Village is desirable. Or you could buy a weekend home. Or travel. This is a wonderful thing she did for you."

"I know! I'm completely fa-klept."

"Verklempt."

"Spell it," she said. I spelled it. "Okay. That's what I am. Are you?"

"Yes," I said. "Not for what your grandmother left you. She obviously adored you. It's the cop. Just when I thought it might go someplace, it fell apart. This afternoon. It was my fault. I said some stupid things." I reached out and covered her hand with mine. "I'm so glad you were home tonight."

"Can't you make it better? Say something smart to counteract the stupid thing? What did you do, anyway?"

"I was defending someone I hardly know," I said. "That was after I called someone I said I wouldn't call. It's over before we started and I think I'm in love with him."

"You're scared. You sabotaged it because you're scared."

I stared at her, stunned by her words, then realized she was right.

"I'm terrified," I admitted. "What happens if he stills wants to see me and we're no good together?"

"That's stupid," she said. "If two people really care about each other they'll make sure they're good together."

"When did you become so smart?"

"When it's right, it's right."

"You're talking from your vast experience?"

To my surprise, Louisa nodded.

"Not vast, but from recent experience, yes. The oboist." She smiled a smile I'd never seen from her before. "If a man cares for you, really cares, he'll show it, however you need it."

"So he's good in bed?"

"Yes, because he cares."

"I never got that far with Antonio," I said. "Just a few kisses. I really screwed up. It's over."

"I don't think so. I have a feeling it'll work out. It's your time. And I'm not remotely thinking of moving from here. With Jonathan living uptown and Betsy spending more and more time in Queens, I won't leave you here alone with Patrick. I don't trust him."

"You don't think I'm safe alone with him? With all the crap he's done, he never laid a hand on me."

"I don't trust him for a minute. I don't think Jonathan does, either, and we can't give him reason to worry. Not just when he's starting college. So you're stuck with me."

"And the oboist."

"And the oboist."

"Maybe Betsy and Eduardo can live here, too," I said. "I'll condo the house and they can buy a floor."

"They'd never be able to afford it," Louisa said. "Me neither, even with my inheritance. Not with the prices downtown. But you should do that and sell a few floors. Eventually. You'd make tons of money."

"If you sold the East Village place and cashed in your stock, you'd be able to buy a floor here." Suddenly the idea of condoing the house felt appealing. Exciting. I put Cecilia's papers in separate files, labeled and stacked them. Then Louisa and I went downstairs and channel-surfed for something we could agree on. Just as we settled on *Room at the Top* with Simone Signoret and Laurence Harvey, Patrick walked in.

"Hi," he said. "I was with my partner. He's going through something."

"Who isn't," I said. He plopped down in his armchair. He looked tired.

The movie was as good this time as the other times I'd seen it. At one-thirty Louisa went up her staircase and Patrick and I went up ours. When he leaned toward me in the hallway for a good night kiss and it landed on my lips, I was too tired to push him away.

"Goodnight, Patrick."

"Goodnight, sweetheart."

CHAPTER SEVENTEEN

I awoke on Sunday feeling overwhelmed. Exhausted. It was crazy of me to have gone to bed so late. I had a fitful dream and was in a terrible mood. I was equally dreading and anticipating the trip upstate. I dressed in linen slacks and a long-sleeved T. The day promised to be hot, but the bus would be air-conditioned. I packed my large canvas shoulder bag filled with a carefully folded dress, shorts and T-shirt, a shawl, better shoes than the sandals I had on, sneakers and some toiletries. I was having a light breakfast of melon and tea when my cell phone rang. A caller from Paris. Marielle and her significant other were models who had been recommended to me by people whose names didn't ring a bell. She and Philippe planned to be in the city the second or third week of September and hoped to see a few properties with me. Large lofts where they could work as well as live, two bedrooms, chef's kitchen, industrial feel. They promised to be in touch once they firmed up their schedule. Patrick walked in as I was finishing the call.

"Paris," I said. "New buyers."

"You look nice," he said. "How about spending today together," he said. "The Met, the Guggenheim..."

"I'm meeting a friend upstate. I'm taking a bus around noon."

Patrick seemed startled. He asked when I'd be back. I told him probably tomorrow, possibly Tuesday. I understood his surprise. I couldn't remember the last time I spent the night away.

"Where will you be?"

"Ulster County," I said.

"A, uh, girlfriend?" he asked. I was surprised to be touched by his obvious vulnerability.

"Yes," I said. "A beautiful friend. You'd find her irresistible."

I realized how curt I sounded. We sat in the garden, reading the *Times*. I started the puzzle but couldn't concentrate. I looked at Patrick with his long, thickly muscled, hairy legs in khaki shorts. His head of wavy, almost black hair with streaks of silver. I felt something then and it shocked me.

It was time to leave. I went inside to gather my things and walked to the Port Authority. Two miles straight uptown. People have complained about the bus terminal for as long as I could remember, the same way they complain about Penn Station. Perhaps I'd feel the same way if I had to use it daily, but for this rare visit I found its lack of charm comforting. It was much cleaner than I'd remembered it and as I found my gate and boarded the bus, I felt a sudden eagerness to be on the road. I settled in my seat and took out the puzzle.

"In pen?" The man in the aisle seat asked in amazement. "Wow! Are you a professor or something?"

"I don't like pencils," I said. He left me alone for the rest of the ride.

I took a cab from the New Paltz bus depot through the hippie college town of New Paltz. Through the town to the road on the right, the split off to Mohonk Mountain House. Marveled anew at the enormous Victorian folly as I had the first time I'd seen it emerge, the sprawling, fantastical, eccentric hotel by the lake. The large front porch with people seated in rocking chairs, Valeria among them. I placed my bag on the floor and sat in the vacant chair at her side, hesitant to disturb her. The sheer beauty of the place. The peace of it, despite the crowds. Soon her hand reached for mine. Squeezed it. She smiled, thanked me for coming.

"Do you want lunch," she asked. I did, but I wanted to freshen up beforehand. We went to our room. The beds set apart by a night table. A small balcony faced the mountains. "I hope you don't mind sharing. It's all that was available."

"I don't mind," I said. I looked around the room, a decent size with antique furnishings. An armchair and two straight back chairs. I went onto the balcony. Two rocking chairs overlooked the lake. I could feel a calmness take over, almost shield me from the hurt of Antonio's words the day before.

"Today's my birthday," Valeria said. "Time to be on my own. That's why I rented a car and drove up by myself, to prove that I could." Her words pulled me away from myself and I looked at her, saw the small, quiet smile of pride on her face and realized what a large step forward she'd taken.

"It's brave of you," I said. Her look of gratitude touched me deeply.

What was there about this woman that pulled me to her? That made me feel protective of her? It was no longer simply an imagined comparison of her looks to my dead sister's. Who knows what Sally might have looked like had she lived? She was long gone and Valeria was alive. Alone. Ready to give life a real try. The miseries I had suffered over the last few years were minor compared to the deprivations and disappointments she'd lived with so long that I felt ridiculous for my own self-pity.

My former self-pity. I was fine. Totally in control. I had a house large enough to function as an army hospital. An orphanage. A small, private school for the extremely privileged. Plus a son, a job, my own bank account that would hold me for years if I showed care. A cheating husband was simply a disturbance. I had roots. Valeria's were flimsy at best, yet here she was, taking her first giant step while I couldn't get myself to file divorce papers.

I don't know how long we sat in comfortable silence before I realized I hadn't told Valeria about my visit with Max. I reached into my bag and handed her his book. She looked at it in amazement, held it to her breast.

"You saw him?" I nodded. More surprise on her beautiful face, then nothing. Nothing. After a long silence she said that was good, we could talk about it later. She'd look at the book later.

I nodded. "I'm sorry. It wasn't so long ago and..."

"Never mind. You went and found him for me. It's just a shock."

She suggested we go rock scrambling during our stay. It surprised me that she would be interested in that, even though Mohonk was famous for the Labyrinth and Lemon Squeeze. I'd done it with Patrick early in our marriage and again, on several visits with Jonathan when he was old enough. I said I'd love to. But we should wait until Monday, after the weekend day hikers disappear and with them, the long lines leading up to the rocks.

"That's what I heard people saying earlier today," she said. "So tomorrow's better. Did I ever tell you that I went to school across the river? The Culinary Institute. I never came here, just heard about it and how lovely it was, but I promised myself back then that one day I would visit here." She turned to look at me and I couldn't help but see the pride on her face.

"It's a real milestone," I said. "And I'm impressed about your graduating the Culinary Institute. I had no idea you were that accomplished."

"I'm good," she said, "but I had no confidence in anything when I moved to the city. And I'm not cut out for that kind of life professionally, at least not there. There are so many people with so much talent. I can't compete. I don't know how to. I don't want to. I don't know how you do your job. What happens when you lose a deal? Do you lose confidence in yourself?"

"I lose a commission," I said. "I'm not happy about wasting all the time I'd put in but I don't let it keep me from the next. I can't."

"If I had more faith in myself I probably could have worked in a good restaurant, built a career. But what if I applied and didn't get that job, or the next. I can't take more rejection. The city's too hard and I'm not cut out for it. In a place like this, it's different. I'm a country girl at heart. This town is a nice mixture. It's country with a busy town, lots of college kids. After I accepted that my time living with Kevin was coming to an end, this was the place that came to mind. Well, also Kingston or Hudson, but it didn't seem as much fun as here. I checked out some real estate online and realized I could afford to buy something modest. Something that would be mine. I could have my own place and still have money left over, if Apple stock doesn't tank again." I nodded, said real estate was a much safer bet than the stock market.

"I think I could maybe even be happy here," she continued. I looked at her. She seemed surprised at her own words, but they made sense to me. "I found a local broker. I was hoping you'd look at a few places with me tomorrow. You don't have to, you can just stay here and enjoy the lake and the views, but I hope you'll go with me." I said that of course I would look with her, that I never tired of looking at properties. I felt her relief as I said those words.

"I'm curious," I said. "You're from upstate, you went to school here. You met Max in New England. So how did you end up in the city?"

"When he kicked me out I went straight to the bus station. I was shaking, hardly thinking. I was numb with sadness, terrified that Max was dead. I was like a crazed person and decided I'd take the first bus I could, no matter where it was headed. It was to New York City. I knew no one there, had only the money I'd taken from Max. The entire ride I slept or cried. I was horrified when we arrived at the Port Authority. What a weird place! The whole area around it felt dangerous. All I knew about, mostly from Max, was Greenwich Village. He'd done poetry readings over the years, had friends there, so that's where I took a cab. I told the driver, Greenwich Village and he said where in the Village, lady. Lady! What came to my mind was The White Horse Tavern. Max must have talked about it, I don't know, but that's where I ended up." Valeria stood up. "Enough of that. Let's go into town for a while, okay?"

She drove us in her rental car and I made an oath to myself to take the bus back to the city no matter when she decided to leave New Paltz. She drove slower than I could walk, her foot off and on the brake. A pregnant woman probably would have had a miscarriage.

"I'm a good driver," Valeria said. "But I'm used to stick shifts from when I used to drive. Before the city. This car feels like it will run away from me. We'll be fine when we get off these twisty roads." And we were. She vindicated herself as she fought for and won a just vacated parking space in town, backing into the tight space with only inches to spare on either side. It was impressive, as though a different person had taken over her body. A parking person.

We walked around and did some shopping. I bought wind chimes for my backyard. In another store window I saw something that caught my eye, a small gift for Valeria's birthday. She followed me in, which wasn't going to make it easy to surprise her. When she walked toward the back of the store I stayed up front and typed what I wanted on my iPhone and showed it to the salesclerk. She was young, with a shaved head and five silver studs on her right ear. She winked at me, then I looked around while she found the items, quickly removed price tags, wrapped the gifts all together in a compact bundle of bright yellow tissue paper and placed them in a small paper bag that I placed in my bag. She jotted the sum on a piece of paper and I handed her cash without taking back the three dollars plus change. A tip for discretion. I smiled my thanks and called to Valeria that I was done. John Le Carré would have been proud of me.

We went for a walk through the town, found a comfortable looking restaurant and went inside. Once we were seated in a booth I brought out the present.

"Happy birthday," I said.

"You think I didn't notice," Valeria said, grinning. "You both thought you were being so cool. The salesgirl reminded me a little of Lisbeth Salander. You know, from *The Girl with the Dragon Tattoo*."

"She looked nothing like her," I said.

"Yes, she did."

She opened the paper and held up the items. Two matching bright yellow, red, blue, pink, purple, green, orange tie-dye T-shirts and two pair of earrings. Long rows of tiny colored beads hung from elongated silver findings.

"What a perfect present!" she said, a huge smile on her face. I'd never seen her look so happy. "We'll be like twins. Let's put them on now, okay?" And she proceeded to slip the T over her long blond hair and simple white T shirt. I did the same. We each took off our earrings and put in the new ones. We looked like we were ready for Woodstock. "It's my birthday," Valeria said to the room, looking around. A few people clapped. A few shouted out 'Happy Birthday.' She looked at me. "This is the best birthday I've ever had and it's because of you."

I didn't know what to say. That I could mean so much to her for doing so little was an astonishing feeling. Valeria turned around and tapped the young man in a neighboring booth on the shoulder. She asked him to take a picture of us in our T-shirts. "Of course," he said, and took her iPhone. He had us stand against the bakery counter and took several photos of us. We sat back in the booth and I found myself blurting out to Valeria that I had a sister once. I was ready to tell the whole long story, but a look crossed Valeria's face. A sadness that appeared so briefly I thought I'd imagined it.

"I never had anyone," she said.

CHAPTER EIGHTEEN

We were on the porch, on rocking chairs. It was utterly relaxing. Beautiful. Families, young couples, hikers, boaters, climbers. A little girl approached us tentatively, smiling. We smiled back as she came to stand at the side of Valeria's chair. An ice cream cone was held at an angle in her little hand. She asked if we wanted to share it with her, then touched Valeria's hair with chocolate-stained fingers. Valeria reached her arm around the girl's waist and gave her a warm hug. I would have thought she'd be the last person in the world to hug a child with such spontaneous warmth, but the look on her face as the girl left, the fleeting glance of longing is what really touched me. So did the realization of my disinterest in that child. There was something wrong with me, I thought. Something missing. A basic warmth. I had a sudden, powerful urge to call Jonathan to ask him if I'd been a good mother. A loving mother, or one who just tried to be.

But what if he said no, or even that I was not so bad. It would destroy me. For the first time in my life I wondered if I was worthy of the life I'd been given. I even had a brief vision of taking a boat onto the lake and letting myself fall gently over the side. The water would welcome me. I would sink slowly to the bottom of the lake, peace would surround me. A few people would feel sad for a while, but I wouldn't mourn. I'd be dead.

This morbid way of thinking was not who I was. I knew it was because of how things had ended yesterday with Antonio. There was an emptiness inside of me without the promise of seeing him again.

Valeria and I sat in silence for a while, long enough so that I was startled when she touched my arm. Max's book lay open on her lap, face down.

"He has a house near Brooklyn College," I said. "He teaches there."

"He dedicated the book to me," she said, her voice so subdued I barely heard her. "I read it through. It didn't take long. See how thin it is. He hates me. He doesn't want to, but he does."

"He also loves you."

"I think he wants to hurt me. I mean really hurt me."

I thought she might be right.

We had a light dinner on the porch as the August evening darkened and starlight danced on the lake. We barely spoke. I barely ate. We went to our room, washed up and readied ourselves for the night. Valeria emerged from the bathroom wearing a knee-length white cotton nightgown that looked as though it had just been starched. I was in my only pair of pajamas, light blue cotton shorties with small red pagodas all over them. She sat in the wing chair. I was on my bed, propped up by pillows. She pulled her legs up under her and rested her chin on her knees. She adjusted the bottom of the gown to make sure that it covered her. I wondered what I might have felt had she not done that, had she sat there, exposed. Thoughts I'd never had before rushed in front of me, thoughts I didn't want to have.

"Isn't it amazing? We're exact opposites, physically," Valeria said. "Night and day. I think you're beautiful."

"Thanks," I said. "I think you are, too."

"Wouldn't it be great if we were lesbians?"

"It would make life much easier," I agreed.

"Basically, though, I'm not sure I get the point."

"About lesbian love?"

"About life. Anything, really. Who's really happy, Ellie? I'm not. You're not. It shows. But maybe now that we're friends we can both be a little happier."

"Huh," I said, the very word sounding odd coming out of my mouth. I thought back, couldn't remember ever saying huh before. And then, just the way I'd blurted out I'd that once had a sister, I said that I was falling in love with Antonio.

"You're kidding! What about your marriage..."

"It's been over for years. Patrick has cheated on me for so long I can't count the number of women. I bet he can't, either." Valeria lowered her legs then, crossed one knee over the other and pulled her gown as low as she could. When she looked up at me I could swear she had tears in her eyes. I was moved. "Don't feel sorry for me, please. I'm over it. I'm over him. If I'm upset at anything now it's that I messed things up with Antonio."

Because I was defending you. And I don't recall ever telling you that I was married.

"Have you ever slept with a woman?" she asked. I shook my head. "Me neither, but aren't you curious?" I shook my head again. "I guess I'm not, either. Well, maybe a little bit, but it's nice to have a friend to talk to about things like this, don't you think?" Antonio in red satin boxer trunks, sweat glistening on his bronze skin. "It's not that I'm interested," she said, "but if I were to be with a woman I'd want her to be like you. Or you."

"Thanks," I said. "I guess the same here."

"Besides, I'm not made for grand passion, though everyone needs sex now and then, don't they? But I don't feel closer to the person afterwards. Do you? When it's over, it's over." She didn't wait for an answer. "Max was a thoughtful lover. Kevin was okay. He's fixated on a woman he's known for decades. Oh, I already told you that. She does what she wants with whom she wants and has, for decades. He suffers."

"It must have been difficult living with him like that."

"He needed help with his female characters. Not so much anymore, he writes almost automatically by now. I needed a place to live. He loves my cooking so it worked fine until it didn't." I sat there and listened, tried to not think about Antonio.

Thought of ways to make things better, but nothing seemed feasible. I'd disappointed him twice in a short period of time. I'd destroyed whatever chance we might have had. "Have you read any of his books," Valeria said. "If you haven't, don't bother. They're dreadful." She sat with her head against her knees. "I've depended on others for too long," she said. "Lived off them. That's why I have nothing now except for my stock and that almost doesn't seem real. Well, I have two things from my father and a locket from my mother. That's all she had in her miserable life. Me, the locket, a husband who drank rotgut. Cancer. That's what she had. That's how I grew up. With nothing, in a place more depressing than I could describe. It damaged me. That's why I held on to the stock and lived off Kevin. Fear. But I'm stronger now. I have to be."

She rose and opened a dresser drawer, took something out, sat back down. Lit a match to a fat joint and took a hit. Handed it to me. It had been years. That familiar sweet smell. Years fell away as I inhaled. I sucked in.

"You do this often?" I asked.

"With Kevin, all the time. This is his." I was pretty sure she hadn't asked him if she could take his stash. Silence as we admired the lake, "We should be on the balcony."

"We certainly should." We moved to the rocking chairs outside. After another joint, Valeria started to giggle. "It's really funny, isn't it?"

"What is?" I said, smiling at the sky.

"Wait. I'll think of it in a minute." I let out a laugh that startled me.

"I have to find something. Wait."

"I'm not going anywhere."

Valeria left the patio and opened the top drawer of the single dresser. The moonlight illuminated her slender figure through her white nightgown. She was so graceful and her breasts so firm. I placed my hands over my own breasts in comparison. They were too full for my hands. I close my eyes and imagined Antonio's hands on them, his large square hands. My nipples hardened in the hot summer night, just thinking of him. I felt moist, just thinking of him.

It's the grass, that's all.

"You're someplace else, aren't you," Valeria said, startling me. She sounded almost normal, but she and Kevin smoked regularly. When had I become so boring?

Valeria handed me a white pastry box. "Here." I took off the thin red string and opened it, looked inside. Brownies! I grabbed one. It was incredible.

"Oh god, that's so good," I said, my mouth full. I reached for another. "These are the best brownies I've ever had."

"I didn't make them. They're from a bakery in town."

"Let's go find them and thank them."

"They're closed now. And they're for us to share, Ellie. Can you please give me one?" I stared at her. She was smiling at me. I realized I was holding the box. There were still six brownies inside.

"You can have three," I said.

"Thanks." I handed her the box. She took one and ate it delicately. "Look at that moon," she said. "Isn't it amazing that it's even there? I mean, how did it get there? And the sky. Imagine if there was no sky."

"I can't. There would be nothing to look at above eye level."

"If the moon wasn't there there'd be nothing to see."

"Stars. And airplanes."

"Could there be stars without a sky? What would hold them up?"

"Birds."

"I don't like nuts in my brownies, do you?"

"These don't have nuts."

"That's why they're so good," I said.

"I like nuts."

At some point I began to nod off. With what felt like a lot of effort I left the chair and fell onto my bed. Valeria walked over and kissed my cheek.

***

I'm in Newark International Airport with two hours to spare before meeting Jonathan at Gate 55, Terminal C. I was extremely early. With time on my hands I decided to store my bag in a unisex locker/ bathroom. The lockers were wooden, which seemed odd in the high-tech terminal. I walked around the airport, realized I'd forgotten the lock combination. I was frantic; I had exactly one hour and forty-five minutes left and couldn't find the locker/bathroom. I ran all over the airport. Huge clocks everywhere ticked the minutes down. An hour thirty-five, an hour twenty-seven. I went to different levels of the terminal, some of them totally empty of anyone. It felt eerie. Ominous. I raced up to the check-in area and asked redcaps, pilots, anyone who seemed to know their way around to help me. No one knew of a bathroom with wooden lockers. We were now a small group, we ran, faster and faster, as enormous minute hands ticked by. One by one the people helping me had to leave. I was alone again. I had to meet Jonathan but first had to find my bags. I was wearing maroon plaid pajama bottoms which kept falling down, and a trench coat. I ran around a curved, glass brick corner and knocked into Sam Waterston and his wife. I told l them to fuck off before I realized who they are. "I'm sorry," I said. As they fell to the ground I saw that his nose was bleeding. I wondered if he'd sue me. His wife gave me hate looks from her prone position. They were both so long. I felt tiny and insignificant in comparison. Scared. I was almost out of time for Jonathan. There couldn't be anything worse than the way I felt. I started to sob, felt around for a tissue but it was hard because I had to keep holding up the pajama bottoms. I called Patrick. He picked up and I heard a woman's voice laughing in the background. He said he has another call and put me on hold. Eventually the line went dead.

***

I woke up sweating. I turned to look at the clock on the night table. One-ten a.m. Something had happened to Jonathan, I was sure of it. I thought of calling Patrick but if there was no answer

I'd be more of a mess. If something had happened to Jonathan but he was unable reach either of us...

I couldn't stand the thought. Reached for my cell phone. It was charged and I had no messages. I kissed it for being there for me. I was pathetic, but it was the middle of the night and that forgives a lot of things. It also doesn't. All I had to do was go back to sleep and give my dream a happy ending and I sort of managed it. Around dawn I fell back into the dream semi-awake, found the locker, saw Jonathan in it, happily reading a Nancy Drew mystery. My pajamas never fell down and Sam Waterson didn't hate me. I knew that because he didn't put me in jail on *Law and Order.*

CHAPTER NINETEEN

Valeria was still asleep when I awoke. She took up no space at all in her bed and her long, wavy blonde hair was spread out like a halo. She looked like someone out of a fairy tale, not that I had ever been much into them. I thought they were stupid. I dressed, wrote her a note, then left the room. I walked around the near side of the lake to the hiking trails.

After half an hour or so I came across a young woman holding a clarinet. She smiled at me just before she began Schubert's *Trout*. I sat on the ground and listened to one of my favorite pieces of music, thanked her, then returned to the room. Valeria was dressed, waiting for me. I grabbed my bag. We had a light breakfast of fruit and tea during which time Valeria called the real estate broker she'd mentioned the day before. She confirmed a noon appointment to look at a few houses. We could go climbing later.

It was so lovely here, perfect for a short visit but there was no way I could live in the country. Seriously. Years before I met Patrick I visited a college friend in New Hampshire, over a school holiday. One night I decided to take the garbage out to the bins in the garage. As I crossed the gravel driveway, a large green garbage bag in each hand, a small skunk crossed in front of me. A baby. I dropped the bags and started screaming at the top of my lungs, which only brought the mother snarling from out of the bushes and coming towards me. I was terrified. I knew I was going to get rabies and die, stranded in semi-wilderness where drivers had "Live Free or Die" on their license plates. I couldn't imagine there being a hospital anywhere nearby and was certain that the rabies I would get would be a fast-moving kind. My friend finally heard my screams and raced outside in her L.L.Bean pajamas just as I was running into her mudroom, racing rabies against the clock. I collapsed on the mudroom floor amid Wellingtons and lumber jackets and a floor to ceiling storage bin filled with paper goods, canned foods, dog and cat food, firewood, charcoal and cans of gasoline.

Who has cans of gasoline in their homes?

"Why are you screaming," she asked.

"Rabies," I sobbed.

"Oh my God, you were bitten by something? Here?"

"I wasn't, but I could have been." I said. I told her about the baby skunk.

"You scared Myrtle and her babies," she said, staring at me in disbelief. "She just gave birth. She's being protective, that's all."

"You name your skunks?"

Now, in New Paltz, I confronted the possible dangers of country living by asking Valeria if she would feel safe in a house by herself, in the middle of nowhere.

"This is hardly nowhere, Ellie. I'd live near town. Walking distance, probably. That's if I move at all. I may end up in a little studio with a big kitchen, somewhere in the city. I just don't know, but looking at a few homes will be fun."

We had about an hour before we were supposed to meet Jan, the broker. She was going to pick us up at a pastry shop/restaurant that Valeria knew and liked. We drove back into town and then walked the few blocks to a sweet building with all the outside tables taken, but several inside were free.

"I love this place" I said, looking around. There was a large display case filled with good-looking desserts. "You could work here. Bake for them."

"Or maybe I could have a place like this for myself," she said. We ordered coffee and rugelach. I looked at the other customers. No one looked like Valeria or me. "I feel comfortable in this town, Ellie. I did years ago, when I went to school across the river."

"What if the broker finds you a place you really love, but it's not right in town. Walking distance, but still country-ish, because this is the country."

"This is a college town, with stores, and restaurants. But don't worry. I always carry protection."

"You have pepper spray?"

"Don't you?"

"No. I don't."

"I have other protection, too, so don't worry?"

"You mean condoms?" Valeria looked at me like I was insane. Someone snorted a laugh from the booth behind ours. I ignored it. "Have you ever actually bought them?"

She shook her head.

"Have you?"

"No. I don't have sex. I'm married." Another snort and then a giggle. I turned around to see a young man seated directly behind me and a girl seated across from him. She grinned at me as I turned. I tapped him on the shoulder so that he, too, was facing me. "You can laugh all you want, but you better use condoms," I said. "I have a son about your age. He better, too." Valeria lost it. Her laugh sounded like wind chimes in a breeze.

"You're putting me on, aren't you," the boy said after looking at me. "About no sex. Because you're pretty great looking for an older person." He turned to his girlfriend. "Isn't that right, honey." The girl was still grinning. She nodded her head.

"Yes. You are both beautiful," she said. "I hope to look so good when I'm as old."

Old?

"Well, would you have sex with me," I asked the young man.

"Ellie." Valeria reached across the table and grabbed my arm. "Don't embarrass them."

"It's okay," he said. "I assume you're just being hypothetical?"

"I am. I'm not usually like this. It's just because I'm out of the city and probably won't ever come back here. It's so liberating to be out of Manhattan."

"I know just what you mean," the girl said. "I'm from the Upper East Side."

*

Jan was a tall woman with dark hair worn short. She had several houses to show us in New Paltz and one hour in which to do it. There were others she thought might be of interest in Rosendale and Stone Ridge but if Valeria wanted to see those it would have to be another day.

"Here's enough for today," Valeria said. "And it's where I'd want to be."

The first house was an uninspiring ranch house with aluminum siding. I didn't even want to go in. Fortunately, Valeria didn't like it and we went on to the next, which wasn't bad except that the neighbors used their lawn for cast-off car parts. The third house was a ten minute walk to town, a small brick house with a sweet back yard. Despite low ceilings and small rooms, there was character to it from the moment we entered the entryway. The living room and screened sunporch were to the left and the dining room was to the right, with a real country kitchen beyond. Upstairs were two small bedrooms and one large bathroom with a clawfoot tub. It was the kind of home that feels welcoming from the moment you step into it. Where the vibes were good. I felt it and couldn't help but see the small smile on Valeria's face.

"The kitchen would work," she said. "And there's room for a decent-sized vegetable garden."

"If you want, we can see it again tomorrow, along with a few others," Jan offered as she apologized for the short amount of time she had that day. Then she locked up and offered to drive us back to Mohonk but Valeria reminded her that she had a car. Jan drove off and we walked around the area and the neighboring homes.

"What do you think," she asked me as we walked.

"It's a perfect little house. You'd need an inspector to check the mechanicals, the foundation, the roof. Find your own. Don't use someone recommended by a broker. Ever."

"If I decide to buy it I'll have to hurry, unless Kevin gives me an extension. What do you think of the price? It's asking two hundred twenty thousand." I had no idea of prices in the area but it seemed ridiculously low compared to anything I'd seen in Manhattan, ever.

"It seems extremely reasonable," I said. "It's a good location and it feels safe."

"I never feel completely safe," Valeria said. "I've learned to live with it, with a little help. Here, let me show you something." We weren't far from Main Street when she stopped in the middle of the street and opened her bag. "Look inside. I can't take it out."

I looked inside the bag, then at Valeria, in disbelief.

"What the hell," I said. "What is that thing?"

"It's a Glock. It was my father's."

"It was in the room with us last night?"

She nodded. "It's always with me."

"Is it loaded?" She shrugged.

What did that mean? This lovely day in the country changed for me in a split second. Guns are for cops and cowboys. People from red states who like to kill things. There was no way I was going to spend another night in a room with a gun-toting woman I barely knew. Not to mention that Max had kicked her out. Kevin was kicking her out. Antonio felt there was something off about her and simply telling that to me just the day before and there I was, sharing a room with her and her six-shooter. Or whatever it was.

"Do you know what to do with it," I asked.

"You put in bullets and pull the trigger."

"Do you have a license for it?"

"Well, no, but my father did."

That was comforting. She could show her father's death certificate if she was ever stopped by police for murder.

"I did renew my driver's license," she said. Then she noticed the grim look on my face. "That was a joke."

"You could have shot me last night," I said.

She looked at me as though I were insane.

"Why would I do that? You don't even snore."

If that was a joke it was a good one, but I wasn't laughing.

"Wouldn't pepper spray be enough protection," I asked.

"What would happen if I made a mistake and spritzed it in my own eyes by mistake?"

"Oh, I don't know, Valeria. Nothing as bad as shooting yourself in your own head, by mistake. But what do I know? That's just a wild guess."

"I never had anyone to protect me, like you do. The gun makes me feel safe. And you heard the hostility Max has for me in those poems." I stopped and turned to her.

"So you have this gun as protection against Max?" That sounded somewhat sensible.

"It was about the only thing that was in my house that wasn't destroyed by the fire, so I kept it."

"So you have it for sentimental reasons. How sweet. Oh, by the way, the hostility you read in Max's poems. That was caused by pain."

"Pain?" Valeria looked puzzled.

"Yes. Because you never came back."

I was upset. Angry. I started to walk faster, away from her.

"He kicked me out! He told me he never wanted to see me again," Valeria yelled, running after me. Catching up.

"People say all kinds of things when their foot is impaled on the floor."

"Oh my God." She grabbed my arm. I tried to wrest it away but Valeria was stronger than I'd thought. Her slender arms held mine as she faced me. Okay, I'd stand there and listen to what she had to say, then I'd find the depot and wait for the next bus back to the city. I had a feeling of unease, strongly reminiscent of the one I'd experienced the day I first visited her on Jane Street when I'd left the loft to wait for the elevator and she blocked my way. Pleaded with me to stay. That day, if only I'd pushed her aside instead of staying, of allowing myself to be drawn into her life, I wouldn't be here now. I wouldn't have grown to like her. I wouldn't be standing in the middle of a street in Ulster County facing a woman with a Glock.

I wouldn't have met Antonio.

"I'm going back to the city," I said.

"Please understand, Ellie," she pleaded. "I've had to take care of myself since I was a kid. I don't think my desire for self-protection is unreasonable." Her perfect face was empty of emotion and that was almost more frightening to me than the gun in her purse. I watched her mouth form the words. "All I have is me and some stock. The market could implode again and I'd have nothing, absolutely nothing. Now is the time for me to do something with my life. To start something I can be proud of. I'll protect myself any way I can. This gun is a safety blanket to me. I keep it to remember I came from somewhere. What's wrong with that?" Her eyes were pleading with me to understand. "You, with a mansion in Manhattan, a son who needs you, a husband who loves you. A career. Security. People like you will never understand people like me." She paused. Sudden, powerful emotion crossed her face. It crumbled, briefly, but she fought it back. "People like you are what I want to be."

I stared at her, felt my anger subside.

"You're right. I do have a lot," I said. "I can't begin to understand what it's been like for you, but that doesn't mean I don't know loneliness. It's pretty damn lonely, being in a marriage with a man who sleeps with every woman he sees. I've worked like a maniac so there was no time to feel the pain, or to feel less pain, but then the day is over and it smacks me in the face. Knocks me into a stupor of misery. That was my life for years. It's over now, because I'm making it be over. I'm fighting for *my* life. I can't be caught up with your problems now. Your gun. I just can't."

I saw the disappointment on her face and part of me wanted to reach out and hug her. The other part won.

"Antonio has a gun," she said.

"You know the difference. Besides, I haven't shared a bedroom with him. I doubt I ever will. Not after yesterday." I started once more to walk away.

"Maybe your husband went to other women because you're so cold," she said, stopping me in my tracks. "You're like Kevin. People who don't need anyone, except when they do." I turned and stared at her. Her face softened. "You scare people off, Ellie. I was surprised when you came up here. I wasn't sure what it would be like, but it was fun, wasn't it. I like you, so much. I really wanted us to be friends."

I looked at her face, the clear, delicate loveliness of it. I had such mixed feelings towards her. "I had a great time, too," I said. "I guess we are friends, but I'm going home."

"Would you have stayed if I didn't have the gun?"

"Yes. Gladly." She hugged me. I hugged her back.

"We didn't even have time for Lemon Squeeze," she said.

"You do. What about Max? Are you going to get in touch with him?"

"I called, while you were in the shower. A woman answered so I hung up. I called again and he didn't answer me for a long time, then he said he doesn't want to see me, at least not until he gets used to the idea."

"I'm sorry."

"Would you mind if I wait with you for the bus?"

"I don't mind at all."

*

I was fortunate to have a seat companion who wanted nothing more than to read a big, fat physics textbook, but the two young women in front of me were talking politics. Specifically, the slate of Republicans candidates for President.

"I can't believe it," one said. "Ben Carson? It's a joke, right?'

"And Ted Cruz? I can't even look at his face."

"What about Trump?"

"Oh, please. Have you ever heard of anything so silly?"

The ride felt endless. I tried to empty my mind, count the trees, the red cars that we passed or that passed us. The blue cars. The out-of-state license plates, the way we did when Jonathan was little. I thought back to the worst days of my depression, the days when I'd look in the powder room mirror unable to recognize the woman with the sad face. The woman whose face broke into pieces, until it vanished. Until, finally, it came back together, feature by feature, into a face of utter sadness.

Those days were gone, except for now and then, each time shorter and easier to conquer because I had tools to deal with them. Dreams. Longings.

I had come back.

CHAPTER TWENTY

The wheels of the bus on the New York Thruway. The gentle breathing of my academic seatmate.

The thought of work intruded. The needs of the buyers. The demands of the sellers.

A second bathroom, for my cat. *But of course.*

The husband who wanted pre-war for the charm. The wife who insisted on post-war for the larger closets.

Uptown. No, downtown.

East Side. No, West Side.

Condo. Co-op. Doorman, no doorman.

Manhattan. No, maybe Brooklyn, and why not throw in Queens. Might as well see everything that's out there, Ellie won't care.

I love real estate. I really do. Every weekend, the first thing I do after the puzzle is read the Real Estate section in the *New York Times.* I check out listings, websites, everything I can. I dream about some of the properties. I make lists for special clients and for clients I'd like to have and sometimes simply because I like to make lists. I remember every interior of every place I've ever shown, except for the utterly forgettable ones. The layout, the furniture, the feel of it. The light. The views. The asking price, the selling price. The commission. Clients with enough money to buy any place they want. Those with almost enough. Those just starting out, so proud, nervous, difficult to deal with. They all matter.

None of them matter. None of it matters. After twenty-odd years of it while dealing with a failed marriage was too much. I was burning out. Burned out. The early morning calls. The late night calls. The showings, walk-throughs, board packages, calls, texts. The need to be 'on.' To be sympathetic, understanding, patient. It had hardened me to those in real need, who didn't know where their next meal might come from, who didn't have a roof over their head. I used to care about such things. Care deeply. I used to volunteer, but I didn't have it in me anymore.

The satisfaction of finding the right home for someone.

The camaraderie at work.

The clients who have become friends.

The commission. Always the commission, figured out to the penny before the contract was signed.

Kevin should know that Valeria had a gun. He should have told me. She would be staying with him until she moved out. Probably, if she pleaded, he'd give her another week, another month. I didn't see him as a man who would kick her into the street, at least if she was making an honest attempt at finding a place, but the longer she might stay, the longer he would be living with a weapon. He had to know. I called and left him a message, then gathered my courage and called Antonio.

"Hi, it's Ellie. I was upstate with Valeria. I was planning to stay longer but found out she has a gun, so I left. I thought Kevin should know, if he doesn't already. Left a message for him."

"Where are you?"

"On a bus."

I ended the call, checked for messages, then turned off my phone, wondering why I'd felt the need to call Antonio. I sat in my seat, unable to do anything but fight a rising depression that increased as we neared the city. I felt my strength weaken and my mood grow grimmer.

The bus reached the terminal, pulled into its berth. The door opened and passengers reached for their belongings, rushed out towards their lives. I stood in the aisle to let my seatmate out and then sat down again until I was the last on the bus. I flung my overnight bag over my shoulder and walked toward the door like it was a gangplank. I squared my shoulders and walked toward the exit doors, through them, breathed in and out, in and out and there was Antonio. He was waiting, but there was no warmth coming from him. He just stood there. His arms, muscled and tan, were at his sides.

"Why are you here?" I asked.

"I have no idea," he said.

My heart almost exploded with feeling but I had to stay strong. We took the elevator up to the main level and walked out the Ninth Avenue exit past a barricade and a door that said 'Police.' I tried to imagine him as a young cop in uniform, with a gun and a billy club and those walky-talky things. What I saw instead was him the first time I went to his loft, shirtless and barefoot, sweat glistening on his body. We walked in silence down Ninth Avenue, stopped so that he could make a few purchases along the way. He greeted the owners, hugged an elderly cashier. His gang in Hell's Kitchen. In a few short blocks we were at his corner.

"Now what?" I asked.

"I don't play games, Ellie. We either have something or we don't and if we don't, this is where we say goodbye."

"What if we're no good together," I said.

"Don't be ridiculous."

He started walking and I followed him, past the security guard and into the elevator. Down the long corridor. I stood mutely as he unlocked the door and went inside. I stood in the threshold and watched him put away the perishables, open a bottle of Pellegrino and pour it into two tall glasses, add ice, cut a few slices of lime. He took his and walked towards the sofa, placed his glass on the trunk and went over his phonograph. His LP record collection.

An almost forgotten sound – *Echoes of Spain.*

I walked into the loft, closed and locked the door behind me and went to him. Stood in front of him as he sat on the sofa, legs splayed the way guys do. I looked at his face, the planes of it, the beautiful, angular severity. I wanted him with an intensity that stunned me. All of me wanted all of him and I wanted him to know it, even if it was only for this one time. I kept my eyes on his as I undressed, methodically folding my clothes as I removed them, then I stood, stark naked.

The surprise, the desire on his normally inscrutable face only made me want him more. I walked without shame to the back of the loft and lay on his bed, my head on his pillow and my legs crossed at the ankle. He followed, undressed with a grace I wouldn't have though possible, then walked over to the bed and lay down beside me. Kissed me gently on my mouth. My nipples. Between my legs that I opened without a thought. Kissed me as deeply as he could, then he entered me slowly, exquisitely. He filled me. I heard moan after moan. My moans, mingled with Miles Davis. When he pulled out it felt as though I'd lost part of myself, but he only wanted to explore me at his leisure. His leisure and my pleasure. No attempt to withhold anything, either of us. I opened to him with an abandon I wouldn't have believed were I not experiencing it.

We were perfect together. Insatiable, until every part of me screamed enough, anything else would be too much. He lay on his back. I rolled on top of him, exhausted. We might have slept. It might have been a dream. After a while I began to rub against him, barely aware I was doing so.

"I can't," he said.

But he did.

"Let's sleep like this," I said.

"You're kidding, right?"

We stayed like that, him inside me longer than I would have thought possible, neither of us moving.

"I don't think anything could be more perfect," I said.

"I knew it would be."

"Do you miss being a detective?"

"I like this a lot more."

"What about Benson and Stabler. They're great, aren't they?" I licked his lips, which made it awkward for him to answer. Finally he said that he absolutely loved them. We slept for a while, me on my stomach on top of him. Much later, well after sunset, we made pasta and vegetables. Cooking together was as natural as our lovemaking had been. As naked. He sat on the sofa and I brought over the large pasta bowl. He took it from me as I lowered myself onto him. That's how we ate supper, more or less. A bottle of wine and a single glass on the trunk behind me. I reached for it and poured some into the glass, the slight backward motion enough to create a sensation that was so enjoyable I repeated it several times. Lean back, twist my body, turn forward again. Oh god. He drank from the glass, then I did, some of the wine dripping onto my breast. He licked it and sucked at it. I thought I'd go insane, the entire time him hard inside me. I took the glass and replaced it on the trunk, took the empty bowl and put it there, too, then started to bounce up and down.

"Is this okay?" I asked.

"You'll kill me."

"It's fun, isn't it? Did you really think we'd be as good as we are?" He grinned. It lit up his face, softened the planes. I leaned over and kissed him. "You better say yes."

"Then okay. Yes."

"I think this might be the best time I've ever had. You don't have to say so but I bet you feel the same way."

He grinned even more broadly. "I feel the same way."

"Do you want me to stop?"

"Talking?"

"No. This."

*

His shower was large, with a rainforest showerhead. A bench. Eucalyptus soap that he lathered me with. That I lathered him with. For me, a lifetime of unmet desire washed away.

"I could probably fall in love with you," I said later.

"What can I do to make it more probable?"

Despite the tenderness of my body, I wanted him then as much as I ever had. More. I looked at him and smiled.

"You're not serious," he said.

I stayed the rest of that day. That night. We never left the loft. Never dressed. We played chess, listened to music, did the crossword puzzle together. I was happy he did it in pen, like I do. Only when a delivery boy delivered our supper from a local Greek restaurant did he put on his jeans.

He told me about the course he was going to teach at John Jay College of Criminal Justice. He showed me the Police Manual he was helping to update. I looked at the eclectic collection of books in his floor-to-ceiling bookshelves.

"You've read them all, haven't you?"

"I don't think I could ever have enough of you," he said.

The most erotic time of all was when I was making a frittata the following morning, my breasts bouncing as I beat the eggs. He stood behind me, hard against my ass while his hands reached around me, his fingers pleasuring me until I dropped the whisk into the bowl.

On Wednesday afternoon he walked me to what was becoming our parting place, the quiet, nearly deserted block of the Penn South houses near West 28th Street, a block past the church with its lines for the soup kitchen.

I took his face in my hands.

"There will never be another man like you, for me. Never."

He leaned against a lamp post, looking at me.

Say something. It took him a while.

"I can't imagine there'll be another woman like you for me, either. Ever."

"It's impossible to tell, with that inscrutable face of yours."

He took my hand and placed it on his heart.

"This is not inscrutable."

CHAPTER TWENTY-ONE

I walked the rest of the way home alone, the feel of Antonio so strong that I felt weak. As I neared my house, I prayed Patrick wouldn't be there. I hardly ever pray but this time it worked. I threw my overnight bag on the wrought iron bench in the hallway, poured myself some ice water and went to the garden. Lay on a chaise lounge and let the August heat flood my sated body. Relived every moment of the last two days, from the moment Antonio met me at Port Authority to every moment of intimacy we shared.

My body. Now, finally, I knew the incredible pleasure it was capable of. I remembered his words, that he didn't think he could ever have enough of me. That's how I felt toward him. I craved him with every inch of me and when it wasn't sex it was simply being with him. Near him. I'd never experienced such feelings before, even with Patrick in our early, happiest days. I'd never even imagined such feelings existed before. Such feelings of satisfaction, of wanting to satisfy. Of being exactly where and with whom I should be.

Later, when the sun proved too strong, I went inside and stretched out on the sofa. No movie, no music, just me trying to keep the passion of the last days inside me. The incredible happiness.

It was impossible. Now that I was in my own home, a pervasive sense of guilt took over. Guilt and dread. I thought of the countless nights over the years when Patrick came home late and barely talked to me. When he mumbled words like 'hi, honey, boy am I tired' and fell into the exhausted sleep of the sexually fulfilled. Now I understood. Sleep as an alibi. Sleep as a way to keep guilt away and satisfaction inside. I fell asleep on the sofa so I wouldn't have to face Patrick when he came home.

I couldn't sleep. I could barely relax in my own house. I went to freshen up and change out of the clothes I'd been wearing. Four days away from home with two outfits. I threw everything in the hamper and walked back to the guest room. Just as I finished putting on fresh underwear I heard the front door slam. Heard Patrick's tread on the old wooden stairs. I hurriedly closed the door.

"Ellie?" he called. "You there?" I opened the door a bit. Said yes, I was here. He took that as an invitation and walked in. He looked at me in my bra and panties for an uncomfortably long time before speaking. "There's a few messages for you on the machine downstairs, in case you haven't heard them."

"I haven't. Anything important?"

Why was he looking at me that way? I grabbed for my robe, but he took my arm, stopped me from reaching it.

"A woman called, wanting to know that you arrived home safely. She didn't leave a name, or at least I didn't hear it. The connection was terrible, a lot of static. An 845 number. I checked. It's the exchange for New Paltz. That's where you were, right?"

Oh, shit. Valeria. I couldn't think why she left a message on my home number until I remembered turning my cell phone off. Kept it off the entire time I'd been with Antonio. Realized it was still off.

"Yes. I met a girlfriend there." He was still looking at me strangely, which made me feel incredibly vulnerable standing there in my underwear. "What is it, Patrick?" I asked, with a sense of foreboding.

"That call was two days ago," he said.

I forced myself to meet his eyes but was unable to stop the flush that spread across my face.

"You've been with someone, haven't you?" he said.

Here it was.

"Yes. I have. For the first time in our marriage." We faced each other in the small room and for the first time in my marriage I felt physically threatened. I also felt angry. I wouldn't let Patrick destroy the joy I'd experienced. I absolutely wouldn't. He slapped me. It was the first time he'd ever done that, the first slap I'd ever received. It would be the last.

"That's spousal abuse," I said as I rubbed my cheek and tried to stay calm. "I'm not going to lie to you the way you lied to me so many times I can't count. And I'm not going to apologize. This was the only time in twenty years. Twenty years, Patrick! That's how long it took for me to experience an orgasm. Oh wait, that's not quite true, is it? I had a few, sometimes, after you and I used to make love. I gave them to myself, remember? 'That was so good, sweetheart' you'd say after you were done. Every single time, the same words, followed by 'I'm so tired.' But you weren't too tired to watch me pleasure myself, were you. You know how disgusted I felt? With myself? With you?" Patrick's dark eyes, always so expressive, looked startled. "Is that what you do with your women? Satisfy yourself, then watch them finish your job? Or do they lie to you, tell you how great it was? What a considerate lover you are?" I knew I was treading dangerously but stood my ground as I recalled years of pain from unmet desire. The smells of other women on shirts I'd bought him. "So who cares if your feelings are hurt now. If your stupid macho ego has been damaged. I don't care, but if you ever slap me again I will kill you. While you're sleeping."

He stared at me as though I were insane. When he finally talked, his voice was low. Too low.

"You're a ballbuster, Ellie. You were the one who was always too tired for me. Too tired or too busy. I had to practically plead with you. You used to talk about your deals while we made love. It's amazing I was able to function at all."

"We never make love. You jerked off inside me."

This was ugly. Really ugly. Patrick's face turned dark with anger. I'd never seen him so mad. He grabbed the bottom of my bra and yanked it up over my breasts. The underwire cut painfully across the top. Then he pushed me onto the narrow bed so that my head almost knocked into the wall. He yanked down my panties and pulled them off, pulled my legs apart so that I was spread open in front of him. He bent over and slid one of his thick fingers into me. Then another. I tried to scream at him to stop but nothing came out of my mouth. I tried to kick him, but it was impossible from that stupid little bed.

Think, Ellie, think. But here was nothing I could do to fight him off.

"Get your fingers out of me," I finally hissed, barely recognizing my voice. "I know a cop."

"You know a cop, honey. Sure you do." I kicked at his head, jerked my body away from him with all the strength I could manage. Tugged at his hands to get his fingers out of me.

"That's who I was with for the last two days. A retired detective with lots of friends still on the force. So do whatever you plan to do with me before I have you thrown in jail for spousal abuse and rape. And don't think I won't do it. Here, I'll make it really easy." I reached behind my back and unhooked my bra, tossed it onto the floor. My breasts were free. It felt great. I lay back, raised my knees and opened my legs as far apart as the space allowed, in a perverse desire to shock him. Taunt him. He stared at my exposed crotch and pulled his fingers out. I stared back at him, saw the desire in his eyes. He looked almost mad with it.

"I almost forgot how gorgeous you are," Patrick said, his voice a whisper. "How lush." But there was no more aggression from him. Instead he sat on the end of the bed and held his head in his hands. I sat up, swung my legs over the side of the bed and grabbed my robe off the hook on the door. I put it on as I walked downstairs, tying it as I walked into the kitchen. I pulled a partially finished bag of Mint Milano cookies out of the cupboard and ripped it open, ate a few piled one on top of the other before I sat down. Cookie crumbs fell down the front of my robe, between my breasts. It was a beautiful robe, red, pink, lavender and saffron flowers. I'd ordered it from a catalog after tossing the hideous pale yellow and green kimono in the trash. It was hard to believe that was just a few months ago. I brushed at the crumbs, ran my hand across my mouth. I had both my cell phone and the land line on the table in front of me. Also an eight-inch Sabatier chef's knife. Never had I felt as unsure of my life as I did that night, not only of what Patrick might be capable of but what I might do to him. There had been a moment upstairs when I would have killed him if I'd had the chance. I thought of Valeria's Glock.

But. There was more than a moment when I'd enjoyed the feel of his fingers inside me. Of spreading myself open in front of him and having him stare at me. Let him see what he missed by sleeping with all his bimbos. Let him suffer for the satisfaction I'd experienced with Antonio.

Patrick walked into the kitchen and I reached my hand toward the knife. He raised his hands in the air.

"I've never been so sorry about anything, El, but the thought of you with another man made me crazy. Please, don't hate me." He sat down. "I don't know what to do. I'd check into a hotel but with the kids coming home tomorrow...I took the day off to pick them up. We can't have them see us like this." He sat across from me, pointed to the knife. "You really don't need that. I'll never lay a hand on you again, I swear."

"You practically raped me. In fact I'm sure that what you did is considered rape. All I need is one little phone call to have you arrested."

"Forgive me," he said. I was barely able to take my eyes from his handsome, anguished-looking face. We sat for a while in silence. As slow as fog my anger lifted, was replaced by sadness. Acknowledgment. "Maybe you don't remember things the way I do," Patrick finally said. "Even in our early years. The times we were making love and you took a phone call. Made an appointment. A deal. You'd leave our bed and say you'd be right back. Sometimes you never came back. When you did, you were rarely fully present. There was always something. A buyer. A seller. You made me feel secondary. Impotent." Tears filled his eyes as I watched, mesmerized. "I'm flesh and blood. I need intimacy. You gave so little, physically and emotionally. But that's no excuse for how I behaved upstairs. It won't happen again. I'll sleep in the garden apartment tonight. I'll call an all-night locksmith so you'll feel safe. There's a good one on Seventh Avenue South."

"How about getting castrated instead," I said, but there was no more hostility. Patrick even cracked a smile.

"Funny. But seriously, you can change the front door keys for everyone but me. I'll just use the street level entrance. Also change the inside lock from the hallway to downstairs. Whatever you want. I'll enter downstairs from the street. You won't even know I'm there."

I wasn't interested in changing the locks, at least not at that moment. I was more interested in me. How Patrick saw me. Everything he said had been true. I had been driven to succeed. Maybe it was simply the love of the deal. Or maybe I was as dead inside as I'd thought I was in New Paltz when Valeria hugged the little girl. The only child I'd ever hugged or wanted to hug was my own. Maybe I'd never loved Patrick enough to put him before work.

But I wasn't dead inside. Not even mildly asleep, at least with Antonio. I'd never felt so alive. Been so satisfied. So desired.

I had to not think of him, not now. I went to the stove and filled the kettle with water.

"There hasn't been another woman for a while, El. I've been trying to make things work between us."

"When was the last one?" I asked. "The truth."

"A month or so before the party. More to have someone to talk to. Her, too."

"How long?"

"Once or twice. Maybe three times. The sex was secondary."

"To you or to her?"

"Both of us. I need to explain something to you. The night of my party I was late because of an emergency. A teen-aged boy had his front teeth elbowed out in a mosh-pit. I didn't even know there still were mosh pits. The kid was in agony. His mother was already a client. I wasn't about to let her son suffer. He was a kid, like ours. I felt so bad about being late for the party that I stopped in Barney's to buy you a present. A bottle of perfume. The saleswoman spritzed some on me to see if I liked it. Then more. She was out of control. I practically screamed at her to stop, just get me a new bottle of anything nice and throw it in a bag and she said to buy Chanel. Every woman likes Chanel. That's why I stank of it."

I stared at him, wondering who would make up a story like that.

As if he heard my thoughts, Patrick said he still had the gift upstairs. Said he'd run to get it. I said it wasn't necessary, at least right then. That I believed him. "As far as being late recently," Patrick continued, "I've been volunteering for emergency work. Like work on that kid. People in accidents. Mostly to give you space." He paused. "Give us a chance."

"It's hard to believe," I said, but I did. It's what he would do.

"That's why I hadn't mentioned it."

Our eyes met. His were swollen. Now I knew with certainty that I had been a big reason for Patrick's infidelities. But still. There was Cindy with the bowling ball breasts and the woman at the Obama call party and how many more that I never knew about. That Patrick might not even remember. I remembered the long, lonely nights. Painful, yearning nights. I looked again at him and felt a deep sorrow for us. A wave of shame for the hours of ecstasy with Antonio. And, God help me, I felt lust. My body, sore and sated from Antonio, penetrated by Patrick's fingers, was primed. I walked over to him and looked into his eyes. Large, dark pools of feeling. I discarded my robe.

The shock on his face. The realization. This moment, or no moment. He pulled me to him and cried against my breasts. His hands held me at my waist as though I were made of gossamer. Then, slowly, of flesh and blood. His hand reached up, caressed my nipples already so tender that the mix of pain and pleasure was profound. He lifted me onto the far, empty edge of the table and raised my legs to his shoulders. Kissed me with a longing that moved me beyond words. I lay back, closed my eyes and expected nothing. Received everything I'd ever wanted from him and then he did it again, in our bed.

CHAPTER TWENTY-TWO

1'm a slut.

That was my first thought when I woke up the following morning. Two men in two days.

Wrong. Two men in one day.

Super slut.

I lay on the king-sized bed and recalled the improbable evening. After making love to me on the kitchen table, Patrick had lifted me, carried me upstairs as though I was weightless, a porcelain doll. I used to break the heads off dolls when I was young. I thought they were stupid. I didn't feel stupid being carried but what I thought of was Rhett Butler and Scarlett O'Hara. Patrick placed me gently on the bed and I looked at him. We smiled at each other and months and years of anger and disappointment were washed away. *Gone with the Wind.* Those were my thoughts as I fell into guiltless sleep – mint juleps and big white porches and my body, sated beyond belief. It was Patrick and me, in the same bed for the first night since his party. Two long months of sleeping on a narrow twin bed in a miniscule room. Suddenly I missed my old bed. The size of it. The large, airy corner room. I wanted it back. I said so to Patrick but there was no answer. That was because he wasn't in bed. He wasn't in the bathroom. I slipped into my kimono and went downstairs.

French toast waiting for me on a covered plate on the table. A note, a heart with our initials and the fact that Patrick had gone to meet Jonathan and Maggie at JFK.

I ate slowly, my body still a bit tingly, then went upstairs, showered, dressed in shorts and a T-shirt and left the house. At West Side Market I bought a rotisserie chicken, corn on the cob, salad, brownies, ice cream, limeade and a beautiful quarter of watermelon. Then I went home, satisfied with myself, and sat in a chair by the large front bay windows. I closed my eyes and relived my recent hours of pleasure. I felt fulfilled. Desired. Ashamed. I wanted more.

A silver Lincoln Town Car made a U-turn in the middle of West 14th Street. I applauded the nerve. It pulled up to the curb and Patrick emerged first, paid the driver and took a duffle bag and a roll-on from the trunk. Jonathan and Maggie climbed out soon after. I went outside, stood on the steps and hugged them all as the approached. The look Patrick gave me was that of a high school boy with his first crush and I felt myself blush. I couldn't help but notice the look of surprise on Jonathan's face.

We had a picnic in the garden. It wasn't long before words began to tumble, one over the other, from the kids.

"My relatives live in a thatched cottage near the water," Maggie said. "It's totally romantic."

"I liked Penzance best."

"The weird gardens."

"The wild coast."

"The people."

"Just being with each other."

"The weather wasn't too bad," Maggie said. "It only rained about half of every day." Jonathan looked at her so fondly that it was clear how they'd spent the rainy parts of days. "What about you guys," he asked, salting an ear of corn.

"We're good," Patrick said.

"That's almost how it seems."

By six o'clock Maggie looked like she was about to pass out. Patrick and Jonathan put her in a cab to her home on Avenue B, a duplex above her family's modest restaurant. By ten o'clock Jonathan decided to call it a night. Patrick and I cleaned up and went into the living room. We were in the midst of an awful movie on Lifetime when I felt an urgent, burning need to pee. I went to the powder room but only a little bit of urine dribbled out. It burned. Even afterwards it burned. As soon as I went back into the living room the urge returned. As I sat on the toilet a third or fourth or fifth time in just minutes, the burning trickle was accompanied by an almost existential shiver. Not a cold shiver, just a strange sensation that I felt first in my arms. I hugged myself, hunched over as the shiver took over my entire body for a few brief moments and then stopped after a few drops of urine forced their way out, each drop feeling like a flame.

Over and over again. It was exhausting. I assumed it was a urinary tract infection from complaints I'd heard over the years. Almost every woman I knew had complained of them, some just once or twice, others too many times to count. If that's what I was suffering through, it was as dreadful as I'd heard it described.

An hour of it. Two hours. When I sat on the sofa, the only minor relief was pressing my hand tightly against my crotch.

"What's wrong?" Patrick asked. I glared at him.

"I think I have a urinary tract infection. I'm going up to take a bath."

I ran warm water in the master bathroom tub. I sank into the water as soon as there was enough to cover the sensitive part of me. I let the few hot drops of pee dribble into the tub whenever I felt the urge. Each time, I experienced those weird little shivers. It was exhausting. I threw one leg over the edge of the tub and pressed against my crotch. I didn't care if droplets of pee ended up on my hand, I just hoped there'd be enough, cumulatively, to end this awful discomfort. My hand was at my crotch and my head was against the back of the tub when Patrick walked in.

"Feeling better?" he asked.

"Go to hell," I said. He asked me a few questions and I snapped answers at him. He opened the medicine cabinet and took a pill out a bottle. Filled a glass of water and handed it to me.

"This will help," he said. "Two pills a day for three days."

"What is it?"

"Cipro. Take it and drink lots of water. Cranberry juice, too."

"You keep these handy for all your women?"

"You'll thank me soon. You should probably call your gynecologist."

"You call my gynecologist. No one's going to touch me there, ever again. I have this because of you."

"Or not," Patrick said, glaring at me. He left, slamming the bathroom door behind him.

*

Cipro was my savior. It began to work within an hour or so. After several glasses of water and before too long, symptoms eased. I actually peed. Pee-ing is easy and fun for me! I was even able to have a decent night's sleep. I took another pill with breakfast and by noon felt good enough to want to do something with Jonathan. He didn't feel the same way. He just wanted to hang around the house. Patrick had one appointment, a touch up on a bonding for a groom before his wedding in the Brooklyn Botanical Gardens. Before he left, he reminded me to take another pill and to hydrate. I wondered if all cosmetic dentists knew as much about UTIs as he did. How many women had suffered through this because of him.

Jonathan was sprawled out on the sofa, reading *Steppenwolf*. I was in an armchair doing the puzzle when I received a call from Linetta Wilton. She was in town for a client, then leaving for three weeks to travel through Vietnam. She said she realized that a summer in the Hamptons followed by almost a month abroad might not be the best business plan for an attorney with a small practice, but we only live once, don't we. She also said that if I had no plans I could drop by her office, she was there the rest of the day and part of the next before her trip. Paperwork. I had taken my morning Cipro, had peed normally, or at least comfortably, I said okay, even though I felt strange agreeing to see a divorce attorney after the night Patrick and I had. I felt like a traitor.

It was just for a talk, I convinced myself. I told Jonathan I'd be back in several hours, he grunted okay, that maybe he'd feel like doing something with me later.

I walked down Seventh Avenue South to Bleecker, then zig-zagged my way to Broadway and south. The sidewalks of Lower Manhattan were jammed with pedestrians in too much of a hurry for the end of summer. It was obscene. I stopped in a coffee shop and grabbed the only vacant booth. The red pleather seat was ripped and grey stuffing crept out. As long as that was all that crept out. I ordered a grilled cheese and tomato sandwich on rye and a cranberry juice, but the combination seemed disgusting, so I changed the beverage to a Coke. As I waited, I took one of my red notebooks and drew a line down the center of a blank page. Asset and Liability columns. I listed our assets, estimating wildly in places. House, furniture, jewelry, my bank account, our joint account. IRAs, my Keogh, Patrick's retirement fund. My estimated income this year. I had no idea of Patrick's income, only what was deposited weekly into our joint account. There was Jonathan's college fund, joint savings and checking, rental income. Our debit column was basically our mortgage and tax bills, water and fuel costs and my credit card debt. I also had no idea of Patrick's credit card debt. He had a bookkeeper. We looked good on paper.

A few blocks past the coffee shop I entered a small lobby in a twelve-story office building. I signed in with the guard then rode a slow, crowded elevator to the eighth floor, walked down a nondescript corridor to Linetta's office. I entered a small front room covered with flowered Mario Buatta wallpaper. A desk with no one behind it and nothing but a phone on top of it. This was so unlike the Linetta I remembered I had trouble believing I was in the right place.

An inner door opened and there she was, a welcoming smile on her face.

"The wallpaper," I said, smiling back.

"My partner's choice. She's on maternity leave." I followed her into a second room, much more suited to the Linetta I remembered. Pale walls the color of smoke, adorned with several black and white photographs. The Five Corners. The Staten Island Ferry with Lady Liberty in view. The old Madison Square Garden. The former Women's House of Detention. An ebony desk, filing cabinets, black leather chairs and couch. Linetta was dressed for the room, in dove grey slacks and blouse, an ivory-colored lace camisole peeking out. Even her eyes were grey. Her lipstick was magenta.

"You look good," she said. "A little tired. Everything okay?"

"I didn't sleep enough," I said. "I had my very first urinary tract infection. Have you ever had one?"

She nodded.

"Sure," she said. "Who hasn't?"

"Nuns and me, probably, until last night. My first. They're brutal. What do you take?"

"What did I take. I haven't had one in years. I think it was Macrobid."

"Not Cipro?"

"No. But that works too. Christ, that'll cure anything. Remember the anthrax scare after 9/11? I carried Cipro with me for years."

"Patrick keeps it in the medicine cabinet, probably in case one of his bimbos needs relief."

"He's that bad? I'm surprised you stayed with him so long."

"Me, too. Now he swears that's all over and wants us to work things out."

"You believe him?"

"I believe he wants that, but I can't trust him."

She walked over to a small refrigerator and handed me a bottle of Evian. "Drink lots of water. Cranberry juice, too, if you can stand it. How's your kid?" I told her he was starting Columbia soon. She congratulated me, then told me her cat recently died. I said I was sorry, that must have been hard for her. She said, no, it was just a cat. I should tell her about Patrick's business.

I told her what I knew, that it was both cosmetic and general dentistry, that he had a partner, they rented an enormous space a few blocks east of Barney's, uptown. They built it out, rent the extra spaces to an orthodontist, endodontist, periodontist.

"That's a hell of a lot of -ists."

I smiled. "Their combined rents more than cover the partners' share. By a lot."

"Smart. What's the setup? An LLC?"

"I should know that but I don't. I'll find out. Does it matter?"

"Yeah, maybe, if you go ahead with divorce. Even with no-fault things can get nasty and then we might want to go after part of it. Dissipation of Assets." At least that's what I think she called it. It was more than I wanted to think about.

"I wouldn't want anything from his business," I said. I showed her the rough net worth statement I'd put together. She commented on the fact that there was nothing related to Patrick's income or debt.

"Find out what you can. I'll do the same. Just because." She looked at the rest of the statement, shook her head. "I'm pretty sure you undervalued the house by a couple of million. The market's still solid, isn't it?" She looked at me. "At least that's what I've been reading. Prices are through the roof."

"It's inflated. It won't hold up. And we have two rent-stabilized tenants, which devalues it."

"Buy them out if you decide to sell. Don't worry, we'll nail the bastard, if and when you want to."

The bastard. What I'd thought of Patrick for so long, yet it annoyed me to hear Linetta talk like that.

"He's been trying," I said.

"Don't kid yourself. That's what men do. They want what they don't have. They can't stand not having it. You know what I'm saying. By the way, I'm not charging for today so tell me the good stuff. There's got to be something."

An image of Antonio and me together on the judo mat. I felt myself blush. Couldn't hold back a smile.

"I met someone," I said. "A retired detective, about to start teaching at John Jay. I don't know, maybe classes already started. We spent two nights together." I leaned back on her leather couch. "It was amazing."

"Ergo the UTI," Linetta said. I blushed, thinking of Patrick and me just hours after Antonio and me. "What? What aren't you telling me?" I shook my head. Changed the subject.

"Remember the first time we met? Ten years ago. Maybe more. The first thing you said to me was that I'd better not be one of those jerks who's gonna waste your time. You'd know it in five minutes."

"And you told me that if I was one of those stupid divas who wanted a penthouse on Lower Fifth for a steal, go find another broker." Linetta laughed.

"Are you seeing anyone now?" I asked.

"Francie. We've been together almost five years. She's a chemist."

"She's a she. I guess that's why you don't get UTIs anymore."

She nodded. Then she stood. So did I, ready to leave, when a sudden, weird weakness overcame me. It was terrifying. I sank back down into the softness of the sofa. A sense of disorientation, as if I'd been hit abruptly with the flu or a stomach bug. Or heart failure or a stroke. As though the world was closing in and suffocating me. I felt light-headed. I even thought I might be dying. But I couldn't die, because of Jonathan. I couldn't die until he finished college. Was married. Had his first child. I had no power over what was happening to me. I clutched the cushion beneath me with both hands, just to know that I could. A grip on the pillow meant I had a grip of myself.

No, it didn't. But it did mean I was alive. I wanted to ask Linetta if I seemed okay but I was afraid to move my mouth in case I couldn't.

"Oh Christ," Linetta said. That was good. I heard her voice clearly. I nodded so that she would know I'd heard. Nodded again because I was so relieved that I could. I could sit on the sofa and nod my head. I could be a bobble doll. "Should I call an ambulance?" That was Linetta, asking me if she should call an ambulance. Her words were clear but I nodded yes, then wondered what hospital it would take me to. What ones are this far downtown? I shook my head. "Yes hospital or no hospital?"

"Which one?" I asked. Linetta walked over and sat down next to me.

"Does anything hurt," she said. I shook my head. She handed me the bottle of water. "Sip. Slowly." I sipped, touched around my mouth after to see if I'd dribbled any water. No. Oh thank God I hadn't dribbled. I drank more. I was supposed to anyway. I made a mental list of what to do that seemed sensible. Breathing seemed like a good idea so I did, breathing in through my nose, out through my mouth. Or should I be doing it in through my mouth, out through my nose. Don't be silly, I told myself. I'm breathing, that's all that matters. I decided to talk, to hear my voice. I spoke the words with deliberation.

"Watch me talk."

"Okay, good," Linetta said. "Go ahead." I almost cried with relief that she'd understood me. It wasn't a stroke. I looked up at her.

"Is my mouth moving normally?"

"Yes. Say some more."

"What should I say?"

"I don't know. Anything. How about how now, brown cow."

"How about how now, brown cow," I said. "Was that good?"

Linetta nodded. "It was perfect. Your face isn't lopsided or anything. Stick out your tongue."

"Why?"

"I'm not sure. I think I read it." I stuck my tongue out. She told me to say how now, brown cow again, faster, twice in a row.

"Oh, c'mon," I said, but I did it.

"Well done! Now roll the r's."

"What?"

"Roll the r's. How now, brrrrown cow." I did it. She laughed.

"I want to hit you," I said. She laughed harder.

"Breathe."

"I've been breathing, idiot. If I hadn't been, I'd be dead." She nodded and I could sense her relief.

"I think you're having an anxiety attack. They're terrifying, but they pass. Once you have one you'll have more, but they won't ever be as scary as this one, or maybe they will be just as scary except you'll know what they are. Trust me on this. C'mon, let's go outside. Fresh air helps." Linetta took both her bag and mine, slung them on her shoulder and pulled me up from the couch.

"Like there'll be fresh air on lower Broadway in August," I said.

"That's my girl."

She locked the door and we walked to the elevator, Linetta's hand on my elbow. I leaned against the wall of the small, airless, crowded elevator car and felt I would pass out if it didn't stop soon. It felt simultaneously that my heart was racing and also that I could hardly breathe. For a split second, when the elevator stopped, I thought my heart had stopped with it. Then we were outside. I leaned against the building and took in deep breathes of hot, stale city air. Cars honked. People pushed. When a cabbie screamed out his open window to a bicyclist weaving in and out of traffic, "Fuck you, asshole, I hope you die," I felt stronger.

"I love this city," I said.

"Me, too," Linetta said. "Did I ever tell you about my first panic attack?"

"No."

Hers happened in Paris. She was traveling alone. She was in a small room in the Louvre that was filled to the brim with Japanese tourists, everyone trying to politely edge their way closer to the Mona Lisa, which was much smaller than she thought it would be. When she finally reached the front line of viewers she found herself, in an instant, struggling to quiet a rapidly beating heart. A weakness. One minute she'd been fine, the next she thought she might be having a stroke. She felt dizzy. Weak. Disoriented. She'd eaten gravlax earlier, in an outdoor café in the baking heat of summer. Maybe it was food poisoning, she'd thought, so she looked for a ladies' room but there was a long line and it didn't really feel like she had to go. She felt like she had to sit down and lean against a wall. She determined she'd rather have diarrhea on a floor in the Louvre than pass out standing in line for the bathroom because what if she hit her head and then also had diarrhea. That would be too much for anyone but then she realized this feeling had nothing to do with her stomach. She felt odder and weaker with each passing second so she sat against a wall outside the ladies' room until a guard told her to move. She shook her head. He took her hand and pulled her up, walked her outside, asked if he should call an ambulance. She shrugged. She had no idea. She remembered to breathe. It helped. She felt a little less weak, a little more in control. His eyes were blue, his shift almost over. If she could wait a few minutes he'd walk her to her home. She shook her head. To her hotel? She nodded. Managed to tell him it was near Rue Princesse. He said his apartment was closer.

"Don't tell me that that was the end of the story," I said. Linetta grinned.

"I stayed with him for the rest of my trip," she said. "It was sweet. He was the last man I ever slept with before switching sides." She looked at me. "Listen to me, Ellie. As a friend now, not a divorce lawyer. It's all about self-preservation. Do what makes you feel happy. And safe." I nodded. I was in total agreement with her words. "There's a ton of jerks in this city. If you think you can salvage a marriage that seems to be on the rocks, go for it. On the other hand, when you talked about your cop, you glowed like a Chinese lantern, lit up from the inside out."

"I glowed?"

"You sure did."

"So what do I do now?"

"Whatever it takes."

CHAPTER TWENTY-THREE

Jonathan and I went shopping for his dorm room. Every time I walk the few blocks of Sixth Avenue and pass TJ Maxx, The Container Store, Staples, Bed Bath & Beyond I recall my dismay when the big box stores began to appear in Manhattan. They are clumped in a few short blocks just minutes from our house. But now, with my son headed to college, their convenience couldn't be denied. Sheets, comforter, pillows, towels, soaps - bought and delivered to our front door within a few short hours. Afterwards, we had lunch at the nearby Rubin Museum. Jonathan seemed disengaged, fidgety. I assumed it was nervousness about starting college, even though he would only be a short subway ride away.

Later that afternoon Patrick took him clothes-shopping at Macy's. When they returned home, Patrick took me aside and said that Jonathan didn't seem himself. Patrick grilled lambchops and corn on the cob, I made salad and we had dinner in the garden. Jonathan was biting into an ear of corn when I asked him if anything was wrong. He didn't say anything at first. Then he threw down the corn and got up from the table. He glared at Patrick with a hostility I'd never seen. Patrick seemed stunned. This should have been a day of excitement, the day before heading off to one of the finest colleges in the country.

"Is anything wrong?" he asked. His voice cracked with anger.

"You really want to know?" Patrick started to stand up but I put my hand on his arm. Jonathan stood and faced us, his shoulders back, hands clenched. "The last ten years of my life have sucked, that's what!" He almost spat out the words. "I've dreamed of the day I could leave for college, out of this hellhole of a home with Dad's cheating and lying and Mom's misery. I almost made it out of the city. I worked my ass off to get top grades and you know why? So I could get the fuck out! Go to Berkeley. Chicago. Duke. Brown. But I couldn't leave Mom alone with you, Dad. I couldn't trust you. I still don't. So even though I'm going an Ivy, one of the best schools in the country, I wanted to be out of the city and away from you! God damm you, Dad! And you, too, Mom, for putting up with his shit for so long!"

He left. Patrick and I sat at the picnic table as flies settled on our food and mosquitos settled on my neck and bare arms. I started shaking. I took one look at Patrick's stricken face and left the table, went upstairs to the guest room and closed the door. I stared at the globe in the corner and wished I were anywhere else. Cambodia. Swaziland. A polar ice-cap. The next day we straggled into the kitchen one by one. I made breakfast but no one had much appetite. I called our car service of choice and ordered a minivan to take us to Columbia. We loaded it with Jonathan's belongings and drove up the West Side Highway. It would have been in silence had it been just our small family, but the driver kept up a steady stream of conversation. Oh, Columbia, you must be very proud of your son. What are you studying? Do you have a girlfriend? I looked at Jonathan but he just stared straight ahead.

Maybe he was just nervous, I thought. Taking it out on us.

No, I had set a terrible example of motherhood by putting up with Patrick's behavior for so long. And Patrick had been a pig. Jonathan had every right to be upset, but not now. Besides, nobody grows up in a perfect world.

The driver turned off on West 96th Street for gas at one of the few stations left in Manhattan. Then we drove across 96th to Amsterdam Avenue, uptown to West 114th Street. The driver helped us unload and wished Jonathan good luck. His middle daughter was starting her first year at Princeton on full scholarship. Maybe she and Jonathan could meet one day. His daughter was beautiful but most of all she was very smart. A Columbia boy would be a nice match with a Princeton girl. He took out his wallet and showed us a photograph of a thin girl with long dark hair. I congratulated him. So did Jonathan. Patrick didn't say a word. He seemed broken.

There were sign-in tables, I.D.s. Teens in shorts and T-shirts, some excited, others blasé or trying to seem so. Probably the city kids. We walked to Jonathan's dorm, took the elevator to a high floor and found his room. A single with a twin bed, a desk with shelves above it and nothing else but his belongings. I said I was surprised he hadn't wanted a roommate. He said he was used to having his own room. He liked it. This was a new Jonathan and I had my first feelings of what it would be like, now that he was in this new phase of his life.

Patrick and I would matter less and less to him.

"I'll help you make the bed," I said, starting to open one of the Bed Bath & Beyond bags.

"I'll do it later, Mom."

Patrick took him aside. I knew he was giving him money. Jonathan also had a credit card, MetroCard, bank account. In an absolutely dire emergency he could walk the hundred blocks home. Five miles was nothing to a healthy teen. An angry teen.

"Let's go," I said to Patrick.

"You don't have to," Jonathan said, turning to us. "There's a lot going on here today. You can meet some of the parents. If you feel like it." But I wanted desperately to be home, away from his anger toward us. His words from yesterday stung even harder today than they had when he'd said them. Then, it had been an unexpected shock. Today, hurt had settled in. Shame. Truth.

I was hopeful that he would soon become happy with Columbia. When he saw that we were serious about leaving he reminded us that he'd be home in a few days for our annual Labor Day picnic. We followed him into the long corridor. Arriving students, boxes dragging, rolling suitcases, parents, excitement, toilets flushing, a hive of activity.

"There's kids from all over the world. We can at least let them know we're here for them," I said.

"We can be there for them?" Patrick asked. "What are we, a youth hostel?"

He was trying, but Jonathan wasn't around to see that. He had left us to introduce himself to other students. He was carrying a large duffle for someone. I was trying to forget last night. I wasn't sure I ever would. I went into another room, where Jonathan was talking to another freshman, a smile on his face. It seemed a good time to leave.

Patrick and I left. I looked around at the activity in the dorm. On the lawn. At the buildings and the grounds and a memory rushed back to me. Years rolled away, back to when I had been a student at New York University downtown. I was a mediocre student, preferring to spend my time enjoying Greenwich Village or playing tennis uptown, in Central Park. Pick-up games. While I was waiting for a court one day, I met a Columbia student named Sato. When a court became available we played singles. We were well matched, both decently strong players. Both sophomores. After our game we walked together up Broadway to the college. It was on a patch of grass close to where Patrick and I were standing all these years later that Sato had tried patiently to teach me Go. We dated for a short time. We were both virgins and he was shy and scholarly. One day he said he didn't want to have sexual intercourse until he was married but added, very matter-of-factly, that he would be glad to lick me "down there." I'd stared at him, embarrassed. Lick me? Down there? Like an ice cream cone? When I didn't say anything he suggested another Go lesson. A lick, a lesson, it all seemed the same to him. A year later, I met Patrick, lost my innocence and fell in love, and here we were twenty years later, sending our son, who wanted no part of us, off to the rest of his life.

"He can be home in twenty minutes, whenever he wants. If he ever wants to," I said. I felt numb.

"Closer to half an hour," Patrick said. He shook his head. "How did the years go by so quickly, El?" He put his arm around my shoulder and we walked a bit, looking for Jonathan. We found him standing in a group of both students and parents. "Let's go introduce ourselves. Then we'll leave." So that's what we did. We were welcoming, assuring out-of-state parents that we were just a short subway ride away, a home away from home for anyone who needed it. But inside, I was still stunned at Jonathan's anger toward us. When I told him that we were ready to leave, all he said was okay, he'd be home for the picnic.

Patrick and I entered the subway, stood on the crowded, airless platform and waited for the downtown local. A Chinese musician seated on a three-legged stool played the same few notes over and over on an instrument I'd never before seen and never wanted to hear again. The continuous, grating sound, the increasingly crowded, airless platform began to feel like a bad joke. I willed the train to arrive. When it finally did, I pushed in and found an empty seat, slid into it before anyone else could. I'm good at that. Patrick grabbed an overhead strap and stood in front of me.

I was squeezed between an overweight man in a dated, sleeveless Rally to Restore Sanity T-shirt and a young man trying to grow facial hair. He was absorbed in a coverless paperback. Patrick stood next to a tall, thin man trying to read the *Times*, its pages a mess that he wasn't able to control on the crowded train. He refused to grab hold of the overhead strap and with every lurch of the train I was sure he'd fall on top of either me or the teen. At West 96th Street a few people stepped off the train and a lot more entered.

"We should get off here and transfer to the express," Patrick said, but I didn't want to give up my seat. The doors closed. Staying on the local meant we had ten extra stops before ours. On the express we would have had only three more. The difference was a matter of a few minutes that felt much longer. We walked from the subway to the house in silence, lost in our own thoughts. Patrick seemed a world away. He went into the kitchen and poured two glasses of iced tea, carried them into the living room and handed one to me. He plopped down in his armchair. I was in my favorite corner of the couch.

"Now what?" he said. "Jonathan doesn't need us anymore."

"Who can blame him?"

"What about you, El?"

"I don't need you."

"You don't need anyone," he said. "You never did. I'm curious. Did the other night mean anything at all to you?"

I looked at him, hoping he didn't expect a repeat.

"Of course it did," I said.

"Do you love me at all?"

"I don't hate you."

"This whole business. It's torture. Our son hates us. You, I don't know about you." His pain was real. I heard it, saw it on his face. I'd been where he was, a suffering I thought would drown me. I couldn't let anything ever pull me back down there again. "My God, El, what happened to us? I loved you so much, but you acted like I was invisible. For years I was sure you had someone else. Why else were you so distant?" I looked at him sitting in his chair, his thick, muscular legs spread wide. He was appealingly masculine. Powerful. "I was building up my business. But you. You let yours take over your life. Our life."

I couldn't have this conversation about why I'd worked so feverishly, not then, less than an hour after seeing our son off to college. Not with his words repeating themselves over and over again. His hostility to us. His disappointment in staying in the city, because of me.

"I'm going for a walk," I said.

Kate texted me as I was walking. She had been invited to a friend's villa in Tuscany for a few weeks and was leaving in two days. She would be back by mid-September but I could have the photographer over whenever it was convenient. There was a key for me at her gallery. I reminded her that I hadn't yet sent the Exclusive Agreement and said that without her signature I couldn't do the shoot. She told me not to be silly, to fax it to her in Italy, she was too busy to deal with anything else before she left. She'd text me the number as soon as she knew what it was.

I called France. Mariella and Philippe planned to be in town after the Jewish holidays. I checked the calendar and wrote down September 23rd, the end of Yom Kippur. They wanted to see no more than five properties and were extremely set on their requirements, except for location. That didn't matter except that it had to be Midtown or further downtown. They needed three thousand square feet or more, with character, lots of light, some outdoor space. It had to be a flexible building, a legal live-work and to please email the possible properties at least a week before their arrival. No more than five million dollars.

The sense of relief I felt from not having any solid commitments for a few days was almost overwhelming. Maybe I could have more time with Antonio. Then I realized he'd be busy with classes and fought the desire to call him. He'd call me when he could. I walked home, trying unsuccessfully to forget Jonathan's words. He'd stayed in the city only for me. My misery had, in essence, imprisoned him at a time in his life when he should be most free.

It's Columbia!

That's what I told myself. You can't do better than that. Obama went there. Jonathan will thrive there, or if not, he could transfer.

He will be fine.

CHAPTER TWENTY-FOUR

Antonio held a take-out menu in his hand. "What do you want on your pizza?"

"Mushrooms, red pepper and sweet sausage," I said. "A large."

He punched the numbers, placed the order. About fifteen minutes later he greeted the delivery guy with a smile and a generous tip.

I grabbed a slice. So did he.

I leaned over and licked a bit of tomato sauce from the corner of his mouth just before I reached for my second slice.

"I love a woman with a healthy appetite," he said.

"Then you love me."

I'd said it lightly, but when our eyes met, I thought, this is scary territory.

"So. Have you ever killed anyone?"

"Smooth transition," he said, grinning.

"Seriously."

"I was a cop for twenty years."

"So that's a yes. How many?"

"Why? Does the thought of it turn you on?" I felt the blush spread across my face.

"Everything about you turns me on," I said. I loved looking at him. Just sitting in the same room felt like a gift. I was forty-four years old and finally knew what I wanted. What I needed. I stood up and walked over to him. "I'm yours." He pulled me to him and held me close. A hunger, a need, a desire to be one with this man. Our clothes came off. I took and took and took, everything he gave, lost in a world of pleasure. Later, I lay sprawled on the bed, legs wide open. Exhausted. Sweaty. Sticky. Amazingly, incredibly happy.

He was on his side, looking at me. "I could look at you forever."

I placed his hand between my thighs. "Forever sounds perfect."

*

He was the only child of a Mexican artisan mother and a Chinese-Hawaiian martial arts father who left when Antonio was a toddler. He'd never heard from him again. He was close to his mother, though he saw her infrequently. She split her time between Mexico and a small studio in Chinatown. She was a weaver and jewelry maker. He spoke several languages, knew several esoteric martial arts, liked to dance.

"There's a club in East Harlem," he said. "Great music."

"Let's go."

"Another time. We're here, now." He pulled me up off the bed, walked us into the living room and placed a record on the turntable. Leonard Cohen's *Dance Me to the End of Love*. Not much beats dancing naked in a moonlit loft, except being lifted up and entered by a man with perfect rhythm.

It was raining when I left so I decided to take the bus rather than walk home. He went with me to the bus stop. Waited with me a long time as traffic down Ninth Avenue inched along. I was happy for the wait, grateful that we had some extra time together until the bus finally arrived. A line of people exited. More boarded, including two in wheelchairs. The ramp for the disabled descended, the two passengers in wheelchairs went up the ramp one by one, were maneuvered into place and buckled in. The rest of the passengers got on, inserted their MetroCards. There were about half a dozen people in front of me now. I reached out and touched Antonio's face, the strong stubble. We kissed. It felt as though the sidewalk, the world, disappeared. Nothing mattered but him. His lips, his tongue, his strong thighs against mine. After a time, I began to hear the sounds of the city. A dog barking. Cars honking. Voices. A skateboard. A few people clapping.

"Yo, guys!"

"Take it to a hotel."

"Hubba hubba!"

"Hey," I heard. I turned to look at the driver. "You getting on or what. I don't got all day."

I was about to step onto the bus when I turned and told Antonio that I loved him.

CHAPTER TWENTY-FIVE

How do people do this adultery thing? How are they built so that they can do it and keep on living a seemingly normal life? For me it was difficult. Painful. From joy to a dread that invaded me like a parasite as I neared home.

Patrick was in the living room, drinking a Stella and just starting *Casablanca.* He was home every night now. He'd made a chicken dish from Mark Bittman's enormous cookbook. The meal was still warm if I wanted some. I felt unexpected affection for him for not asking questions. For not being angry. It came as an unpleasant surprise when he paused the movie during the "Marseillaise," which annoyed me. It was one of my favorite scenes.

"If you want to be with this cop of yours, go ahead. You have to know what's out there. I guess." I stared at him in disbelief. "I've begun to make peace with you seeing someone else. It may last, it may not. For my sake, I hope it doesn't. I'm trying to see your side, that's all." I didn't know what to say, so I didn't say anything for a while. When I did, it was the wrong thing.

"Will you consider moving downstairs?"

Patrick looked at me, startled. Disappointed.

"*You* move downstairs," he said. He left the living room. I heard the fridge open. Close. I turned the movie back on and settled back into the corner of the couch to watch the rest of the movie. The pride with which Ilsa looked at Laszlo as he sang in defiance of the Nazis. It was a brilliant scene. I paused the film at that point, to replay it when Patrick returned. When he did, it was with a pint of L'Arte del Gelato chocolate sorbet and two spoons. He sat back down, next to me.

"If we divorce, would we remain friends?" His face was impassive, unusual for such an openly emotional man.

"Maybe even best friends," I said, meaning it. "I trust you with everything except your, uh, member."

"It's trying to behave." He smiled, but there was pain in his eyes.

"I was almost destroyed, Patrick. I can't go back there. If I do, I'm not sure I'd survive a next time. I'm serious. I'm sorry."

"I'll never forgive myself for not seeing things more clearly before this. I love you enough to want you to be happy."

"What does that mean?"

"I'm not sure. I hope this cop guy's a decent person and not just in it for the sex."

"Maybe I'm just in it for the sex," I said.

"I'm not sure if that makes me feel better or worse. But if this is your stab at seeing how freedom feels, I guess I'm okay with living downstairs, at least for a while. But he can't sleep here, in this house. I mean that."

"Of course not. Thank you," I said. "I'll make downstairs nice for you."

"Can we have date nights?" I looked at him, so surprised at the unexpected and sweet suggestion that I let out a laugh.

"Your place or mine?"

"I love you, El.

It was the nicest evening I could remember having with him in years, but it didn't stop me from calling Zack, a Queens contractor, the following morning. He said he'd stop by between jobs and that he'd be able to start work after Labor Day.

"I'm surprised you have time to see me today," I said.

"The last days of summer I have time. My men don't. And for all the business you've sent my way over the years I'd make time for you whenever."

He came by during lunch and gave me an estimate for renovating the garden apartment. I gave him a curried chicken sandwich and a tall glass of lemonade. There would be a team of three. The maple floors had to be sanded and polyurethaned, walls sanded and painted. We needed more electrical outlets. New lighting. The galley kitchen would receive a new dishwasher and sink, new tiles on the miniscule backsplash. After he left I called Housing Works and made arrangements for them to pick up everything but the piano, the dresser, a few floor lamps and a rug. Then I called Patrick at work. He had just finished bonding four teeth on a runway model and was through for the day. I asked him if he wanted a Duxiana or a Hästens. He asked if that was a new brand of ice cream.

"They're mattresses," I said, smiling. He said he'd only know once we tried them out, together. He had short days now, just emergencies, so by mid-afternoon we visited both stores. They were a few blocks apart, both near our house. He insisted on going back and forth between the stores and having me lay down next to him, trying out all the king-sized beds. He said it was better with my head on his shoulder. I said sure, honey, and he grinned. The Duxiana saleswoman said we were absolutely adorable.

"We're separating," I said.

"I'm sorry," she said.

"But we'll have date nights," he said.

"I can let you have the floor model of a different style for a better price," the saleswoman said.

"We'll think about it," I said. There was another mattress store nearby that I wanted to visit.

That night as I lay in the guest room I worried about Patrick's sudden agreement to move downstairs. Then I worried about Antonio getting Lyme disease while hiking with Kevin over Labor Day weekend. I worried about Jonathan having well-rounded meals up at Columbia. I worried about my next panic attack. I worried about everything but my business, dreading the rush that usually came in the Fall and if I'd be able to emotionally handle it.

I made a promise to simplify my life. Decided it wouldn't be right to see Antonio until Patrick moved downstairs. There had to be a modicum of decency and control or it would prove too much for me. I wrote the following in one of my red notebooks, the one I'd started for the renovations downstairs, with the names of the contractors, the sources, the delivery dates for various items. I also made a list of what was left to purchase, including towels, bedding, plates, glasses, though I probably had enough of those upstairs to bring downstairs. I titled the page "The Decorum of Illicit Love," and followed it with lines of wisdom such as the following:

Cheating with decorum

Adultery without admonishment

Abstinence while decorating

Restraint while redecorating

Delay passion with patience

Don't frolic while furnishing

I almost tore that page out of the book because it was infantile, but I hate to tear pages out of notebooks. It's a sign of defeat and also spoils the notebook, unless it's a spiral. My red notebooks weren't spirals.

Downstairs would be finished in a few weeks. I could wait a few weeks to see Antonio. He'd be busy with classes and his Police Manual revisions after his Labor Day weekend in Maine, doing outdoorsy macho things with Kevin. I called and made him promise to use a lot of bug spray with DEET and he laughed harder than I'd ever heard him laugh.

I'd miss him, but I never was and never would be the kind of woman who couldn't be without a man. At least I didn't want to be that kind of woman. Besides, I had too much to do. There was the Labor Day party to shop for, overseeing the downstairs renovation, faxing the Exclusive to Kate as soon as she sent me the fax number from Tuscany, searching properties for the French models.

Patrick suggested spending the day together. The look of hope on his face was too difficult to deny.

"Okay," I said. "Whatever you want."

"What I want is to spend it in bed with you," he said.

"Next idea," I said.

We ended up taking the subway to the Staten Island Ferry, the way we had on our first date. We stood on the deck of the ferry and he put his arm around me. Without thinking, I leaned my head on his shoulder. He kissed my top of my head. It was nice. Too nice.

"Patrick," I said, turning to face him.

"What, sweetheart?"

"I'm confused." He held me against his broad chest and hugged me.

"We'll be all right, sweetheart. Whatever happens, I'll be there for you."

"And I'll be there for you, if you behave yourself."

My feelings were conflicted once we were back in our great big house at the very northern edge of Greenwich Village. It was almost as though the years of depression hadn't happened. As if this little interlude was the true example of our life.

Patrick went out to pick up some beer. I called Jonathan.

"How's Columbia?"

"It's just been a few days, Mom. So far, so good."

"Have I been a decent mother?"

"The best. Seriously. I'm sorry about what I said. I like it here, like being in the city for school. I'll see you soon, at the picnic."

"You can go to graduate school out of state. Or transfer."

"I'm fine here. So far at least. Look, I have to run."

"I met someone, honey. An ex-detective."

"You're dating? A cop?"

"Yes. He's retired. He's teaching now, at John Jay."

"That's some news. I want to meet him, make sure he's good enough for you." He paused. "Does Dad know?"

"Yes."

"Wow!"

"I love you so much, Jonathan."

"I love you, too."

Patrick wanted to watch a ballgame. I didn't. He kissed me good night and I went upstairs, surprised that we were able to end the day and evening with such easy civility. I propped myself up on pillows on the narrow bed and picked up from where I was in the last of Stieg Larsson's trilogy. I couldn't concentrate, even on the end chapters of the final book. I began to feel that creeping dread take over, invading me inch by inch. I tried to fight it, find refuge in the novel, but I found myself re-reading paragraphs. Sentences. Single words, over and over again. Wondered how I would get through the night, the next day, the rest of my life. Was it simply guilt? Should I end things with Antonio and try again with Patrick? But what if I did and Patrick returned to his old ways. I'd never trust again. Anyone, even myself. My instincts.

I sat up straight, away from the pillows that had been propping me up as my head started feeling fuzzy. Deep breaths. Three in, six out. Three. Six. In, nose. Out mouth. Touch toes, move South. My head felt both empty and heavy and weak and weird. My heart was racing. Breathing didn't help, but it had to.

It had to.

I closed my eyes and tried as hard as I could to empty all thoughts and just breathe. After a while it worked, a little. I wanted to stand up and see what that felt like, but I was afraid. What if I fell. Patrick wouldn't hear me.

Patrick.

Partridge.

Partridge in a pear tree.

Partridges in pear trees. Pears dropping from trees, plop plop plop. Worms in ripe pear trees and snowshoes in winter, walk on bare floors and you'll get a bad splinter, roses and tulips and sapphire rings, these are a few of life's wonderful things.

Breathe, Ellie. Just breathe.

It was time to deal with this. It was ten p.m., a time I usually wouldn't call anyone, unless it was the West Coast. I texted Linetta, my new go-to person and asked if there was anything to take for panic attacks. She called me right back.

"Are you kidding me?" she said. "There's something for everything. A doctor for everything. I'll give you a few names, though most shrinks are out of town now through Labor Day. But maybe someone will be around. Ready?"

"Ready," I said, reaching for the pen and paper always on my nightstand. She rattled off the first name and phone number and I scribbled it down. "Okay, got it. Go on," then wrote down the other names and numbers of the psychiatrists she suggested.

"Just remember, it's August. If you do get lucky and find someone available, none of them take insurance. None of the good ones do. Don't even ask."

I fell asleep with the list in my hand. It was comforting. The next morning I called the names on the list, mostly to no avail. But Dr. Louis Lewison was in town and would see me on short notice, only because Linetta was in his poker club and she would hit him if he didn't make time.

His office was on the ground floor of a pre-war co-op on lower Fifth Avenue. There was a small waiting room in which I didn't have to wait before he led me into a large room lined with filled bookcases. I immediately felt at home. I sat in a chair that reclined all the way if I wanted it to. I wasn't sure yet if I wanted to be that comfortable. That vulnerable.

"It's panic attacks," I said. "Probably because I'm an adulteress." He let out a laugh and then apologized.

"I'm sorry. That wasn't professional."

I asked him if anyone ever called him "Louie Louie." No, he said and I shouldn't ever try, even though it was indeed a great song. He had questions for me. How long had I been having the attacks. A few months, I said. But only a few attacks. What meds was I on. Absolutely none other than Cipro for a few days. How have I been feeling physically? Fine, thanks. Was I allergic to anything? Not that I knew of. How do I sleep? On my side, I said and saw him try to hide a smile. How's my appetite? Non-stop. Age, name and serial number. Then, with that out of the way, he asked me to tell him how I really felt. His voice was soothing. Maybe it was a requirement for being a shrink. I relaxed into the chair, took a few deep breathes and let it all out. My parents' aloofness, how I pushed myself at work, Patrick's affairs, the unexpected celibacy that had become the main characteristic of my twenty-year marriage, depression. Meeting Antonio and the power of my attraction to him. Our affair. Dr. Lewison answered with a few non-committal grunts that were somehow comforting and made me want to talk more until he said, "Time's up. I hope Linetta told you that I don't take insurance. All I need is your first-born."

I looked at him, startled, then laughed so hard I almost choked.

"No wonder she speaks so highly of you," I said, wiping away a few tears. Laugh tears. This shrink stuff was all right. No wonder so many people had one. He told me that anxiety attacks are suffered by an enormous percentage of the population and can be helped by a mild sedative that should not make me tired. That I shouldn't feel overwhelmed by guilt for wanting to experience passion and affection. It is something we all deserve. To be with people who nourish, not demean or belittle in any way. A lot of sensible words, all in the last few minutes of our session. I felt so good after speaking with him that when he handed me a prescription for diazepam I thought I would probably never use it. I told him so and he said to fill it anyway. He told me to call him in mid-September and we'd set up another appointment, that he just happened to be in town for a few days before heading to Cape Cod for two weeks. Truro. Did I know it? I nodded. Did I love it? I nodded again. I made out a check for three hundred dollars and we shook hands. I thanked him profusely and practically waltzed down the street because I felt so relieved. I called Linetta to thank her. She said she couldn't talk because she was standing on her head.

"So how did you turn the phone on," I asked. "With your nose?"

"Don't be a smartass."

CHAPTER TWENTY-SIX

Labor Day

Jonathan showed up for our annual picnic with Maggie and two friends from his dorm, one from Ghana and the other from Idaho. They set the picnic table with paper goods while Patrick started the grill.

Betsy brought Eduardo, her fiancé. He was a tall, thin elegant man with a slight limp. She looked magnificent in a turquoise dress and silver and turquoise earrings, the perfect color against her bronze skin, not unlike Antonio's.

Patrick barely had time to mingle, busy as he was shaping hamburgers, splitting hot dogs, grilling chicken and shrimp that I had marinated. He loved this. Loved to be a gracious host, fully in charge of the chores he enjoyed.

Louisa walked down the steps that led from the sliding glass kitchen door and waved to everyone. She was with a tall, almost skinny man with a mop of light brown hair. The oboist from the East Village. His name was James and I looked down at his feet, extremely long and narrow in his brown leather sandals. We all have something. His face was bony, his smile wide. He was the kind of man who would grow into his looks, I thought. The kind that gets better with age.

"Oh jeez, I almost forgot," Louisa said. "A woman was sitting on the stoop. She said she's a friend of yours, so I let her in. Hope that's okay. She said she'd wait for you in the kitchen." I looked toward the kitchen just as the glass door slid open. Valeria stood on the small deck that led from the kitchen to the garden. She looked ethereal in pastel summer dress, sandals, a straw hat. I walked over to her, surprised to see her back in the city. She handed me a package wrapped in tinfoil and intricately tied with a thin lavender ribbon.

"My zucchini and chocolate loaf. I'm back at Kevin's. He's not there, he's hiking with Antonio for a few days and I have one or two things to take care of. Besides, I wanted to see you. Can we go inside?" She gazed at the guests. At Patrick, standing by the grill with his back to everyone, spatula in hand. Murmured that she was sorry not to have called first. That it was a bad idea and what had she been thinking. She turned and walked back to the house and I followed, leaving a garden full of curious people wondering who the woman with the straw hat was. Everyone but Patrick, too happily occupied to notice her or anyone else.

Valeria sat at the kitchen table with a sense of familiarity I found astonishing. She untied the ribbon, neatly unwrapped the tinfoil. I brought over a knife and two glass art deco dessert plates. She took the knife from me as though we had done this a hundred times before and sliced the loaf. Identical thin slices.

"I repaid the money I borrowed from Kevin, plus. I put it on the dresser." She laughed, or rather, she tried to. Her lower lip trembled. "I'm sorry. It was wrong of me to come here. Very wrong." I felt torn. I wanted to be outside, with family and friends, but she seemed desperate to talk.

"You're welcome to stay for our party," I said.

"I can't. That's one of the reasons I'm here now, to explain. Also, I don't know what to do about Max. He said he wasn't ready to see me, he needed some time but that he understood there was unfinished business between us." She looked at me. "It sounded frightening, the way he said that. Unfinished business. But I need to see him. It's really important. To me, at least. And the fact that he sounded so cold..." She paused for a brief time. I didn't know what to say so I ate another slice of her cake. "I can barely think of anything else until I see him," she continued. "When I asked your help in finding him I really didn't think you would and when you told me that he's here, in the city, I didn't know what to think. I was happy, surprised. Scared. When you saw him and he said he didn't want to see me, the hurt was enormous, but I also felt this relief. I don't know what I want anymore. I don't know where I belong anymore. My life doesn't matter to anyone, and why should it." She looked around my kitchen. Stood up and looked out the window to the garden and then back to me. "See how much you have. Your family. Your guests. I have no one. I've messed up what few relationships I had."

"No you haven't. We're still friends." But were we? I was puzzled by her, by her visit, but felt no ill-will toward her. "Your Glock was a bit of a glitch, but without that in your bag, we're okay. You didn't bring it here, did you?"

"I didn't. I promise." She smiled at me, a tentative smile, as though she was testing it out. "Anyway, it jammed when I tested it after you left New Paltz. It's a piece of garbage. Like my father was garbage. I threw it in the lake. I made sure no one was looking. Not the hotel lake. Minnewaska. Do you know it?"

"I know of it. I've never seen it."

"It's lovely."

"What's happening?" I asked. "With the real estate situation?"

She had no idea. After the owners of the cute little house had received her offer they decided they weren't ready to sell. They would rent it to her for a year with an option to buy, but Valeria wanted more stability. A place, finally, of her own, and a safer place for her money than the stock market. She looked at a few more places before realizing she might be happier in a studio in the city, a less expensive area than the West Village. Maybe the Upper East Side or some place in Brooklyn. She felt adrift.

"I need to make amends to the few people who matter to me. Max and you matter to me. Kevin, too. I owe him a lot." Her hands shredded a napkin into little pieces, a habit of hers now familiar to me.

This was not the time for such discussion, not with the party going on.

"Join us, outside," I urged again. "You'd be welcome."

"No, I wouldn't. I haven't told you everything."

"I don't need to know everything."

The sliding doors opened and Patrick came in.

"El, c'mon..." He noticed Valeria sitting at our kitchen table and his face paled. Hers flushed a deep crimson. They stared at each other until she looked away.

Oh my God.

From the discomfort so evident on both their faces, from my familiarity with my husband's predilections, it was clear that Patrick and Valeria knew each other, perhaps intimately. Probably intimately. I fought back nausea as Patrick lashed out at her.

"How the hell do you know my wife?"

"How the hell do you know Valeria?" I said to him, hearing the rise in my voice and hating the sound of it. I felt as though I'd been punched in my solar plexus. I closed my eyes and tried to control conflicting emotions. In three, out six. Three, six. Three, six. Happy little pick-up sticks. Tons of bricks and sharp ice picks. Om.

Patrick was speechless. Valeria wasn't. She said Patrick had been her dentist for several years. A few months ago on a lovely spring day, the kind of day that makes you love New York and wonder why anyone in their right mind would want to live anywhere else, she happened to be his last patient. She needed the bonding on a front tooth touched up. There was a teeny tiny chip and it upset her. It was, coincidentally, shortly after Kevin told her she had to move out by the end of September and she was upset enough by that. To have a dark spot on a front tooth was too much to cope with, so she had pleaded with Patrick's office to fit her in, because she was extremely upset despite the happy tulips along Park Avenue.

They fit her in at the end of the day. It was a short appointment and the two of them walked out of the office together.

Even with the wild co-incidence of my husband and Valeria knowing each other, I had to give thought to that last bit. In all my years of going to all the doctors I've ever been to, I'd never walked out of the office with one of them. I began to have a really sick feeling in my stomach.

"I needed someone to talk to, Ellie. That's all," Valeria was saying. I heard the words through my rising nausea. "After he touched up my tooth we went for drinks. It's not like we were strangers. I was feeling so vulnerable about my living situation that it was good to have someone sympathetic to talk to."

"Of course," I said. "Patrick is known for his sympathetic nature." I shot a look of disgust at him. His face seemed green. "I understand. You had a few drinks and became tired from all the talking. It can do that to you. So wait! Let me guess. The Carlyle Hotel is just blocks from his office and it has a bar. And hotel rooms upstairs! So thoughtful a hotel. How fortunately convenient. Patrick reserved a room so you could talk, and also rest!"

"Ellie, sweetheart, it wasn't like that."

"It wasn't," Valeria agreed. "He didn't have to reserve. He already has a room." ·

I thought I would throw up. I ran to the kitchen sink, my mouth wide open, but nothing came out, just a few heaves and unpleasant sounds. I looked out the window and saw flowers, food, people, all oblivious to the hell going on inside my head. Inside my house. I turned around and wiped my mouth with my arm, even though there was nothing to wipe away.

"Go to hell," I said. "Both of you." I looked at Patrick in disgust. "You keep a room at the Carlyle?"

"It's a business expense," he said, his face ashen. I hated him then so much that I could have shoved each of the knives in the wooden rack into a different part of his body, one by one. Relished the squish of his skin as the blades penetrated.

"I had no idea how much I'd like you," Valeria said to me, a slight tremble in her voice.

"But you liked my husband more."

She looked at me, at Patrick, then back at me.

"No. Not really."

"Most of the time we talked about you, honey. About us."

"That's true. Ellie. He talked so warmly about you that I knew we could be friends."

I stared at them in amazement.

"Just shut up."

The shame on her face. The sorrow on his. Fuck the sorrow on his face. It was old by now. This was *crazy*. I had guests outside, any of whom might walk into the kitchen at any moment. Jonathan and his college friends. Maggie. Eduardo. Louisa. The oboist. I had to set an example. With my hands clenched into tight fists I said as calmly as I could that what's done is done.

Oh, no. Now Valeria was crying.

"Stop it," I said. "Just tell me something. Why did you get in touch with me the first time? To see what I looked like? To gloat that you slept with my husband? You were just one of many, you know. But I told you that already, didn't I? At Mohonk."

"I needed a place to stay," she said. "Patrick mentioned that you had a vacant garden apartment. That's why I called you but when we met for lunch at Moustache, I liked you so much that I wanted our friendship to be based on trust. I couldn't even consider living in your house after sleeping with your husband." The way she said it, as though her innocence made it all right, made me want to smack her. I stared at both of them in disgust. The fact that Patrick had been ready to rent to Valeria without even discussing it with me infuriated me almost as much as his sleeping with her. But no, he said, that wasn't the case at all. He'd mentioned the empty apartment then gave her my business card, complete with photo on the front. A very flattering photo. My wife is a great broker. Call her! You'll like her! We even have an unused unit in our house. We could have sleepovers.

Even with what was going on, it surprised and touched me that Patrick carried my business cards with him. I didn't carry his. In fact, when anyone asked if I had a dentist I could recommend, I told them no.

"Please don't tell Kevin," Valeria said.

What?

The kitchen door slid open and Jonathan joined us. "Hi, guys, the party's in here now?" He looked at us, at our stricken faces. "Uh, should I leave?"

"Hi, sweetheart," I said. "Please stay. This particular party is over." I introduced him to Valeria. "She and your dad had a fling, but it seems as though it's run its course." Patrick had the grace to look ashamed. Maybe he was ashamed of me, of my words. They weren't exactly an example of good parenting. Jonathan glared at his father, shook his head in disgust, told Valeria to have a nice life, looked at the dessert plate and grabbed a slice of the zucchini loaf.

"This is delicious," he said, taking a large bite.

"Valeria made it," I said. "Just for us. Wasn't that lovely of her?" It felt good when he threw the remainder of the slice in the garbage can, just as Louisa walked in.

"This is Louisa," I said to Valeria. "She's a tenant and a friend. Louisa, this is Valeria. She and Patrick had a one-nighter, or maybe it was two or three. They're confused about how many times because Patrick was so busy telling her how wonderful I am."

"I want to pour boiling wax over your stupid head," Louisa said, glaring at Patrick. I explained to Valeria that Louisa worked at a nearby men's salon and among other services she did body waxing. She could, conceivably, drown a person in hot wax. Valeria sat immobile, looking like a porcelain doll with dead eyes. Patrick said nothing. I looked out the kitchen window. Jonathan's friends, Betsy, Eduardo, and Louisa's oboist were sitting and talking outside. Valeria, Patrick, Jonathan, Louisa and I were sitting inside and barely talking. Valeria was dabbing her eyes delicately with a pink handkerchief embroidered with tiny red roses. I looked at it in amazement.

Who carried embroidered handkerchiefs anymore? Who carried unembroidered handkerchiefs?

"I'm sorry, Ellie," she said. "You're the last person in the world I wanted to hurt." She looked at Patrick. "You don't deserve her. She's the best and only friend I've ever had and see how I messed that up. By the way, that last time we were together? In May? You gave me a urinary tract infection." She stood and took her purse. She turned to Jonathan. "Your mother is a very special person. Your father, not so much."

CHAPTER TWENTY-SEVEN

I walked Valeria out of the kitchen, through the hallway and opened the vestibule door. While I was unlocking the front door I saw her reach into her straw bag for something. For a split second I feared it was her gun. It wasn't, so I paid no attention to it. She stood by my side as we stepped through the door onto the landing. Traffic was light on West 14th Street. The lull before people began to return to the city from Labor Day weekend. An ambulance, its siren blasting for no reason, as there was little traffic to slow it down, raced east. A driver drove by in a convertible, blasting Otis Redding's *Dock of the Bay*.

"If I stood in the middle of 14th Street right now and a Mack truck ran me over, no one would care," Valeria said. "Not even you. Not now. What you must think of me." She grabbed my arm. "What's it all for, Ellie? What is any of it for? Believe me when I tell you I never meant to hurt you."

"You couldn't hurt me if you tried," I said.

I had an overpowering desire to push her down the steps, all eleven of them. I felt an equally strong urge to hug her. I did neither. She descended with her usual grace. Once she was on the sidewalk she turned to look at me, waved and called goodbye.

She looked extremely sad as she stood at the curb for a minute or two, then squared her narrow shoulders, looked left and right and walked into the street, straight in front of an oncoming eastbound crosstown bus. Its impact threw her into the middle of the street. She landed with her body almost perpendicular to the road just as a delivery van across the street peeled out of its parking space and rolled over her head, crushed it first with the left front tire and then with the rear, even as people screamed in horror and banged on the van windows. I stood mesmerized by the blood, the bone, the brains. The angles of her broken arms and legs. A loud "NOOOOOOO" emerged from deep inside me, yet I couldn't look away. Couldn't move. Like a horror movie where you cover your eyes with your hands but open your fingers because you absolutely have to see.

I turned my head and threw up in one of the two long flower boxes filled with almost dead geraniums that sat on either side of the landing. Then I wiped my mouth on my bare arm and turned back to look at the mess in the street. A small crowd had surrounded her and people halted traffic coming from both directions. Across the street a man unbuttoned his white dress shirt, took it off and placed it over Valeria's smashed head and face. His shoulders were shaking, I could see that, even from my vantage point through the gaps in the growing crowd. People held phones at random angles, taking pictures. Of course they were. Hopefully one of them had the decency to call 911.

I started to walk down the stairs but my legs felt weak, my head light. I stood one or two steps from the top and grabbed onto the wrought iron railing. The next thing I knew someone ran up the stoop, blocked my view and pushed me down, forcing me to sit. I looked into a face stained with tears.

"I thought you were going to fall down the stairs, señora," he said. He was a large man with a gentle voice. He sat on the step below me, his head in his hands. I could see over him. The bus driver had emerged from his vehicle, plus some of the passengers. I couldn't see the delivery van. Either it was blocked by the bus or had driven away. I hoped someone took down the license plate number, but this was no one's fault.

Two cops joined the man and me on the stoop.

"I saw everything," the man said to the cops. "My name is Oscar Gonzalvo. G-O-N-S-A-L-V-O. You can call me Sal." He pointed at me. "I saved this woman from falling down the steps and probably breaking her neck." The policewoman looked at me. I nodded yes, he might have. I thanked him. I asked the cops which precinct they were from. This had a certain relevance as we live on the south side of West 14th Street, which is in the Sixth. The north side of West 14th Street is in the Tenth.

"We're from the Sixth," the male cop said. "Most of the deceased's upper torso is in the Tenth. I guess the rest of her is ours, but the Highway Unit handles this kind of thing."

There's a Highway Unit?

He and his female partner were trying hard not to show how shaken they were by what had happened. They seemed so young, not much older than Jonathan. I assumed they had seen what had been Valeria's head and face. You'd have to be dead not to be deeply shaken. Maybe have nightmares for the rest of your life.

"What's the Highway Unit?" I asked.

"The Collision Investigation Squad. They're on the way."

Cliff should be here, I thought. He was a detective in the Sixth. He knew Valeria. I asked the young cops to please call him and ask him to come over. I didn't know his last name but he was a Detective in their precinct and they said, yes, of course they knew him. The woman cop said she would call. I told her to tell him that it was Valeria, and for him to please call Kevin and Max. The male cop wrote down the names while she called. I left them outside and walked unsteadily into my house. There was a thin, white letter-sized envelope on the vestibule table, propped against the wall. I took it inside and put it with the bills in the bamboo bill holder in the kitchen, then went into the living room and sat on the sofa. Someone, I had no idea who, brought me a cold drink. The woman cop. Then she asked me if I was married. If my husband was here. I said yes, he was probably in the garden, grilling hotdogs and hamburgers. We were having a party for Labor Day. To please not upset him or he'd burn the food and there were teenagers out there who didn't need to know what had happened.

"But your husband should know..."

"I'll tell him," I said, wondering why she thought he should know. Because he was my husband? The man of the house?

"Let the lady of the house calm down," Sal was saying. "I can talk for both of us. I saw everything. *Everything.* These two señoras, this one here and her friend, were on the steps, talking. I couldn't help but notice, they were so beautiful." He looked at me and nodded. "*Es verdad, señora.* You so dark and *la otra, rubia,* her hair like gold." Tears started to fall down his face but he continued to talk as though his life depended on it. "*La rubia* she walked down the steps like a goddess and stood still like she was waiting for a break in the traffic. I thought she was going to jaywalk and I wanted to tell her not to, it's illegal." He looked at the cops as if for approval. "But she didn't. She waited, then she walked straight in front of the oncoming bus. The 14D. That's the one that goes across 14th, then through Alphabet City and ends up at Delancey. That one. Not the regular crosstown, you know, the one that just goes across 14th. Not that one."

Images of Valeria's face and head swam in front of me. Images etched into my memory. Blood and guts and brains and the hideous flatness of her head and face. I started to tremble.

"What was the deceased doing here? Do you know that?"

"No. What does it matter? She's deceased," Sal said.

"She was visiting," I said. "We're having a picnic in the backyard."

"You have this whole house?" The male cop was looking around.

"There are tenants."

"Did they know the deceased?"

"No. Well, one met her briefly."

Patrick walked into the living room. When he saw the cops he looked startled.

"What's going on," he asked. The cops looked at me.

"This is my husband," I said to them. "Valeria was hit by a bus," I said to Patrick.

"The 14D crosstown," Sal said, holding out his hand to shake Patrick's. "I'm Oscar, but everyone calls me Sal. From my last name. Gonsalvo. She's dead like a doornail."

"Shut up," I said. "Not another word." Patrick stood there, a look of total confusion on his face.

"Valeria's dead?" His face turned white. He gripped the back of the sofa to steady himself. I had nothing to give him. Nothing. It took all I had to keep myself together.

"You knew the deceased?" The female cop looked at Patrick and he nodded.

"She was beautiful like an angel, then there she was, her brains scattered all over the street," Sal said.

"I told you to shut up," I said, hearing the anger and distress in my voice. I took a few deep breaths and then looked at the policewoman for help. She understood. She took Sal by the elbow and walked him away, toward the front door. I heard her thank him for his help.

I leaned my head against the cushioned back of the sofa and closed my eyes against the images that forced their way forward. Pushed them back. They would have to wait until later. Until the cops were gone. Until my son and his friends were gone. Until the house was quiet and then I could let myself go. Patrick stood behind me, gripping my shoulder as if for support. I knew he must be feeling great guilt. Too bad. Maybe if he'd learned to keep his zipper closed he wouldn't be feeling that guilt.

Anger pushed away horror once again, helping me. Patrick, spared the visual horror of it all, came from behind the couch and sat beside me. It was the last thing I wanted. I wasn't there to comfort him and there certainly was no way for him to comfort me. The confrontation between him, Valeria and me such a short time ago came back vividly. Almost as vividly as her brains mixed with blood and bone and long, blonde hair. I barely noticed as Louisa walked into the living room.

CHAPTER TWENTY-EIGHT

"We're out of paper plates," Louisa said. She looked at our faces, at the cops. "Want to tell me what's going on here?" I stood, partly to be away from Patrick and partly to try to keep busy. I took her to the front of the room by the bay windows and told her what happened just minutes after she'd threatened to pour hot wax on Patrick's head. My voice sounded steady to me. Even and steady. "What are you saying? She's dead? That woman in the kitchen? Oh my God."

I told her, in impeccable detail, how Valeria had calmly committed a hideous suicide. I felt the need to describe all of it as Louisa gazed out the window, at the bus, the van, the cops, the crowds. How she had walked gracefully down the steps and stood at the curb. Looked both ways.

Louisa shook her head in disbelief. "What a hideous way to die. Patrick must be a super lousy lover." I stared at her and she stared back. "That was a stupid thing to say. I'm sorry. It just seems so, I don't know. Out there."

"She timed it for me to see," I said. Anger again, invading me. Almost obliterating the horror. I asked Louisa to take Patrick back to the garden. To keep him away from me. She hugged me and started to walk away, came back and asked if I was okay.

I said no but that I would be, even though I wasn't sure. She walked over to him, still seated on the sofa, a stunned look on his face. She grabbed him by the hand and tried to pull him up, but he shook his head. I heard him say he had to stay near me, that I might need help. Skinny Louisa wouldn't take no and they finally left the room together. With him out of my sight I felt slightly calmer. I sat in an armchair to await whatever happened next, which was Cliff's arrival. He walked in with the man who'd placed his shirt over Valeria's face.

"He needs a shirt," Cliff said to me in greeting. "He has to get to Grand Central Station and can't go shirtless."

"Yes, please. The cars are air-conditioned and I don't want to come down with a summer cold, plus I probably wouldn't be allowed on the train. If I could borrow a shirt, anything at all, I promise to have it dry-cleaned and returned by the end of the week."

"It was extremely kind, what you did," I said. "Of course you may borrow a shirt."

"I couldn't leave her like that," he said. "Did you know her?" I nodded. He said he was sorry.

"How are you holding up, Ellie," Cliff asked. I was so surprised at the kindness in his voice that I began to tear up. I couldn't. Not yet. Not with a house and garden filled with people.

"For now I'm okay, thanks. My son and his friends are in the backyard."

"Our son," Patrick said. He had re-emerged from wherever Louisa had tried to take him and his presence only caused me to tense up. He looked at me, the shirtless man and then at Cliff. A long look at Cliff. "Are you her cop?"

"No," I said. "He's not. Please take this man upstairs and give him a shirt. A good one."

"I'm Samuel," the man said. "Thank you."

Patrick didn't move. He seemed fixated on Cliff, so I told Samuel to come with me and led him upstairs to the master bedroom. I went into the walk-in closet and from Patrick's section I pulled the most expensive shirt I had ever bought him, a Turnbull and Asser dress shirt.

"I don't need such quality," Samuel said. "Just something for the train."

"I know it's too big for you," I said. "Anything of Patrick's will be, so it might as well be nice." He put it on, was tucking it in when Patrick and Cliff entered the room.

"My James Bond shirt?" Patrick looked at me in disbelief. Cliff grinned. "You bought that for me for our anniversary, El." Samuel started to unbutton it. He looked dazed.

"I'm sorry," he said. "A T-shirt would be fine."

"Maybe there's something in my son's room," I said.

"Our son's room," Patrick said.

I went into Jonathan's room and opened his dresser drawers. They were mostly empty but for a few T-shirts, some loose change and a package of Zig Zag rolling papers. I made a mental note to ask when he'd started smoking pot. I didn't care, as long it was an occasional thing. He was a good kid, a good student. A few joints here and there... and that's when I thought of Valeria and me at Mohonk, taking hits and eating brownies. The pure pleasure of it. The fun. Her head, like a melon someone dropped on the ground and stomped on while wearing combat boots. I sank to my knees.

Cliff walked in and saw me there. It took all I had not to fall apart in front of him. He squatted down and put his hands on my shoulders. I grabbed his arm and he pulled me up and as I rose I leaned over to shut the dresser drawer. The last thing I needed was for Cliff to see the rolling papers and arrest my son for pot. Or was it legal in the city now? I wanted to ask, I wanted to cry, I wanted to sleep.

"No, wait a second," I said, remembering why I'd come into the room in the first place. I opened the dresser drawer again and pulled out one of the T-shirts Jonathan had left behind. Cliff and I walked back to the master bedroom and I handed Samuel a black Mötley Crüe shirt. "Your choice," I said. "This or James Bond."

He smiled, rebuttoned Patrick's shirt. He turned around to tuck it into his trousers and wandered over to look out the window. He turned back to me in surprise.

"You're having a party," he said. "In the middle of all this you have to be hostess. I'm sorry." He paused. "Did you know her?"

I nodded. "We both did. There's nothing for you to be sorry for. It's just my son and his friends, plus my tenants. Our annual Labor Day picnic."

"Tenants?" he said, sounding surprised.

"Two of them. Rent-stabilized."

"Oh, too bad," he said. "Otherwise it's a great house. If you ever consider selling, give me a call." In spite of the situation, I almost laughed. So did Cliff. He could barely hold back. Patrick stared into space, on the face of it he was the most affected of us all. Was it deeper feelings for Valeria than he'd admitted to? Was it guilt?

Samuel reached into his back pocket, took out his wallet and handed each of us an embossed business card. He was a senior partner in a top law firm. I looked at him with renewed respect, that he of all the people on the street was the one who had given his shirt to Valeria. He asked if it was all right for him to leave. He hadn't seen the actual accident. He'd left a private luncheon and was walking east to Union Square to take the subway to Grand Central when he saw the crowd gathering around Valeria. "No one had covered her. They were too busy screaming or pounding on the delivery van or calling 911. You wouldn't believe how many were taking pictures with their phones. Sick." He turned to Cliff. "So I'm not much of a help, I just did what I could." Then he sank down on the edge of the bed and put his head in his hands. His shoulders began to shake and soon the sobs started. "Oh God, that poor lady. What a hideous, bloody mess."

I looked at Cliff, he looked at me. We knew what he'd seen. We'd seen it too.

"How bad was it?" Patrick asked. "Honestly."

"Bad enough so that I'll never forget it," Samuel said. Cliff nodded. I looked out the window to the garden, to the sight of happy people oblivious to the horrors in front of the house. Or were they oblivious? Surely Louisa had said something, to prepare anyone for when they went inside and saw the police. The somber faces in the street.

"It's okay," Cliff said. "You can leave." He pocketed Samuel's card.

"You can't go to Grand Central like this," I said to Samuel. "Stay as long as you need to. Overnight if you want. And if you need food or something to drink, there's plenty in the garden." Patrick looked at me as though I'd lost all semblance of sanity. "Why are you looking at me like that," I asked. "How do you expect Samuel to get on a train to Westchester while he's so upset? What's wrong with you?"

Samuel looked up, his eyes red, said he'd be all right if he could just have some more time to compose himself. He really did want to be home. His wife was in Peru, climbing Machu Picchu with some senior Outward Bound type group so he had to feed and walk the dog. He really had to. It was an old dog with a weak bladder. During the week he had a dog-sitter but since it was Labor Day weekend, well, we know how it is, don't we?

"Sure, buddy," Patrick said. "I understand. Take all the time you need. Keep the shirt. Would you like to be alone for a while?" Samuel thanked Patrick for his understanding. Thanked all of us. It was all quite civil and under control. Cliff asked Patrick to stay with Samuel while he talked privately to me. I was surprised, but led him down the hall.

"What's this, the maid's room?"

"My room," I said. "For months now."

A flash of surprise crossed Cliff's face. "Oh. Well, Tony and Kevin are on the West Side Highway, not far from the George Washington Bridge. They'll be here soon." Of course. They'd know to beat the holiday traffic back to the city.

"You need to call Max," I said. "Valeria's husband in Brooklyn. I have his number somewhere."

"First thing I did," he said. "He's on his way. I didn't give him all the details. Kevin, the husband and Tony. They'll all be here. It might get interesting. By the way, did your husband know Valeria?"

"Biblically," I said, unable to hide the bitterness that crept into my voice.

"Aw, for Christ sakes, El," Patrick said, startling both Cliff and me. He was standing in my doorway, his face a chalky white. "Samuel's throwing up in the bathroom. He messed up my shirt."

"So give him another."

"You're sure you're not her cop," Patrick asked a second time.

"Patrick gave Valeria a urinary tract infection," I said to Cliff.

"That's hardly reason to walk in front of a bus," Patrick said, sounding defensive.

"Tell me about it after you've had one," I snapped. Cliff tried unsuccessfully to hide a grin, then apologized when he saw me see the grin. His phone rang.

"The Medical Examiner's on his way," Cliff said. "This should be cleaned up soon. That's lucky. You never know, on a holiday weekend. Traffic is still being diverted, but it'll all be clear after CIS leaves."

"What's that," Patrick asked, then said never mind, he'll check on Samuel again.

"Look, Ellie, the reason I wanted to talk to you alone," Cliff said as soon as Patrick left. "It could be awkward for you with Tony here." He paused. "Even more awkward than things seem to be." His tact surprised me. So did the realization that I liked him. I looked him in the eye.

"I want Antonio here," I said.

Cliff nodded. "I think maybe I underestimated you."

"I think maybe I did too, for many years." I led the way back to the master bedroom.

"Your husband's been very kind," Samuel said. "I vomited on the first shirt, the Casino Royale. I'll have it cleaned, along with this one." He now had on a pale blue shirt with the collar open, the sides billowing on his slender frame.

"Forget it," Patrick said. "And whenever you're ready, I'll walk you to the subway, make sure you're okay." I saw the faintest flicker of surprise cross Cliff's face before we all headed downstairs. I wasn't surprised. Patrick had a heart that was generous and kind, almost as generous as one of his other organs. I went to the kitchen, looked out to the garden. Eduardo was grilling more burgers and everyone seemed to be having a good time.

What did they know?

CHAPTER TWENTY-NINE

Two worlds, inside my house and outside.

There was now just Cliff and the young female cop left and she seemed anxious to depart. I went out to the garden. Jonathan walked over. "Louisa told me what happened to that woman in the kitchen. That's pretty heavy. You okay?"

"I'm holding on."

"Dad's not. He told me he's going to walk someone to Union Square, but he's just wandering around. Inside, outside."

"He'll survive."

"He's not as strong as you are, Mom." I looked at Jonathan in surprise. "I mean it. With what you went through over the years you kept all your appointments, made sure there was food in the house, clothes for me. You never let yourself go, not completely. Not ever. It sometimes seemed superhuman, forging ahead through your depression. And look at you now, keeping it all together."

"I'm trying," I said. I hugged him and went to wait for Max. A few minutes later, there he was, standing in the hallway and staring into the living room until his eye caught mine. He walked over, looked around like a lost soul. His face seemed on the verge of falling apart. I led him to the sofa. Sat him down. Asked if I could offer him anything to drink.

"A bottle of vodka might help," he said, trying to smile. He told me he'd been outside, talking to someone named Antonio. An ex-cop. The Coroner had arrived and told him he'd have to go to the morgue in the morning. I didn't mention that it would be impossible to identify Valeria. I wondered if someone could spare him that horror. "She called me twice. The first time, the woman I've been seeing now and then answered the phone. Valeria hung up without identifying herself, but I knew it was her. The second time, I answered. Hearing her voice after all this time, it did something to me. All my feelings, the hurt, the love I had for her, the rage. It came pouring back, overwhelmed me. I even thought of how I might pay her back for the pain she'd caused me, terrible thoughts about how I might hurt her. I said I'd call her back. I never did. I was afraid to. Afraid of myself." Max paused. His face was ashen. "She almost destroyed me once. If she did it again I knew I'd never recover, so I ignored her." He put his head in his hands.

Even as I hurt for him, felt some of his pain, Max's words hit me like a blow. He had practically repeated to me the words I'd said to Patrick such a short time ago. I'd thought of hurting him. Physically doing something terrible to him for the pain he'd caused me, because there really is just so much we can take before it's too much, no matter how strong we are. If we take a second chance with the same person and it turns out to be lousy or a repeat of the same, it could change us forever and not in a good way.

That was my fear. How much can we trust before we might never trust again.

"You saw it happen, didn't you," he asked. I nodded. If they showed him Valeria's smashed skull he'd never get over it. He said he needed to eat something because of the pills he was taking, even though the thought of food made him nauseous. I offered to bring him something from the picnic in the garden, some fruit perhaps.

"You're having a party," he said. "Doesn't it seem barbaric to eat at a time like this? I don't mean for your guests, of course. For me. But I'm feeling awfully light-headed." He stood up and grabbed my arm as we walked through the dining room, the kitchen, out to the small deck. He stood there and held onto the guard rail. Looked at the small gathering below. I walked him down the stairs and introduced him. Betsy gave him her chair and I asked her to make him a small plate of food. She soon returned, holding a plate with a grilled chicken thigh, a hamburger, fruit salad and a brownie on it. Max nibbled at each offering, then sat the plate on the grass as tears pooled, spilled from his eyes.

"Nice garden you have," he said.

"Thanks. It's mostly because of Betsy, the woman who gave you the food. She spends hours on it. If you want to, you can rest upstairs." He shook his head, said it was better if he was near people. I walked over to Louisa and asked her who knew about what had happened. She said that everyone did, sort of. She'd told them there was a traffic accident outside the house but that things were under control.

"Who's that guy with you," she asked? "He looks like Sam Shepard."

Kevin was on the small deck, looking at me. He waved me over, took me aside and told me that Antonio was outside. That the street was clearing out and cops were beginning to leave. I took him to Max and made the introductions. Max the husband/professor/poet this is Kevin the sort of lover/roommate/romance writer. Kevin surprised both of us when he held his hand out to Max and said it was a pleasure to finally meet the man Valeria had always loved. Max let out a sob. Then he thanked Kevin for his words. I left the two of them alone and went over to Jonathan and his friends.

"This is some introduction to life in the big city," I said to the boys from Ghana and Idaho.

"I'll say," the Idaho boy said.

"We better help move the food inside," Jonathan said. "We're splitting for a party in Greenpoint pretty soon." He looked at me. "It's seems obscene, doesn't it? After this to go to a party."

"This was a party," I said, "and life goes on."

"Obviously not for everyone," he said.

I walked back inside. Patrick and Samuel weren't around so I assumed they'd left for Union Square. Cliff was in Patrick's armchair, looking through an issue of *Architectural Digest*.

"I was just waiting to tell you I'm off," he said. "No need for me to be here any longer. By the way, Tony's outside." He stood and held out his hand. "You're all right."

"You are, too," I said, shaking his hand. Then I hugged him, surprising both of us.

"Stay strong," he said.

Strong. I guess I was. I watched out the bay window as he walked down the stoop to where Antonio was talking to one someone in the middle of the street.

"Max is staying with me for the night." I turned around. Kevin was standing there with Max. The new odd couple. "I'll go with him to the Medical Examiner's tomorrow."

"I want her ashes," Max said. "I bought a niche years ago. In a beautiful white building with a cherry tree outside. I thought I had melanoma, that's why I bought it. I didn't have it but I have the niche. It's big enough for the two of us, when it's my turn. Until then, Valeria stays with me."

Like Louisa with Cecilia, I thought, but a very different kind of love. I told him it was a lovely idea and that it was what Valeria would have wanted. To be near him.

"It's hardly the reunion we might have had, had I not been such a fool." I saw the misery in his eyes. "No one knew her vulnerabilities the way I did. I should have..." His knees buckled and Kevin caught him. Shot me a look as if to ask, 'what do I do?'

"She always loved you," I said. Then I felt sorry for Kevin. "She loved you, too," I said. "Just not as much."

They left. I wondered why we do what we do to each other. Then I walked outside. The bus and the delivery van were gone, but the Chief Medical Officer and Highway Unit vehicles were still there. There was a white outline where Valeria's body had been. The earlier gawkers were gone, replaced by others walking down the street, wondering what had happened. But there was no dead body in the street, nothing of interest to see, so they walked on. I sat on the stoop and waited for Antonio. It wasn't long before he joined me. Sat close to me and held my hand.

"How are you holding up," he said.

"She and Patrick slept together. I just found out today."

"Who's Patrick?"

"My husband."

"Valeria and your husband?" I nodded.

"She showed up today while we were having a party. We were in the kitchen when Patrick walked in. I knew immediately, from the looks on both their faces, though I hadn't known that he kept a room at the Carlyle. I walked her to the door. I wanted to kick her down the stairs, but she descended with her natural grace, stood at the curb and timed it perfectly. For me to see. Every horrible second of it." I was as angry as I was shaken. "For me to remember, always." I heard the bitterness in my voice. "Then I had to deal with all these people in my house, my guests."

"I was wrong about Max," he said.

"What?" I said.

"I thought that if anything bad ever happened to Valeria it would be because of him. I had a bad feeling about him from the time I found out he was living here. I didn't trust him, and then reading his poems. The anger. Christ, was I wrong. We spoke for a while. He's a good guy. Never stopped loving her. He loved her so much it almost destroyed him."

"That's what I think, too," I said.

"It never occurred to me that she'd kill herself."

"Me either. Deep down I thought she and Max would get back together. One day." We sat there for a while, side by side, my hand in his. He was so solid, so strong and yet even he was shaken. "I can't stay here tonight," I said. "Not after all this. Would you mind if I stayed with you?"

He looked at me, his face unreadable.

"Anytime," he finally said. He looked as serious as I'd ever seen him. "I think all the time might be okay with me." I felt the catch in my throat as he touched my cheek. "I love you, too."

My heart tumbled over itself. I stood and took his hand, led him into the house. We entered the kitchen just as Betsy was carrying in some of the remaining plates from outside. She saw my hand in Antonio's, looked shyly at him and couldn't hide a small smile. I introduced them just as we heard the clunk of shoes coming down the dining room stairs. Jonathan and his friends.

"I thought you guys had gone already," I said.

"Not yet." He looked at me, then at Antonio. At our entwined hands. His friends stood waiting for him but Jonathan seemed in no rush to leave. I felt my face flush as I introduced them. I watched, fascinated, as Jonathan held out his hand in greeting and Antonio's hand left mine to shake my son's. It was an odd, special moment. "I approve," Jonathan said, looking at Antonio. "At least so far."

"Thank you," Antonio said. Jonathan then introduced him to his friends. They thanked me for the picnic, said they hoped I'd be okay and then they left for Brooklyn.

The kitchen phone rang. It was Patrick. He asked if everyone was gone. I said mostly everyone. He was still at Grand Central and planned to stay until Samuel was on the train. How was I holding up. I told him it was wonderful that he was taking care of Samuel. That I wasn't sure how I was. I told him I couldn't stay in the house that night, that I was going to stay with a friend.

"El, please. It was a couple of times. It didn't mean anything, to either of us. And the room is paid for by the business."

"Nice tax write-off," I said. "But what you said, that it didn't mean anything. As far as I'm concerned, that makes it worse. I need to be away from here now." I hung up and went back to the living room where Louisa, the oboist, Betsy and Eduardo were sitting and talking. Waiting for me. Did I need them for anything. Was I okay. I introduced them to Antonio, told them

I was okay and not to worry. I thanked them. They let me know they would be staying the night in the house, in their respective apartments with their respective partners. They were there if I needed anything. I thanked them and said I would be at Antonio's.

"Oh," said Betsy.

"Isn't that nice," said Louisa.

"Where do you live?" Eduardo asked.

"Hell's Kitchen," Antonio said.

"Oh. Hell's Kitchen. Hell of a lot of construction going on over there now, pardon the pun. Hudson Yards and that other thing, just east of it."

Anything but what happened to Valeria.

I wanted to pack a few things. A change of underwear, my toothbrush. Moisturizer. I went up the dining room staircase. Antonio followed me, a bit confused. He looked in the massive master bedroom. Stepped inside while I walked past him to the little room and grabbed my overnight bag. He joined me.

"What's this, the maid's room?"

"That's what Cliff asked," I said. "It's my room, but not for long. Patrick's moving to the garden apartment. I'm having it renovated for him." I turned to him, felt a rush of feeling so strong I had to sit. He was so perfect for me that I couldn't believe he was in my life.

We went downstairs and I locked the door to the garden. I looked around to make sure everything was in its place. I noticed the bamboo bill holder with the white envelope and pulled it from the pile. A single photograph was inside. Valeria and me in New Paltz, wearing the tie-dye T-shirts I'd bought for her birthday. Huge grins on our faces. I dropped the picture as though it were hot.

"Damn her," I screamed. Antonio picked it up from the floor and looked at it. Turned it over. Handed it back to me.

Please don't forget me.

"She knew what she was going to do," I said. "She wanted me to see." I fell apart then, leaned into Antonio's chest, sobbing.

I wanted to tear the photo to shreds. Stomp on it. I wanted to enshrine it in a sterling silver frame.

"I won't forget you," I whispered. We stood like that for a while, Antonio holding me. Calming me.

We walked up Ninth Avenue to his place. We curled up on his couch and listened to Bach Partitas. We ordered in. Neither of us ate much.

"I understand how she could do it," I said. "Why. I really do. But I can't forgive that she did it in front of me, timed it to the second. She wanted to me see her like that. She needed me to see her like that. Feel her incredible loneliness and pain." I felt a sudden, almost unbearable sorrow. "I'll miss her."

"I know you will. I will, too." I fell asleep in his arms. I'd never felt so at home. So safe. Through a fog of exhaustion I heard him call me darling. My darling Ellie.

CHAPTER THIRTY

Kate texted me about a week later. The September day might as well have been the height of summer as the temperature was in the high eighties. She was back in the city and hadn't received my Exclusive. Had I sent it? I texted back that I'd never received the fax number in Italy. Oh, well, she said. I should send it to the gallery and they'll get it to her. Meanwhile I should do the photo shoot whenever I felt like it, she was in no hurry to move but wanted to get started with the marketing. Fall season and all that. So I called Oliver, the photographer. He said we should schedule soon. He was going in for a mini face-lift so how about Wednesday, which was after Rosh Hashanah and before Yom Kippur. His healing was to be part of his atonement.

"You're Jewish?"

"No, sweetie. But it's a good thing to do."

"You should atone for your vanity," I said. "Forty-year-old men don't need facelifts."

The next days were busy. Two clients called, both ready to sell. One was moving out of the city, the other wanted to sell so she and her husband could buy something cute in Brooklyn. A little carriage house in the Heights. Or maybe a converted fire house in Bushwick. Or Greenpoint. Something unique. What did I think about a Victorian in Ditmas Park. If the price was right they could also swing a weekend home in the Hamptons. Or the North Shore. Or maybe Connecticut. Could I recommend brokers for those places? I told her I'd get back to her with referrals. Then there was Kate's house and the French underwear models. I felt overwhelmed. At one time I would have thrived with all this business but now it was more than I wanted to deal with, which was nothing. For the first time I'd been in real estate I thought of taking on a partner, someone willing to do the research and also schlep to Brooklyn. I decided to ask Trudy. She was energetic, honest and lived in Brooklyn. I called her and she said she'd love to work with me. We would split the new clients fifty-fifty, but Kate and the models were mine.

One of our new Exclusives was a classic six apartment on Park Avenue. Living room, dining room, kitchen, two bedrooms and a maid's room. The other was a thirty-five hundred square foot, first-generation loft in the Fur District, or what remains of the Fur District. The owners wanted to move to Brooklyn, to a tree-lined street in a charming area. Meanwhile, Trudy received a call from the owners of a carriage house in the East Village that was located behind a co-op building that used to be a school for girls. According to Trudy, it was so charming that the ad would write itself. She'd sold it to them about a decade ago and now they were moving to Boulder, Colorado to be near their grandchildren.

This was a lot of work coming in all at once. Trudy and I went to see the properties. The classic six was roomy, airy, immaculate. The Fur District loft was another story. It had been untouched for decades. The single bathroom was an enormous, open, circular space smack in the middle of the loft, surrounded by a hand-painted shower curtain on a round rod that enclosed a toilet, tub, shower, sink and bidet. It was all I could do to take my eyes off the shower curtain. Brightly colored nymphs, satyrs, suns, moons, giraffes, angels, doughnuts all painted on the semi-transparent curtain. The stunner was the toiletries neatly lined up on home-made, crudely painted wooden shelves. Expensive French and Portuguese soaps, lush towels perfectly folded, Molton Brown shampoos. My favorite. The kitchen was a single line of sink, stove, refrigerator, counter-tops covered in exquisite tiles. The rest of the space was airy, high-ceilinged and lined with oversized windows that had to be washed, badly. The only views were of brick walls but somehow, strangely enough, it didn't deter from the space. It was its own world, of another, simpler time. Beds, couches, tables, chairs were scattered throughout, so that anyone could be comfortable, anywhere they chose to be. A true first-generation loft, almost impossible to find anymore. I felt a rush of tenderness toward the space. For the owners, who I never met.

The carriage house was as charming as Trudy had promised. An intimate space with fireplaces in both the living room and upstairs master bedroom. Tiles, brick, a tiny private garden in front to welcome you home. The bathrooms were small and elegant. The roof deck was reached by pulling a thick chain that hung from the second floor ceiling and when pulled hard, released a ladder up to a restful retreat. This would sell quickly. We left brochures and Exclusive Agreements at each of the properties. Park Avenue and the carriage house signed while we were there. The loft owners had theirs delivered to us at the office a few days later. That left Kate's house. I had the date set with Oliver for the brochure shoot and no signed Exclusive. I didn't want to pressure her. Besides, I trusted her and I don't trust so easily.

The Park Avenue and Fur District sellers wanted Open Houses as soon as possible. Trudy and I set them up for Sunday, giving us five days to distribute the news to other brokers and have show-sheets printed up. My contractor texted. The garden apartment was ready for Patrick, I should come and see it and by the way please bring a check.

"I'm at the office," I said. "I'm busy. I can't be there for a while."

"So I'll send the guys home and wait for you on the new couch, maybe catch some TV. Okay with you?"

"Sure," I said. I rushed through some paperwork and about an hour later I walked home. I opened the street level wrought iron gate and unlocked the heavy metal door that lead to the wide downstairs hallway. I was greeted by glistening wood inlaid floors. Gorgeous floors that for years had been covered by old carpeting. Beautiful floors. It was a good sign and my heart started to beat with anticipation. I looked at the door to my right and approached, put my hand on the brass doorknob. So much depended on Patrick's reaction to the renovations that I was almost afraid to open the door. I needn't have been. Everything was better than I could have hoped for. The floors, hidden for years under old carpeting, was the same gorgeous floors that were in the outer hallway. The painted stucco walls, the new furniture, the lighting, all were perfect for the intimate space. The Hästens bed was big and masculine. The kitchen and bathroom with their new fixtures looked great.

"It's perfect," I said, relieved. Happy. There was nothing, I thought, that Patrick would fault. I couldn't hold back a huge grin. Zach laughed with delight when he saw my satisfaction.

"We did good, Ellie," he said. "This is exactly what I'd want if my wife kicked me out."

"Really?"

"Really." We left the apartment for the hallway to the inner staircase and climbed the stairs to the dining area. I wrote Zach a check for thirty-two thousand dollars and thanked him. "Hope it works out, Ellie. Always a pleasure."

I stayed home the rest of that day and waited nervously for Patrick. I made a nice dinner for us. Candles, flowers, lamb chops, a pear tart. He came through the front door, not expecting either dinner or that he would be moving downstairs so soon.

"This is lovely, sweetheart. Thank you."

"You're welcome. By the way, the downstairs is finished," I said. Patrick looked startled. Disappointed.

"So all this here is like my last supper?"

"This is a dinner between friends,"

"You're exiling me." But he didn't sound angry, just a bit lost.

After we finished eating Patrick pushed back his chair, stood up and left the room. I heard the squeak of the floorboards on the stairs as he climbed them toward our bedrooms. My heart sank. I grabbed my phone and keys and left the house, blinking back tears of anger and disappointment. I'd agonized over the remodeling of the garden apartment. I'd spent hours cooking supper and he hadn't even wanted to see go downstairs to take a look. I walked east to Fifth Avenue and turned south. As I neared Washington Square I calmed down a bit. *I would move downstairs.* I would call Linetta and have her file divorce papers, something I should have done when I'd met with her. I didn't want to hurt Patrick, I wanted him happy downstairs. It wasn't as if I was banishing him to a cellar, for God's sake. He'd still come upstairs, just not all the time, and not to sleep.

I was disappointed in his reaction but the more I walked the more I understood that change would take time. He would love what was done in the garden space. I was simply worn down from juggling my feelings for Antonio and the guilt that accompanied it. I hadn't allowed myself to think about him these last few busy days, but as I walked he became all I thought about. How he felt about me. How he made me feel. Then the guilt over Patrick and what he must be going through, how hard he was trying.

And how long would that last? Until I gave in and went back to our marriage? Linetta's words came back to me, loud and strong. Men want what they can't have.

Was she right? What if I did go back to Patrick? How long would he stay faithful? I would never know my future with him. My emotional future. The thought of all his women – Cindy, Valeria, the ones in-between. How many were there? I should sit down with him one day and make a list.

I had to take care of me. I walked to Soho and then up Spring Street and back west. Thompson, Sullivan, Sixth Avenue, Waverly, weaving in and out of streets until I was back on Seventh Avenue South, walking against traffic. A walk to no-where and back. Back home, I sat on the stoop and wondered what was next for me. This thing with Antonio. Was it something solid or would it end tomorrow, or next week. Did I care. At least with him I'd found myself, my ability for pleasure. It seemed it was bottomless, except when the rest of life interfered.

I had to stop thinking about him. I unlocked the door, went into the living room and sat on the sofa, feeling confused and exhausted.

"Oh, there you are," Patrick said, startling me out of what had started to feel like a bad place. He was at the threshold of the dining and living rooms. "I've been looking for you. I'm finished."

"Finished with what?"

"C'mon, El. This isn't easy." He grabbed my hand and pulled me up off the sofa, led me downstairs. "Look how beautiful these floors are," he said. Then he led me into the unlocked lower apartment. "You did a brilliant job, honey. I love it. As long as I can sometimes come upstairs and spend time with you, I'll be okay." I looked at him, so startled that it barely registered at first. He plopped down on his new sofa and I walked into the bedroom. The new dresser I'd bought had its drawers open and his clothes neatly stowed. The bathroom had his toiletries put away. He'd moved in while I was walking off my mood. "I'm not finished. I need another day or so, is that okay?"

"Of course it is," I said, realizing I'd given little thought to how momentous this move was for him. For us. All I'd been thinking about was that he had to agree to it, to like it, to actually do it. He had. I wanted him happy, wasn't sorry he would be close by, at least for the time being.

"Will I see you tomorrow," he asked, almost shyly.

"Sure," I said.

"And the day after that?"

"Patrick..."

"It's all right, El. Whenever. Can I have a welcome home hug before you go upstairs?" He stood up and walked the short distance to where I stood at the door. He held his arms out. I leaned into his embrace and hugged him back, then pulled away to leave. He was looking down at me and somehow our lips met, startled both of us so much that we pulled away, stared at each other in surprise.

"I'm going upstairs," I finally said.

"Okay, honey."

I went upstairs, straight back to the little room and picked up a book. I was staring at the words when my phone rang.

"It's your downstairs neighbor. I love you. Goodnight."

CHAPTER THIRTY-ONE

I picked up the keys from Kate's West Chelsea gallery and headed up Tenth Avenue on the bus. Oliver, the photographer, was outside, waiting for me.

"Sweet little house," he said. "And the block is surprisingly nice. For the area."

"The garden level is off limits for the shoot," I said. "It's Kate's workshop. It'll be clear in the floor plan." At which point I made a mental note to call the floor plan guy. "That's the entrance to it, straight ahead, through the wrought iron gate."

"I can see that," Oliver said wryly.

We climbed the stoop. Nine steps. Kate's four-story house was red brick. Mine was clad in brownstone. Hers was eighteen feet wide. Mine was twenty-five. She had front gardens on both sides of the walkway up to the stoop that made me smile. I unlocked the doors and the surprise of how much she'd changed the interior hit me instantly. She'd gutted much of it. There was no more vestibule. No more floor to ceiling doors separating a wide hallway and the living room. No hallway. She had opened up the parlor floor so that the moment one stepped into the house, it was into one large, open, riotously colorful room. Aside from the staircase to the left, the living room now took up the entire width of the house, the walls painted shocking pink. Wherever there was wall space it was covered with large framed posters. If they weren't posters, Oliver and I were looking at Matisse, Cocteau and Chagall originals. Two small love seats were covered in royal blue velvet, throw pillows were predominantly Mexican yellow and deep purple. Bookcases lined the far wall on either side of a stone and tile fireplace that would have looked at home in Santa Fe. The walls of the dining room were painted cobalt blue. The room itself was as wide as the living room, but not as deep. An enormous vase filled with yellow tulips sat in a pewter vase on top of a long wooden table. Beneath the table was a Persian rug, rich with reds and blues.

The kitchen was a bit softer, painted a buttercup yellow, the round table covered with a yellow and blue Provençal tablecloth. A plate of lemon squares, neatly covered with Saran Wrap, sat on the table with a note next to it. They were for us, as was the limeade in the fridge. I left the Exclusive on the table next to the dessert plate and took a lemon square. I thought it must have come from the nearby Little Pie Company because I couldn't imagine Kate having ever baked. I sat at the table to digest the changes in the house since I'd first seen it, ten years ago. There was such an exuberance to it that made me feel as though I'd entered a fantasy world. I was charmed by Kate's taste, the unexpected eclecticism of it.

I felt at peace.

"This place is crazy," Oliver said. "I better get busy. I'm starting upstairs." I followed him and his equipment to the fourth floor. It had two similarly sized bedrooms connected by a large, mostly all-white bathroom with a claw foot tub, sink, toilet, and bidet. All white but for pale lavender and ivory toile wallpaper and a brand new bar of lavender soap. One bedroom was painted cornflower blue with stark white molding and bedding. The second was plum and mustard color with lime green accents. The third floor had the same layout as the fourth, but all the walls were stark white. One room was set up as a gym, the other had a large loom in the center. A beautiful loom with nothing on it, it seemed a work of art in itself.

I left Oliver and went back to the living room, thinking Kate's house might be a hard sell, with all the color and busy-ness everywhere.

"I'm ready for this floor," Oliver said later as he walked into the kitchen. "Move your ass." I walked through the kitchen to the magenta painted door that led to a small outside deck. It overlooked the garden, which I had barely glanced at from the kitchen. I knew it was there, I knew it would be lovely, but when I stepped outside, into it, Kate's garden turned out to be an astonishment of surprises. She had sectioned it off with stone benches, small statues, chaise lounges and a fountain. Pockets of serene surprises.

A soft wind wafted by, wind chimes tinkled. I lay on a moss-green colored chaise lounge and closed my eyes. Wind chimes. Valeria had bought some for me in New Paltz. The recollection stabbed at me. I didn't even know where they were. I'd meant to hang them in my garden but never did. I had to find them. Water gurgled from somewhere. I rose to find its source. A fountain, almost hidden behind moss and ferns and other plants I didn't recognize. A liquid melody.

I was enchanted. Of the countless properties I'd shown over twenty years, I never once thought in terms of living in any of them. Why would I, with my own big, beautiful house, more than twice the size of Kate's. I went back to the chaise and stretched out, closed my eyes and actually sighed with contentment. The tranquility, the chimes, the gurgling, the colorful rooms made me feel as though I had been transported into another world.

Oliver's voice intruded. He was on the deck to tell me I had to move again so he could photograph the garden. I changed places with him, stood and watched as he looked around the garden, then back at me with an enormous grin on the face that needed no cosmetic treatment. He took the last of the photos for the brochure I would write up and have the company produce and mail out. I walked through the house making sure all lights were out and everything was in order, locked up and then we left.

"That is one weird and delightful home," he said as I walked him to his SUV. He asked if I wanted a lift but I wanted to walk.

I was so absorbed in thinking about the house as I walked downtown that I almost passed by Antonio's street before I realized it. Realized we hadn't spoken in a while. I stopped and called him.

"It's me," I said. "I'm here, on your block."

"It's lousy timing," he said. "I have a class. I was just about to leave."

"I just need you for fifteen minutes."

He laughed. "A quickie on the corner?"

"I wish. It's to show you something. Please. It's right on the way to John Jay." Ten minutes later he loped down the few steps of his building. His easy grace. He had a satchel over his shoulder. A book bag. I thought of all the young women in his classes and felt a sudden insecurity.

"What's up?" he asked.

"You'll see."

We walked the few blocks uptown hand in hand. I felt like a schoolgirl with her first crush. When we reached Kate's street and made a left onto it, toward Tenth Avenue, I realized that her house was almost exactly where Antonio's loft was situated in the block. If one had the power to walk through buildings it would be possible to walk from his building, across the street, through the garage, through the building abutting it on the next block and on and on, until entering Kate's garden.

I unlocked her front door and led him through the house, room by room. I didn't say a word. I didn't waste his time. Downstairs, upstairs, through the kitchen to the garden. "Sit," I said, just as I had with Oliver. He sat on a bench. Unlike Oliver, he was still as stone. At some point I felt him looking at me. Our eyes met.

"It's Kate's house," I said. "The gallery owner we met at MoMA. I had a photo shoot here today. I fell in love with this house."

"I thought you fell in love with me."

"That was ages ago. I'm fickle." He grinned. I wanted to lay naked on the ground on top of him.

"Seriously. Why am I here? I don't have much time." I experienced a sudden loss for words about my reason for bringing him here. My need to show him this house. I took a deep breath and kept my eyes on his.

"I love my house. I never thought I'd want to leave it. With all the places I've shown and sold over the years, this is the first one that touched me so strongly. That's why. I wanted to share it with you."

"You're thinking of moving? Of buying this?" He seemed surprised. So was I. The thought of buying Kate's house hadn't occurred to me, yet I felt a visceral pull towards that I couldn't explain. It was sweet and cheerful, perfect for a new beginning. My house was large, elegant and serious, easy to get lost in despair. I realized then, that is exactly how I had felt, roaming about those large empty rooms during the lowest times of my marriage. It was a magnificent house, but it was somber. Maybe only because my marriage had hit such a low place, maybe because Jonathan was no longer home. Maybe, just maybe it was time to move on. I looked into Antonio's green eyes and opened my heart to him.

"You're only the second man I've been intimate with. In my whole life. More intimate than I thought was possible." Emotion crossed his face that stopped me from saying more.

It took him time to answer.

"That's an awful lot for a man to hear."

"It's a lot for me to say. But seeing this house, I realize that I'm changing. That my needs are changing." I paused. "For the first time in years I can envision myself living somewhere else. Really starting my life again. You've given that to me."

"Christ, Ellie, you know what you're doing to me? How am I supposed to teach a class now?" He pulled me close and kissed me.

"That's awfully sweet," a voice called from the deck.

"Oh God, it's Kate," I said, pulling away. This wasn't good. The last thing I needed was for her to think I was using her house for a tryst. I walked toward her and handed her the keys, embarrassed. Antonio was right behind me. "I was heading back to you to return these when I passed Antonio's block," I said. "He lives only a few blocks away and I love your place so much that I wanted to show it to him."

Kate looked from me to Antonio, then smiled a brilliant smile. I wondered who her dentist was. "So we're not only MoMA fans, we're neighbors, too," she said to him. "I'll certainly know where to go if I need to borrow a cup of sugar." She winked at him. She really did. "So, detective, do you love my place, too?" He grinned at her. Said that he did. That the construction going on around him ten blocks south had made him forget there were still spots of tranquility in Hell's Kitchen. Kate grinned back at him. "I don't suppose you have a twin brother, do you, Detective?"

"Sorry," he said.

"How about a friend?"

"That I have," he said. He kissed my cheek and left.

"Oh my, Ellie," Kate said. "He's what they call a hunk, isn't he."

CHAPTER THIRTY-TWO

My next panic attack occurred a few days later while I was seated between the Parisian underwear models in the back of a Lincoln Town Car. I'd picked them up at their Soho hotel while the driver waited in front of a No Standing/No Parking zone. I waited in the lobby for a good ten minutes before they descended the elevator, both wearing skintight black leather pants and fitted black leather jackets even though it was warm outside. She had coppery red hair worn halfway down her back. He had a blond man bun that worked on him. Both were so stunningly elegant that I felt like their poor cousin from the Ozarks, even though I knew I looked okay. He climbed into the back seat of the car with the relaxed grace of an athlete. Or an underwear model. I followed, then she slid in next to me in a single movement so fluid that I wouldn't have noticed, except how could I not have? Her legs were as long as all of me and I'm not short. I introduced them to Dev, our driver, who wore a turban the color of saffron. It was magnificent against his mahogany skin. He offered us small bottles of water before pulling into traffic.

"Our friends the Silverman-O'Sullivans speak highly of you," Marielle said to me. I had no idea to whom she was referring.

It shouldn't have been a name easy to forget, yet I had. Despite the sudden lightheadedness that had come over me I imagined a redhead marrying a Hasid beneath a chuppah of four-leaf clovers. "They're pregnant again. They'll be calling you. They'll need a bigger space than the Duane Street loft."

Duane Street. View of the park. High ceilings. Small bedrooms. Mattie Silverman and Ollie O'Sullivan. "I bullied them into buying that loft," I said. "They'll make a fortune on it."

Dev drove the short distance to Tribeca, where we saw one property. All brick walls, beams, concrete floors. It was large enough but too dark. The second showing was a few blocks north and west, closer to the river. This was the area Antonio had bought and sold in, years ago. The area where he must have made a killing, price-wise. This loft had vaulted ceilings, large windows, old wood floors, but the bathrooms and kitchen area were miniscule. Dev was driving north on Hudson Street near the Holland Tunnel when I felt the undeniable tinges of dread creep over me. I had to get a grip before it got a grip on me. Now that I knew what it was, what it could become and that it would pass, I knew I'd be able to fight some of the panic I'd experienced in Linetta's office.

But I couldn't. I tried hard but couldn't push back the growing sense of disorientation, of terror. I didn't have diazepam on me, the two milligram pills prescribed by Dr. Louie Louie. I hadn't felt a recent need for the pills so now, instead of being able to reach into my bag to discreetly calm myself while seated between two of the most sophisticated, sexy clients I ever had, I was probably going to faint, or worse.

A closed car. Difficulty breathing. Rapid heartbeat. Dizziness. I probably would have fainted had there been room.

Maybe it wasn't a panic attack. Maybe I was having a stroke this time, or was dying. One of those sudden, inexplicable, unnatural deaths we read about in the *Times* obituaries. Maybe I should call Jonathan and say goodbye, just in case. Patrick and Antonio, also. If I can find the wherewithal to do so. I took a few deep breaths and asked Dev to stop the car, hoped the words that came out of my mouth sounded normal.

"Is something wrong?" Philippe asked. I nodded. Dev pulled over to the east side of Hudson Street and parked. Philippe stepped out and took my hand, helped me out, walked me to the nearby building. I leaned against it, pressed my back into it. There is nothing like brick and mortar. Nothing. "Take deep breaths," he said.

"I am," I said. But I hadn't been. I started. Inhale three, exhale six. Or was it four. It didn't matter. I was breathing.

"Are you okay?" A woman's concerned voice. A kind voice, almost musical. Accented. Of course it was accented. It was Marielle.

Think.

I am leaning against a wall that is brick. I turned my head. The brick is red. The sneakers that are walking by are on some-one's feet. The sneakers are pink high-tops. Bubblegum pink. A miniature dachshund has a camouflage scarf around its neck. A scarf on a dog. In September. Swollen ankles in tight shoes.

Look up. I did, grateful I was able to.

I know that building across the street. St. Luke in the Fields. So the brick building that is holding me up is P.S. 3, The Charrette School. I am near the corner of Hudson and Grove, two of my favorite streets in the Village. I will be fine as long as I lean against this school.

"Does anything hurt?" Philippe asked. "Here?" He touched my head. I shook it as I looked at him. He was awfully good looking. "Here?" He touched my left breast. I figured it was all right since he was Parisian.

"Take some of my water," Marielle offered. I drank some. It was sparkling. I noticed her shoes. The heels were so high and thin they could de-bone a fish. She'd never get far in those, if she had to. I was wearing low-heeled Bruno Magli shoes, comfortable enough to walk to Far Rockaway and back if the urge to do so ever overcame me.

"I'm fine now," I said.

"Can you continue with us today," Marielle asked. I looked at her, saw such unexpected kindness. I nodded.

"There is no need to apologize," Dev said. "You almost certainly had an anxiety attack. I get them all the time."

"I hope not when you're driving," I said.

"We are not meant to live such stressful lives," he said. "I wake up each morning not knowing if this might be the day I'll be robbed or shot. Or stabbed. Or an SUV rams into me on the West Side Highway, so far away from home."

"India?"

"Queens."

"What about on the FDR Drive?"

"This feeling has never happened to me on the East Side."

This was good. Talking was easy and fun for me. That panic attack was over and we climbed back into the car to continue with our tour. I showed Marie and Philippe a property in the West Village. From their lack of enthusiasm I knew that so far I had missed their expectations. I offered to buy lunch so we could further discuss the market but they only ate twice a day. Breakfast and dinner. I was starving, but what could I do?

The last property was in what is now sometimes referred to by some real estate people as West or North Chelsea or Hudson Yards but always was and always will be Hell's Kitchen. It was blocks from Antonio's loft, just slightly further east. As we drove up Tenth Avenue, Marielle and Philippe saw the handful of newly rising glass towers behind high construction walls. She asked hesitantly where we were going and what those buildings were.

"Hudson Yards. It's being built over the old rail yards. Those buildings are the first of many luxury towers to be built here. There will be apartments, offices, parks, incredible views."

"Do you like it, Ellie?"

I hated it. A future city of glass for the extremely rich, complete with elegant stores and world-class restaurants. From what I read, it would even have its own health clinic and a few spectacularly artistic structures for the arts. Anywhere else, but not in Hell's Kitchen's low-rise, low to moderate income neighborhood. It felt wrong. Obscene.

"Somewhere else I might love it," I said. "Not here." Probably not what a broker should say but it was hard to ignore the fact that the city I loved was being devoured by glass towers. Hungry, overpriced fangs, rising into the sky.

"Slaughter on Tenth Avenue," Dev said. "Do you know it? Dum, dum de dum de dum, dum de dudedum, dum," he sang, his voice surprisingly deep. "Richard Rogers. That's what this is. The murdering of Manhattan's soul."

The murdering of Manhattan's soul. It was becoming harder and harder to deny.

"Still. I'd love to see it when it's done," Philippe said. "This area could use something exciting."

Seeing Philippe's reaction, I had to admit that some of the buildings were beautiful. A true vision, just not for here.

Dev parked in front of a fire hydrant on a gritty block lined with commercial buildings. Marielle, Philippe and I left the car and I rang the buzzer of a twelve-story building. After a wait long enough to make me uneasy, we were buzzed in. I felt I'd let the models down with this first outing and hoped this listing was as good as it appeared on the website.

The Deco lobby where we waited for the elevator was nicer than I could have hoped for. We rode up in silence. I sensed disappointment from both Marielle and Philippe and only hoped to have another day with them to find properties more suited to their needs and tastes.

The elevator opened directly to the loft and I knew immediately that it was not wasted effort. A long bookshelf-lined hallway to our left and then an immense open space with perhaps twenty people working at desks towards the far end. Stylish sofas scattered about the center. An open chef's kitchen, a hallway off of which four bedrooms and two baths were cleverly hidden from the main space. Thirteen-foot high tin ceilings, worn, wide-planked wood floors. Brick walls. Massive windows.

Marielle grabbed Philippe's hand as they walked through the enormous space a second time, her high heels tapping against the wood floors. They were careful not to disturb anyone as they received discretely admiring looks. They spent a few minutes on the terrace, long and wide enough for a red Weber grill, a few tables and chairs, small potted plants. I gave my card to the artist owners and we left. Marielle had a thoughtful look, lost in her own world. Philippe told me he knew that look. They had to talk. They were in town for a few more days. If there was anything else as good as this property, they wanted to see it. They also wanted to revisit this loft at night, to experience the neighborhood after work hours.

I probably should have told them this wasn't a neighborhood and nothing happened after work hours, but who knew, with Hudson Yards rising fast just blocks away the entire neighborhood was about to explode. Except probably not this block and maybe a few others.

Dev leaned against the car, looking relaxed. I told him to take Marielle and Philippe wherever they wanted to go, that I felt like walking. Marielle said she admired my aubergine silk pants suit. I told her it was from Bendel's. She asked if that was far from where we were and I said nothing was far in a Town Car. I paid Dev and they drove off.

CHAPTER THIRTY-THREE

It had been over a week since Antonio and I were at Kate's. That we had spoken. It was, in fact, closer to two weeks. He'd warned me that he would be extremely busy for a while. I missed him yet felt hesitant about calling him. When I finally did, I regretted it. He sounded distracted and distant. He said he was glad I called, but I wasn't. The call made me feel worse. Then he mentioned, almost as an afterthought, that his upstairs neighbor had offered to buy him out because he needed the extra space. Buying Antonio's loft would double what he had. He'd have a spacious, airy duplex and as a well-known photographer he felt strongly that his business would increase once Hudson Yards and its monied masses moved in.

"Are you considering it?" I felt strange. Empty. It was obvious that I didn't matter to him nearly as much as I'd thought. Forgetting the power of our physical relationship, didn't my opinion count? As a broker with two decades of experience?

I felt a sense of diminishment that grew with his silence. He said that preparing his classes took a lot more time than he'd thought. He felt very stretched at the start of the term, his first term teaching. He had something in mind and would call me soon. He missed me.

No he didn't. I'd been around this block before. If he missed me he would have made time to call, or at least email or text a few words. I understood he was at the threshold of a new career and had a Police Manual to edit. A dalliance with a married woman would have to wait until he had time. But I wouldn't wait. I couldn't emotionally afford to deal with uncertainty and I wouldn't allow myself to be available at his convenience. Even though his reasons were probably honest.

Even if.

I didn't need him. I'd gotten my self-esteem back, had orgasms I'd never known existed. Most of all, I had my strength back and no one, ever, would take that away from me again. Antonio could call me when he had the time and if I happened to have that time for him, great. I wasn't his convenience. The rest of my life was up to me. Besides, the sex couldn't possibly have been as good for him as it was for me, so if we'd reached the end of our little journey together, I was the winner.

I had plenty of my own work to do. Exclusives. Showings. Deals. My son, who, last time we talked, was having a great first semester. And things were working out at home between Patrick and me. To his credit, he respected that he could no longer just walk into my part of the house without asking if it was okay with me, even though in reality he could. I hadn't yet put a lock on the dining room door leading down to his garden level space. There was just a hook that was so old he could easily unlatch it simply by opening the door a bit and reaching in to lift it up, but he hadn't. At least not often, and only when he called out, "honey, I'm coming up," from the staircase by the dining room. I also hadn't changed the front door locks, out of sheer laziness. It would mean sets for me, Louisa, Betsy, Jonathan. There was time.

I needed a hobby. A pastime, just for me. I would take piano lessons again. The piano was downstairs, in Patrick's apartment. I would leave it there and buy a better one. There was room near the bay windows in the living room. Plenty of room and plenty of time for my limited ability to grow and flourish. I knew it would. I would hold salons in my living room. My parlor. where I would play "Moonlight Sonata."

Okay, that was settled.

Patrick invited me down one evening when he and one of his partners, the one 'going through something' were watching a football game on the new, massive TV. They were drinking beer and eating popcorn that he must have smothered with melted butter the smell was so strong. I stood in the doorway before entering, saw the Patrick I'd met over twenty years ago – young and carefree and handsome as hell. It seemed he was enjoying his man cave. I stayed with them for a while, but football's not my thing.

"Goodnight, sweetheart," he said.

"See ya, El," his friend said.

The underwear models called. They were back in Paris and had been "so busy or of course they would have called sooner." They had decided against the Hell's Kitchen loft even though it had "everything we wanted, Ellie. Everything. It's perfect for us," Marielle said. "Isn't it, *mon cher*?" I heard a grunt that I assumed was a *oui* from Phillippe. She said they'd walked around at night and the streets were practically empty. Empty of people and empty of charm. She said they knew they'd told me that the area wasn't important, but those blocks weren't an area. I said it was an area that was changing by the day, but I agreed it wasn't for everyone. "You are our broker. Find us that loft in a better location and we will, how do you say, jump on it." I told them that such a loft anyplace else except Staten Island or the Bronx would be double the money. I wondered what kind of underwear they wore at home.

My partner Trudy came down with something on the Sunday we were holding our second Open Houses, one on Park Avenue that she was hosting and the Fur District loft, which I was. It was the first Sunday in October. My turnout was decent. I didn't know about hers until she called me later that day. It turned out to be a hideous disaster, as bad as a real estate Open House could be. About halfway through the two hours, she started feeling feverish and sat down for a few minutes to combat an attack of nausea. During this short time one of the guests had apparently used the master bathroom without asking her if it was okay to do so. When he walked back into the living room he walked briskly past her and out the door. There he turned to her and shrugged his shoulders. She sensed something might wrong, that he had perhaps stolen something, so she walked into the master bedroom. She had to support herself holding onto the walls, and not just because she was feeling poorly. The stench from the en suite bathroom almost caused her to throw up. The effluvia that overflowed the toilet onto the bathroom floor, apparently left there by the man who had shrugged, fortunately halted a few inches from the bedroom and its Aubusson carpet.

Trudy felt too ill to handle the clean-up so she locked up the apartment just as other customers and brokers were arriving. She apologized, handed each of them a business card and promised to give them private showings, then jammed in next to them in the elevator, hoping not to faint. She said she must have appeared so shaken that no one seemed upset. One even offered to hail a cab for her. She told the relief doorman that the Open House was over but he spoke only Polish, or what she thought was Polish. He kept holding up his hand with the fingers open, three times in quick succession. She finally realized he was telling her the regular doorman would be back from break in fifteen minutes, but she was too weak to hang around. She wrote a note, left it and her card on the lobby desk, then made a mad dash into cab the broker was holding for her.

That night the owners called me and cancelled our Exclusive. They said they were sending our firm bills for both the cleaning and emotional distress. I pleaded with them not to say a thing to my manager, Trudy and I would pay for the cleanup. I explained the circumstances, that Trudy was incredibly responsible but that she'd taken ill. Everyone who entered the apartment had signed in. I would figure out who caused the mess. Meanwhile, was there anything I could do to regain their trust? I practically groveled to keep the Exclusive, when the last thing I wanted was to work at all.

"At least the idiot could have used the powder room," the husband said.

"No, honey," the wife said. "Then the mess would have been near the entrance hall. We might have stepped on it, slipped, and broken our necks. Or hips."

"Yes, dear. You're right, as usual." They were each on a land-line phone extension. I wasn't the only one still using a landline.

"The super came right up," the wife told me. "We gave him five hundred dollars but Stu said it was worth more than that to clean the mess. Disease and all that. We're sleeping in the guest room tonight until the smell dies down. As long as we can work exclusively with you, we'll re-sign. Won't we, honey. Only Ellie can be here from now on. Okay?"

"Okay."

"Okay."

I thanked her and insisted on taking them to dinner. For them to name the place. Two nights later I met them in my best little black dress and paid for champagne, caviar, Chateaubriand. Some fancy dessert tray. It cost me almost six hundred dollars, all because a buyer had diarrhea.

"Shit happens," Stu said after another his third glass of champagne. I spit up a little of mine.

"I told you there was something wrong with the flusher," the wife said, turning to her husband. "Men never listen."

They thanked me for a delicious meal and walked home.

CHAPTER THIRTY-FOUR

Lights were on in Patrick's apartment but none anywhere else in the house. Not on my floors, not on Louisa's or Betsy's. It was a house meant to be filled with people and it always had been that way, until now. Now it appeared dark and deserted and enormous. I unlocked the doors and sat on the sofa, checked my phone. No messages from Antonio. No texts. No hi, Ellie. I miss you. I checked the answering machine in the kitchen. Nothing there, either. Once again I had a sense that something had changed with him, maybe a gorgeous grad student in her twenties who carried no baggage. Why would he want me, anyway, a married woman with tons of it, and just a few years away from menopause. Soon I'd be sprouting long white hairs on my chin. I wouldn't want me.

I turned on the TV and watched a few *Law and Order: SVU* reruns. I couldn't concentrate even on that. I tried to busy myself with work details but it was impossible. All I could think of was how I'd opened my heart and soul and body to Antonio and for what? To be disappointed. I should have known. Men's passion is cheap. All they need is a place to put their erections.

I thought of Kate. I'd left several messages for her and she finally texted that she signed the Exclusive but hadn't had time to get it back to me, which was total bullshit. She could have faxed it. Mailed it. Sent a messenger. Everyone in the city uses messengers all the time. It's a simple business charge. For that matter, I could have walked over and picked it up. It seemed clear that she wasn't serious about selling. In addition to lost time and the cost of the photo shoot that would come out of my next commission check, I'd put my trust in someone when I should have learned by now that no one can be trusted.

No. That wasn't true. Jonathan, Betsy and Louise could be trusted. Even Patrick, about everything that didn't include his anatomy. I decided to call Kate one more time before I wrote her off, before I let myself give in to the fact that she had no real loyalty to me, at least anymore.

Who needed her or her house with its pink walls and tinkly fountains. It was all too perfect, just like her. No wonder she was alone after all these years.

My cell phone was charging in the living room so I called from the landline in the kitchen. I actually love my landline. It's a 212 exchange and I'll never give it up. I punched in Kate's cell number. I took the handset into the living room, plopped onto the sofa and listened as it rang two times. Three. It was picked up on the fourth ring, just as I was about to hang up.

"Kate's phone." A man's voice.

A voice that had whispered intimacies to me. Laughed with me. A voice that now, upon hearing it, made me almost retch in horror. Antonio, on Kate's cell. I dropped my phone in disbelief and the heavy-ish handset hit my knee before making a soft thud on my Persian rug. As it fell I heard him plead for me not to hang up. Stupid caller I.D. I picked the phone up, walked back into the kitchen, threw it onto the table and pulled the plug from the wall jack just seconds before I made it to the sink and gagged. Wondered why I'd thrown the phone. It had done nothing wrong. I lifted it and apologized. "I'm sorry, phone." I placed it gently back in its cradle.

Kate's words to Antonio came back to me that day in her garden. Her innocent-sounding words apparently hadn't been so innocent. *Now I know where to go if I need a cup of sugar.*

I sank hard onto a kitchen chair. This was a hurt I hadn't felt before, a gut-wrenching pain worse than any I'd experienced in all the years of Patrick's infidelities. That pain had built up over the years, spread itself out, eventually numbed me. This was a sudden, raw, vicious attack. A betrayal that felt too much to bear. A double betrayal.

No, wait. There was a rational reason for his being at Kate's house. There had to be. I was jumping to ridiculous conclusions.

No, I wasn't. Kate was a beautiful, successful, sophisticated woman, completely beholden to no one.

As I sat at my kitchen table I felt a sudden, shocking closeness to Valeria. Her vulnerability, her loneliness. I went to the drawer in the kitchen where I keep odds and ends, where I'd stored the photo of us in New Paltz. I took it out and stared at it. Hugged it to me. I held it close and cried for both of us.

CHAPTER THIRTY-FIVE

My cell phone was ringing. I walked to the living room and pulled the charger out, put the phone on mute. I went upstairs to the guest room and lay on the twin bed, let tears come. Deep sobs tore through me until I sat up and screamed at myself to shut up. What had I really expected from Antonio? I'd known him just a few months. We had great sex. Multiple orgasm sex. He'd served his purpose. I didn't need him any more than he needed me. Fuck him and fuck Kate.

"Fuck you, you fucky shitty fuckers," I screamed. "Fuck shit scum schmuck pieces of crap I hope you die fuckers DIEDIEDIE."

That felt good, so I continued to curse - at the low bookcase, at the globe in the corner of the room. Then I felt terrible. I love books and globes, so I apologized to them as I had apologized to the phone, downstairs. "I'm sorry, bookcase, I'm sorry globe, I didn't mean to yell at you." Then I realized I might be losing my mind because who apologizes to a globe.

I'd lived through deceit before, I'd live through this. It had just been a surprise, that was all. I walked into the master bedroom, shed my clothes all over the floor and once again stared at my body in the armoire mirror. Antonio would never see this body again. Would never touch it again. Never ever again.

I almost doubled over in pain.

I decided to take a shower. Maybe if I sang I would feel better, even though I never sing in the shower. Still, it couldn't hurt. I turned the water on full force and stepped in. Stood under the powerful showerhead and belted out the first few stanzas of "Oklahoma." It failed to relax me and I gave up on singing and started cursing - fuck pig shit on a stick, but the silky shampoo that I rubbed it into my hair was soothing. It smelled delicious.

"I'm Gonna Wash That Man Right Outta My Hair." "Sing a Song of Sixpence." Pocket full of rye, gin, Scotch. I wished I had a waterproof notebook - I could list every alcoholic beverage I could think of. I could think of a lot of them even though I don't drink anything alcoholic except for wine. Then all the non-alcoholic beverages. Then ways to kill liars and cheats.

May Antonio and Kate rot from syphilis.

Syphilis, scurvy, scabies, SARS, sciatica.

I had my lists and I had Molton Brown Ginger Extract shampoo. I was set. I stayed in the shower a long time. Afterwards I put lotion all over myself except where I shouldn't, dressed in jeans, a long-sleeved T and forest-green, ankle-length, fringed suede boots. I threw a change of clothes in my overnight bag in case I decided to go away, because I could. I could go anywhere I wanted. I could do anything I wanted and I would, except I would never ever again believe another two-timing fuckfaced bastard.

This cursing felt good. I realized why people do it. I would be okay as long as I cursed. And what did I have to regret, anyway. I'd experienced heights of passion, a lack of inhibition that had been mind-altering. So thank you, you fucking pile of horse manure, now you can shrivel up and die. Or suffer every second for the rest of your miserable life because you won't have me and that is your loss. You will feel the loss of me every second of every minute of every hour for the rest of your life and I will be happy and carefree.

I packed a plaid vinyl bag with a few things. An ugly bag to match my ugly mood. A single sob escaped me and as I walked downstairs that I swore that it would be the last one out of me, ever. I went to the kitchen and washed the few dishes in the sink, turned out the lights, texted both Jonathan and Patrick that I might be out of town for a few days, not to worry. It was true. I might go somewhere. I texted Trudy to cover for me if necessary but to absolutely stay away from the Park Avenue co-op, though there was no need because I had received an offer and it was accepted. There was a contract out. The owners loved me.

Where should I go? I was open to anything. Nothing. I could stay home and happily watch *Law and Order* re-runs. I could go to New England and see the foliage. It was the time for that, for the leaves, somewhere up north. Vermont. I could stay in a charming country inn, like the house Diane Keaton bought in *Baby Boom*. I would walk to Penn Station, a single mile straight north on Seventh or Eighth Avenue and decide where to go. I wasn't sure that trains to Vermont left from Penn Station and I didn't feel like going to Grand Central, but they did go to Boston. That would do. They have leaves there, too, and the Duck Pond. Or is it a Frog Pond. Beacon Hill. A charming hotel. I ran upstairs and added more clothes. A nicer dress, a warm sweater, then went downstairs and unlocked the inner vestibule door. A folded piece of paper had been slipped through the mail slot. I bent to pick it up. It said *Open the door.*

I was going to open it anyway, so I did. Antonio was sitting on the top stoop. He turned around the instant he heard the door open and stood, walked to me and pulled me back inside. He held my arms and looked at me, concern on his face, as much concern as that face of his could show. He tried to hug me. I pushed him away. I thought of kicking him in the groin.

"Didn't you hear the doorbell?"

"I was in the shower," I said. "It takes time to wash away deceit."

"Deceit?"

"I hate you. I really hate you. Get out of my house or I will start to swear. I've gotten really good at it."

He grinned.

"I'm not really in your house. I'm in the vestibule, which is closer to outside than inside. I've been sitting here for more than half an hour, waiting for you." He took the suitcase from my hand and placed it on the floor. I bent down and took it back. "Going someplace?"

"Maybe, maybe not."

"Where might you go?"

"Anywhere that you aren't." He grinned. All the severe planes of his face softened and there was a different kind of beauty. I hated him for that, too.

"Let's go inside so I can explain," he said.

"You don't have to explain anything to me. I know all about cheating men. I married a pro."

"I could use a drink."

"There's a bar down the block. Two of them. The seedier one's closer." But he was still grinning and looked so good that if I saw him kill a litter of kittens my heart would still turn over a million times.

"One drink." I looked at him, at the grin he couldn't seem to wipe off his face. I wanted to smack it off. Then I decided he deserved a drink for initiating me to the world of fabulous sex. Also, he no longer meant enough to me to deny him a drink out of spite, so I put on the hallway light and led the way to the kitchen. I gave him a glass of water. "I was hoping for something stronger," he said.

"Then help yourself. The liquor's in the dining room." I wasn't about to wait on him.

He came back soon with a squat glass filled with something. Probably Patrick's Scotch. He hadn't taken his liquor collection downstairs yet. Antonio opened my refrigerator and took out a few ice cubes and placed them in his glass, then leaned against the counter. He seemed right at home. I took a sip of the tap water I'd poured for him and waited for whatever he had to say.

"I'm crazy about you," he said.

"Shut up."

"I've been so busy…"

"I don't care."

"May I finish?"

"Sure, finish the drink and get out."

"All right," he said. "If you're sure that's what you want." He put down his drink, lifted my T-shirt and fondled my breasts.

"You can't do that anymore," I said, but my nipples were hard and between my legs I was damp and I wanted him so badly that the kitchen floor looked pretty good.

The front bell rang. I pulled down my shirt and went to answer the door. Kate stood there, a small cake box held in her elegant, freshly manicured hands.

"Hi," she said, smiling.

"So much happiness," I said.

"I come bearing cake and a signed Exclusive." That surprised me. I took her lightweight coat and hung it on a hook in the hall, then led the way toward the kitchen, but she ignored me and entered the living room, looked around. She took her time admiring it and then the dining room. "Gorgeous house, Ellie." We entered the kitchen. Antonio was finishing off his Scotch. Kate gave him a hug, some papers, then sat down at the kitchen table, placing the cake box neatly in the center. "Isn't this lovely, the three of us together."

"Lovelier than I could ever have imagined," I said.

Antonio and I also sat and the three of stared at each other. I glared, Antonio and Kate seemed completely at ease.

"Is someone knocking on a door," Kate asked a few minutes later.

"Don't worry about that, it's just my husband," I said. "He lives downstairs." I went into the dining room and opened the latch.

"Hi, sweetheart," Patrick said. "I got your message that you were going out of town and I still have my liquor up here…"

Antonio stood up and walked over to Patrick and me. I looked back at Kate. She winked at me and we both watched as the two men sized each other up, the way men do. Antonio finally held out his hand, but Patrick didn't take it.

"Are you her cop?" he asked.

"No," I said.

"Yes," Antonio said. "I hope you don't mind."

"I do. And cop or no cop, I'll beat the crap out of you if you hurt her. She's been through hell with me, so if you're playing games here I will hunt you down and hurt you."

I stared at Patrick in astonishment, then shrugged and walked back to the table. Kate looked blasé, which she does well. I sat next to her. Patrick and Antonio joined us at the long wooden table.

"I'm Kate," Kate finally said to Patrick. "I'm a friend and client of Ellie's."

"I'm Patrick," he said, distractedly. "Ellie's husband. And he," he pointed to Antonio, "is her, uh..."

"I know Antonio," Kate said. "He is possibly buying my house." I almost spit up some of the water I had just swallowed.

"A house here, in the city? Like this house?" Patrick seemed confused.

"Much smaller," Kate said.

"How can a cop afford a house in Manhattan at these prices?" he asked, looking at Antonio. "I hate to make assumptions, but you must be dirty."

"I'm retired. But Ellie said the same thing," Antonio said.

"You're not worried about where his money came from?" Patrick asked Kate.

"He did someone a favor," I said.

"It's because of Hudson Yards," Antonio said, talking to no one in particular. "I live right at the edge of it and I don't want to live with the construction. It'll take years. My neighbor wants to buy me out and duplex the units."

Kate opened her oversized bag and slid some papers over to me, said that if Antonio does buy her house, she hopes I would lower the commission to four percent because, really, all I did was have the photo shoot and show him the house, once. I was so surprised to see the signed Exclusive that I nodded. Then I thought about it.

"Only for him. Make him the exclusion and four's okay. Otherwise it's six."

"Five."

"Okay. Five." Kate added Antonio's name on the front of the Exclusive with him as the exclusion, initialed it, did the same to a copy and slid the original over to me.

"Thank you," I said. I turned to Antonio and asked him what the probability of his going through with this really was. He said he was waiting for the Engineer's report, that was what he was doing at Kate's, earlier.

Earlier, as in when I'd had my meltdown.

"Isn't the neighbor who's interested in buying your place worried about the construction?" Patrick asked.

"He's a photographer, pretty well-known. Those Hudson Yards condos are for the wealthy. He thinks it'll be great for his business, and he'll be doubling his space. Besides, he has a place in Paris. He's there a lot."

Patrick turned to Kate. "So if this goes through, where do you go?"

"One of the new buildings along the High Line. Near my gallery."

Kate had her bag on her lap and she placed her hands on top of it. The movement was subtle. The look on Patrick's face was anything but. He looked at her hands as though mesmerized, and who could blame him. She could have been a hand model they were so beautiful. Only when Patrick saw me watching him did he look away. I took a look at the Exclusive. The asking price was two point nine million but there was no signed Contract of Sale so I didn't know what the agreed upon purchase price was. Whatever money I might receive would be the easiest commission earned in years, if I discounted my earlier hysteria.

Patrick went into the dining room and returned with a bottle of Scotch. Antonio held up his glass. Patrick shrugged and then brought over glasses for the rest of us. As he handed Kate her glass she glanced up and took what was probably her first good look at him. He met her gaze and it was remarkable. It was the first time I'd ever seen her the slightest bit uncomposed and also the first time I'd seen Patrick look with interest at another woman without lust in his eyes. He simply seemed surprised. Both of them did. It was all so weird that I couldn't sit there doing nothing. I started rummaging through the cabinets. The refrigerator. I put up a large pot of water, then went over to the long counter and started chopping gorgeous tomatoes I'd bought at Union Square market. Antonio soon joined me, began crushing a few garlic gloves and tearing fresh basil leaves. There was some zucchini. I sliced them. Then a red pepper. At one point Antonio stood behind me just long enough to whisper in my ear that it had been more fun doing this naked together in his kitchen.

"A lot more fun," I said.

"You're smiling, aren't you," he said.

"Yes."

"Are you happy?"

"Yes."

I'd never prepared a meal alongside Patrick in all our years together. With Antonio it was as though we were born to it.

"I'd love to see the rest of the house," Kate said. "From what I've seen on this floor it's quite a place."

"I can't show you the top two floors," Patrick said after an awkward pause. "We have tenants. But if you want I'd be glad to show you Ellie's floor and also where she's exiled me." I looked at him, surprised at his words. More surprised at his tone. At his manner. He was smiling. "How long has it been, honey? I forget."

"Days," I said.

"That's all?"

"Maybe a few weeks."

He and Kate left the room.

"This situation should feel much more awkward," Antonio said, a bemused look on his face.

"Why are you doing it," I asked, turning to look at him. "Buying Kate's house."

The water was boiling. He added the pasta. He said the offer for his loft was not only fair, it was more than he thought it was worth. So while he hadn't thought of selling until the offer, he had been dreading the nearby construction that would take years to complete. When he saw my reaction to Kate's house, he looked at it from my eyes. A broker's eyes. A charming house on a quiet street, in his neighborhood. He loved Hell's Kitchen, the small ethnic restaurants, the store owners, the location. And it was even closer to John Jay than the loft was.

"But a single guy doesn't need a whole house."

"And I don't need to be crazy about a married woman, but I am," he said.

He drained the pasta, dumped it into the sauté pan with the vegetables. Added a bit of olive oil and flipped the mixture around like a pro. I had a sudden fantasy of the two of us, naked, running through the rooms of Kate's house if it became his, chasing each other from bed to couch to chair, making love everywhere. I looked at him and grinned.

"What?"

"I'll show you one day. If you do end up buying Kate's," I said. He covered the pan with a lid and said we should let Patrick and Kate know that supper was ready. We. I lead the way downstairs. The door to Patrick's apartment was open and I stood in the threshold, watching him and Kate as they sat closer together on the sofa than people who just met each other usually would.

"I don't care if you don't like modern art," Kate was saying. "You're coming to my new show next month. I won't take no for an answer."

"Then of course I will," Patrick said. "I'd be delighted."

Really? I managed not to let my mouth hang open in surprise. I turned to look at Antonio, standing behind me in the open doorway. He grabbed my hand and squeezed it.

"Supper's ready," I said.

"Oh. Listen, honey," Patrick said as he turned to us. "Kate's on a no-carb diet so I said I'd take her for some steak. The pasta can keep if you want to join us. We'll just be at Old Homestead."

I couldn't explain the mixed feelings that came over me then. The very place where Antonio and I had been the day we'd met. He must have felt something, too, because he stood closer to me, put his hand on my waist.

"No," I said to Patrick. "That's okay. You two go ahead."

"Enjoy the dessert," Kate said. "I can't eat it yet. I still have two weeks to go on this diet." We all went upstairs to the hallway so Kate could retrieve her coat and bag. Antonio and I went back to the kitchen, looked at the pasta, then he looked at me.

"We have at least an hour. Probably two. The pasta will still be edible."

"I can't. Not here," I said, but I took him by the hand and led him up to the little room.

"You're kidding. On this tiny bed?" he asked.

Later, we ate all of the pasta as we sat across the table from one another, unable to wipe the grins off our faces.

CHAPTER THIRTY-SIX

A few days later I was in my robe in the living room, watching Lawrence O'Donnell on MSNBC, when Patrick texted me. Could he come up to talk? Without waiting for an answer he was knocking on the door.

"What's up," I said, going back to sit on the sofa. He turned off the TV and plopped down next to me. I waited for him to say something but he seemed tongue-tied. "Patrick," I finally said. He ran his hands through his hair.

"Look, honey, can I talk to you as a friend?" I looked at him in surprise.

"Of course," I said.

"Here's the thing, El. As much as I don't want to know about what's going on with you and this cop of yours, I understand." He paused, looked at me for a long moment, took a deep breath and asked me if it was serious.

"For me it is, at least for now."

"Fair enough. He seems like a decent guy and I'm not an idiot. Anyone can see the attraction between the two of you. The ease you have with each other." I felt a surge of affection for him then. Real, deep affection. "So here's the thing. All those women over the years. They were just bodies. Oh, please, honey. Don't look at me like that. This isn't the time to make judgements. I needed sex. So did they. I never promised anything."

"What a guy," I said, but there was no bitterness in my voice.

"It's good we can talk like this, don't you think," he said. I nodded. "Twenty plus years together, sweetheart. You're my best friend. You probably always will be. I guess what I'm saying is, the other night, with Kate. It felt different. Sort of like a date." I smiled, but I felt funny inside. I nodded again, like a stupid bobble doll. "Those other women, it wasn't the same. Afterwards, it didn't matter if I saw them again or not. I don't think it mattered to them if they saw me."

"Ships passing in the night," I said.

"I guess. So what do I do now? About Kate. She's a whole different ball game." I stared at him. Patrick was asking me for dating advice!

"She's my client," I said, my voice calm. "You cannot screw around with her and I mean that in every sense of the word. She's accomplished. She's connected. She's as decent as they come. If you mess up my relationship with her by acting like a pig, I will never, ever forgive you."

"I swear. I won't. She likes me, El. She said so. I want to do the right thing, but I'm not sure what that is anymore."

"She said she likes you?" Patrick nodded. "As a person, or as a guy she wants to see again?"

"That. The second one. We had a long talk over dinner. She said she has great friends and colleagues but that there hasn't been anyone special for years. That this was a hard city to be lonely in." He looked at me, surprise clear on his face. "A woman like her. It's hard to believe." I didn't know whether to laugh or cry or to punch him in the face. My husband with his portable penis, talking to me about loneliness. "What should I do?"

"I don't know, Patrick. Did you take her home?" He nodded. He did, in a cab. "Did she ask you in?" He shook his head, said that she had taken his hand, kissed his cheek, thanked him for an unexpectedly lovely evening. That was all. "I wasn't sure what I was supposed to do, so I said I also had a nice time, then took another cab home."

"You should have walked. You don't get enough exercise."

"She reminds me a little bit of that French actress you like so much. What's her name? The skinny one with reddish hair."

"I don't know. Oh, wait. Isabelle Huppert?"

"Yes. Her. Don't you think there's a resemblance?" I looked at him, stupefied.

"Except that they're both women, no. They look nothing alike." Then I thought for a minute. "No, you're right. There's a quiet elegance, similar hair color, slender..."

"Yes! An elegance. Kate has that same *je ne sais quoi*, don't you think?" That *je ne sais quoi*? Patrick? His phone pinged. He read the message and his face lit up. He typed something back, his thick fingers awkward on the small keypad.

"What?" I said.

"It was Kate," he said, beaming. "She invited me to dinner next week. I said yes. Is it okay with you? She wants to know that, too."

I was too surprised to answer.

"What should I bring? Wine, or maybe flowers?"

"Wine's always nice."

"Red or white?"

"Oh my God. I don't know. It's just what you do, bring something. Maybe a small bouquet of flowers, but not from a corner deli. They die too fast. From a florist." I looked at him and I don't think I was imaging that Patrick looked as uncomfortable as I felt. He also seemed happy. I felt my insides knot up in a mass of confusion. I wanted him at that moment with a sudden fierceness I could hardly believe. Was immensely grateful that the feeling disappeared as quickly as it had appeared. "Just be yourself," I said. "Not your slam, bam, thank you ma'am self. Your kind, funny, natural self. Don't try to impress her. It won't work. Don't overdress. I'm going out now. I need a walk."

"Thanks, honey. It's great to be able to talk together like this, isn't it?"

"I guess," I said.

"Mind if I sit here for a while before heading home to my Batcave?"

"Very funny. Stay as long as you like." He made himself comfortable and reached for the remote. I felt a surge of affection for him then. I grabbed a light coat, checked that I had my phone and keys in my bag and left. I went to the corner diner and sat in a booth. I ordered coffee and a slice of cake that I ignored. I reached into my bag for a pen and my red notebook, turned to a blank page and drew a line down the center of it. It looked surprisingly straight. I felt a fleeting satisfaction as I labeled two columns.

What I Have	What I Want
Health.	
A son in college.	
Money in the bank.	
A husband.	
Tenants.	
My big, beautiful house.	

I stared at the blank right hand column. And stared. Then I placed the notebook back in my bag and took a ten dollar bill from my wallet. I left it under the cake plate and left the diner, then walked straight up Ninth Avenue with a single purpose. There was something I had to do, to know. It was all I could think about as I increased my pace on the way uptown.

My phone beeped. I would ignore it.

No, I would look to see who was calling. I could at least manage that.

It was Kate. I picked up and was sorry I did. She sounded flustered.

"This is awkward, isn't it," she said.

"What is?"

"You know. Me and your husband."

This was last thing I wanted to do, talk to Kate now, about my husband. About anything.

"He said you remind him a bit of Isabelle Huppert."

"Really? I love her. That's a compliment, isn't it?"

"I would take it as one."

"I hope this isn't improper, Ellie, but I invited him for dinner. He said yes, but I don't cook much. As in I'm extremely limited. Do you mind my asking what his favorite foods are?" I was so focused on my own situation that with anyone else I probably would have hung up, but I found myself giving her advice.

"He's a man with an appetite. Pot roast, Italian. Chicken. Basic food and a lot of it. Rocky Road ice cream with chocolate syrup. U-Bet, if you can find it."

"I'm nervous. I haven't cooked for a man in years. For myself, either." I heard the hesitation in her voice, realized this wasn't an easy call for her. But as we get older, our lives matter on a different scale. We have less time and have to make it count.

"Listen, Kate. Patrick was not faithful."

There was a long pause before she said she was sorry. Truly sorry. I told her I thought he had changed, or at least was trying to. "Small steps. Basically, he's a good guy. Just go online for recipes. Martha Stewart. Someone like her."

I ended the call, more concerned with my life than Patrick's or Kate's. I continued uptown, to Antonio's. I called when I reached his corner and told him where I was. He didn't say anything at first and then said to come up. I would have leaned against the wall of a building for support but there were none. There was just an empty lot with some flimsy construction boards protecting its privacy. I walked to his building feeling more and more hesitant, questioning myself, my feelings. My fear. A bike messenger was leaving as I was entering. He winked at me. The security guard was doing a puzzle. He stopped and smiled at me. I waited while he called up and the elevator came down.

I shouldn't have come. I wasn't ready, not really.

Antonio stood in his open doorway and watched me as I walked to him. No smiles, no hugs. I followed him into the kitchen and leaned against the island. I could look at him for the rest of my life and be happy.

"What do I mean to you?" I finally asked. There was a silence from him that felt unbearable. Then he closed the small distance between us and took my face in his hands. He kissed me gently on the lips.

"Everything," he said. "You mean everything to me."

My relief, my joy must have been obvious because he grinned as he pulled me against him in an embrace. "I guess that was the right answer, wasn't it?"

"Not bad," I said, my head against his chest. The beat of his heart was my private serenade.

The End

Acknowledgments

There are many I want to thank who have influenced my journey to writing this novel. Janet Albaugh, for threatening to end a lifelong friendship if I didn't take a Method Writing class. Kathrin Seitz, for so brilliantly teaching that class and becoming a valued friend. Barry Wallenstein, for his friendship, advice and rather esoteric knowledge. Retired NYPD 1st Grade Detective Bobby Moller, for graciously answering all my questions. Shanna McNair and Scott Wolven of *The Writer's Hotel* for valuable guidance and a great experience. Gay Walley for her wisdom, talent, and incredibly generous support. Janice Eidus for her kindness and much appreciated advice. Linda Langton for her enthusiasm and help in getting this baby published.

My wonderful family. My parents, who instilled in all of us their love of literature, music and crossword puzzles. My sisters, Madelon and Natalie for always - and I mean, *always* - being there for me. My son, Nicholas, for his generous and loving spirit: it's been a remarkable adventure, growing up with you. And my husband, Bob - physicist, writer, editor, tech wiz. You are magnificent.

About the Author

Elisabeth Amaral has designed jewelry, co-owned both a children's boutique and a restaurant in Harvard Square and was a real estate broker in New York City for many years. She is the author of a children's book, *Elodie at the Corner Market*; a collection of short stories, *When Any Kind of Love Will Do*; and a memoir, *Czar Nicholas, The Toad, and Duck Soup*. She curates and co-hosts a reading series at *Otto's Shrunken Head* in the East Village.

CPSIA information can be obtained
at www.ICGtesting.com
Printed in the USA
LVHW011110090720
660099LV00005B/200